Praise for the Sa...

"*Sanctuary Island* is a nov... a crackling fire or on a sun... story of hope and forgive... power of love."
—Susan Wiggs, #1 *New York Times* bestselling author

"I didn't read this book, I inhaled it. An incredible story of love, forgiveness, healing, and joy."
—Debbie Macomber,
#1 *New York Times* bestselling author

"A heartwarming, emotional, extremely romantic story that I couldn't read fast enough! Enjoy your trip to Sanctuary Island! I guarantee you won't want to leave."
—Bella Andre, *New York Times* bestselling author of the Sullivan series

"Well written and emotionally satisfying. I loved it! A rare find." —Lori Wilde, *New York Times* bestselling author

"Fall in love with Sanctuary Island. Lily Everett brings tears, laughter and a happy-ever-after smile to your face while you're experiencing her well-written, compassionate novel. I highly recommend this book, which hits home with true-to-life characters." —*Romance Junkies*

"Redemption, reconciliation, and, of course, romance— Everett's novel has it all." —*Booklist*

"Richly nuanced characters and able plotting . . . Everett's sweet contemporary debut illustrates the power of forgiveness and the strength of relationships that may falter but never fail." —*Publishers Weekly*

ALSO BY LILY EVERETT

Sanctuary Island
Shoreline Drive
Homecoming
Heartbreak Cove
Home For Christmas

AVAILABLE FROM ST. MARTIN'S PAPERBACKS

Three Promises

The Billionaire Bachelors

LILY EVERETT

St. Martin's Paperbacks

This is a work of fiction. All of the characters, organizations, and events portrayed in this book are either products of the author's imagination or are used fictitiously.

THREE PROMISES: THE BILLIONAIRE BACHELORS

Copyright © 2016 by Lily Everett.
"The Fireside Inn" copyright © 2014 by Lily Everett.
"Bonfire Beach" copyright © 2014 by Lily Everett.
"Lantern Lake" copyright © 2014 by Lily Everett.
"Epilogue" copyright © 2016 by Lily Everett.

For information address St. Martin's Press, 175 Fifth Avenue, New York, NY 10010.

ISBN: 978-1-250-07612-0

Printed in the United States of America

St. Martin's Paperbacks edition / February 2016

St. Martin's Paperbacks are published by St. Martin's Press, 175 Fifth Avenue, New York, NY 10010.

10 9 8 7 6 5 4 3 2 1

For my mother, Jan, who loved these
stories more than anything else I've ever written.
I miss you every day, Mama.

The Fireside Inn

Prologue

Miles Harrington lounged back into the deeply cushioned Chesterfield sofa and contemplated the three very different men he'd asked to meet him at the Biltmore Club that afternoon.

Taking a measured sip of his single malt, Miles let the smoky flavor burn down his throat as he silently acknowledged the truth: When he had decided last year to sponsor Leo, Zane, and Cooper for membership to the most exclusive private club in Manhattan, he'd been trying to compensate for his rebellious younger brothers. As if by mentoring some other guys who wouldn't throw it back in his face, Miles would make up for the fact that his own brothers wanted nothing to do with him.

Of course, everything was different now—because of Greta. Miles allowed a soft smile to cross his face at the thought of his bright-eyed, sheltered fiancée. Greta might not have had much experience of the world outside her small hometown of Sanctuary Island, but she'd taught Miles a lot about the workings of the human heart and the bonds of family.

But even though Miles was finally making strides toward real relationships with his brothers, Dylan and Logan, Miles still felt a sense of responsibility for his young friends.

Even if sometimes they drove him nuts.

"Who do I have to screw to get a drink in this joint?"

Zane Bishop kicked his battered black Converse sneakers up onto the gleaming burled walnut surface of the mid-century antique coffee table and threw his dark head back to cast a searching gaze over the quiet lounge.

"The Biltmore Club is not one of your dive bars," Leo Strathairn reminded him, sardonic amusement clipping his crisp British-inflected words even shorter than usual. "You absolute heathen. Don't you understand where we are?"

"The Billionaire Club." Cooper Haynes, always unable to sit still, prowled their private corner of the lounge like a caged tiger.

Miles stepped in. "Biltmore members do not repeat that ridiculous nickname," he said sternly. "When I got you all in here, you promised you wouldn't embarrass me."

"Sorry, Miles." Leo apologized more easily than the others. Miles wondered if it was a British thing, or if it had more to do with whatever had made the son of an honest-to-God English earl ditch his family to live the expat life in Manhattan.

"Hey," Zane protested, crossing his bare arms over his short-sleeved black T-shirt. A T-shirt, at Biltmore . . . but that was Zane. And, to be fair, that simple tee was probably designer and ludicrously expensive. "It's not actually our fault that the whole world calls the Biltmore Club 'the Billionaires Club.' If you think about it, it's really the club's fault for only letting in billionaires."

Miles acknowledged the point with an ironic salute of his cut crystal highball glass, but it was Leo who said, "True. But we don't have to be crass enough to perpetuate the nickname."

"Oh, God forbid we should be crass," Zane grumbled, most of his attention on flagging down the passing waiter to order a drink.

"Besides." Cooper shrugged, propping his broad shoulders against the marble mantelpiece over the cold, empty fireplace grate. "We are billionaires. So what? We should be ashamed of it?"

Miles and Leo exchanged a quick glance. Like Miles, Leo had inherited most of his wealth from his family, and they occasionally found that a weird chasm could suddenly open up between their "old money" ideas, and the way Cooper and Zane felt about their "new money."

What Miles valued about all of them, both the self-made men who worked hard and played harder, and the rogue aristocrat with an actual title and centuries of tradition behind him, was the genuine friendship that had sprung up between them.

But part of that friendship was based on the fact that all four of them had been bachelors, living the single lifestyle as billionaires in New York City. And that was about to change.

"If I could have your attention for a moment," Miles said. He didn't raise his voice, but then, he didn't need to. Three pairs of curious eyes turned toward him.

"Okay," said Zane. "Let's get this show on the road. Why did you ask us to meet you here today?"

"Not that we aren't glad to see you back in the city," Leo put in, crossing his legs in the exact way that would put no creases in his impeccably tailored trousers. It wasn't deliberate, Miles would bet—manners like that seemed to have been bred into the Brit, or drilled into him at an early age.

"You've been gone?" Cooper asked, perking up at the mention of travel. "Me, too—just got back from Bali last night, matter of fact. Man, that's a gorgeous island."

Miles grinned. "As it happens, I've been spending time on an island, too. Sanctuary Island, off the coast of Virginia."

Cooper frowned. "Never heard of it."

Zane grimaced. "Sounds . . . sweet. By which I mean, boring as hell."

And, of course, it was Leo who sat up a little straighter, his piercing gaze sharpening on Miles's face. "Stow it, lads. I think Miles here has something more on his mind than his recent vacation."

Not for the first time, Miles studied Lord Leo. With his tousled chestnut hair, lean, chiseled face, and light gray eyes, Leo looked like exactly what he was: a wealthy Englishman, born of privilege and at home in high society. By all rights, he should be an entitled ass, self-involved and arrogant—but he wasn't. Which made Miles wonder what the hell happened to make Leo so good at reading other people's moods and expressions.

Time to stop stalling. Miles cleared his throat and braced himself for the explosion he was about to set off.

"Leo's right. As it turns out, I met someone on Sanctuary Island and . . . we're getting married."

He squinted one eye half closed and hunkered down for the blast, but all that happened was a long beat of silence. And then Zane was up and off the sofa so fast, his battered leather pants squeaked across the tufted Chesterfield cushions like tires squealing on a racetrack. "What the hell, man? You were gone for, like, a hot minute! This is crazy. You—the head of Harrington International, the coolest guy we know—you can't possibly be marrying some bimbo you met on vacation."

"You make it sound as if I don't know what I'm doing." Miles bared his teeth in a smile that he was fairly sure wasn't the least bit comforting. "Trust me, I do. Greta is amazing. She changed my life."

He didn't miss the alarmed glances zinging back and forth between his three young friends. Reminding himself he'd anticipated this reaction from these commitment-shy men, Miles settled deeper into his chair and finished off his whiskey. The glow from the alcohol was nothing compared to the warmth that suffused his chest when he thought of the woman he was about to make his wife.

"You must admit, it sounds odd." Leo, ever the diplomat, spread his hands wide in an unthreatening gesture. "Ever since we've known you, there's been no hint of a serious relationship. Much less a desire to marry."

"What does she have on you?" Zane demanded, blue eyes flashing with the secrets he usually hid behind his loud, boisterous, party-boy demeanor.

Protectiveness rose up in Miles's chest. No one talked about Greta like that. But before he could get up a good growl, Cooper stepped between them.

"No. It's not blackmail. It's worse than that." Cooper

studied Miles's face with dismay that went deeper than the situation seemed to call for.

Leo's handcrafted Italian loafers hit the plush carpeting with a muffled thud. "What could be worse than blackmail?"

A muscle ticked in Cooper's jaw. Crossing his muscled arms over the battered olive drab of his waxed canvas field jacket, he ground out, "Miles is in love."

Hearing it aloud made something deep in Miles's chest relax. It wasn't nearly as strange as he'd feared. He deposited his empty glass on the side table and laced his fingers behind his head. "That's right. I'm in love, and it's by the far the best thing that's ever happened to me."

Leo averted his gaze as if uncomfortable with the blatant emotion of Miles's statement while Zane openly scoffed. Cooper—well, Cooper smiled a little, but the half quirk that dimpled his scruffy cheek didn't convey much actual happiness.

"No point trying to talk him out of it," Cooper advised the others. "He's got the look. It's going to have to run its course."

"Even when that course runs straight down the damn aisle?" Zane sounded outraged. If it were up to him, he'd probably kidnap Miles and hold him captive until he missed the wedding date.

Miles held onto his temper with an effort. "In this case, my course runs straight down the sand. We're having an outdoor wedding on the beach. And I want you all to be there. In fact, I have jobs for you."

"Um, I've already got a job," Zane reminded him. As head of Whatever Entertainment, Zane owned and ran live music venues across the country.

"Exactly," Miles said with satisfaction. "Which is why you're the most qualified person to help plan the reception."

Zane looked thoughtful, which was better than an outright refusal, so Miles pressed his advantage. He turned to the tall, scruffy man by the mantel. "And Coop, our resident adventurer, is on honeymoon duty. Greta has never been anywhere. I want her to experience something incredible for the first time, and I want to be there with her when she does it."

"That . . . actually sounds fun to plan. A challenge . . ." Cooper's green eyes took on the distance of far-off horizons, his toe tapping with the need to keep moving, to never stay in one place too long.

"I'm almost afraid to ask," Leo drawled, a sarcastic edge to his smile. "What wedding-related business do you have for me, Miles? I eagerly await your will. To business that we love we rise betime, and go to 't with delight."

"Something you're perfectly suited for, Mr. Shakespeare," Miles said, his shoulders relaxing. This was the easy one. "Greta and I would love for you to choose a reading to do at the ceremony."

To his surprise, Leo was the first of the three to tense and frown at the news of his appointed task. The frown lasted only a second, though, before he blanked his face of any expression.

"Of course," Leo murmured, silver gray eyes as opaque as the surface of a mirror.

Hesitating, Miles frowned. "Is that . . . are you all right with that? I've told Greta all about you, the way you pepper your conversation with quotes and lines of poetry—

we're both excited to hear what you come up with for the reading."

Leo smiled, wide and easy and nowhere close to lighting his eyes. "If you want a reading fit for a king, you've come to the right place. Have no fear, Miles. I'll find the perfect piece to read at your wedding."

Miles forced himself to nod smoothly. They'd each agreed to their tasks, and thereby they'd agreed to come to Sanctuary Island and be part of the wedding. In most circumstances, Miles would never have doubted his ability to get his way, but with these three? He planned to take their yesses and run with them.

Standing and rebuttoning the top two buttons of his charcoal wool blazer, Miles gave his protégés a benevolent smile. "Excellent. In that case, I'll be off. Greta is waiting for me."

Leo set down his glass of cognac. "Want to share a cab uptown?"

"No, but thanks." Miles spared a quick glance at his Piaget watch. " I'm not going to the penthouse."

"The helipad." Zane groaned, covering his eyes with his forearm. "Of freaking course. Tell me again, how many generations do you need to go back with this club to get helipad access?"

Miles arched a brow. "Jealous?"

"You know we are." Cooper shook his head. "Man, there are days I'd give anything to dial up my private chopper and have it transport me directly to the Billionaires Club roof. Not that I have a private chopper."

"Not that it matters if each of us purchases a custom-designed, one-of-a-kind helicopter to rival Miles's luxurious craft," Leo pointed out. "Since new members to the club have no hope of being granted helipad access."

"That's the whole reason I haven't bought a helicopter yet," Zane grumbled, ruffling his black waves with a rough hand. "Fine, go back to your precious Sanctuary Island. Try not to die of boredom before we get there."

"You should come down a few weeks before the wedding," Miles said, ignoring Zane's editorializing. "There's a lovely hotel on the mainland, just a ferry ride away from the island. You'll all be comfortable at the Fireside Inn for an extended stay. I want you to have a chance to get to know the island before the ceremony."

"So we'll get there—what? Ten minutes before the wedding starts?" Zane blinked, his big, blue eyes giving him a completely false innocence. "That should give us enough time to see everything your island has to offer."

For a brief moment, Miles almost envied them. There was nothing quite like that first discovery of Sanctuary Island and the magic to be found there. But they wouldn't believe anything he said now, so he limited himself to a mysterious smile, knowing it would drive them crazy.

It did. "Oh, for the love of—" Cooper shook his head. Wanderlust lit his eyes with green fire, the curiosity Miles had counted on zooming to the fore. "What's so special about this place anyway?"

"Didn't you hear?" Zane's lip curled as he slouched deeper into the chaise longue. "Sanctuary Island is perfect."

"Nothing in this world is perfect," Leo muttered.

Miles inclined his head. "That's true enough. Although what I've found with Greta comes damn close."

Cooper muttered something that sounded like, "For now," while Zane groaned and threw himself down full length on the chaise. Miles glanced at Leo, hoping for a little support, but instead, he encountered nothing but confusion—as if Leo literally couldn't imagine being in love.

That did it.

Miles stuck his hands in the pockets of his Brioni suit pants and lifted his chin. "What would you boys say to a wager? The prize: that custom chopper of mine you all love so much, plus—I'll sign over my restricted access to the roof of the Biltmore Club. Are you in?"

Sitting bolt upright, Zane narrowed his eyes. "What are the stakes? Only one of us can win the helicopter and helipad access."

Miles grinned slowly. "I'm betting each of you will find the course of your life forever altered by your trip to Sanctuary Island. In fact, I'm willing to bet each of you will find love there. I watched it happen to both of my brothers in turn, and now all three of us are happily in love. The island is like no place you've ever been, I promise you. What's more, if you travel to Sanctuary Island with me tonight, four weeks out from the wedding, I bet you'll succumb to its lure before I ever say 'I do.' "

Silence reigned thick and exciting in the air. "And whoever doesn't . . ."

"Whoever is still single and unattached by the time I march down the aisle gets the helicopter," Miles declared. "Along with the glory of victory. Who's in?"

Incredulous glances pinged back and forth across their corner of the lounge as Leo, Zane, and Cooper processed the terms of the bet. Miles straightened his shoulders, a sense of rightness settling over him like a warm blanket.

He was going to win this bet.

After collecting nods from Cooper and Zane, Leo stood from the couch and extended a hand to Miles. Serious and intent, his crisp accent more pronounced than ever, Leo said, "We accept your wager. Although I, for one, feel a tad guilty at how simple it will be to beat you. I have no intention of falling in love, on Sanctuary Island or anywhere else."

"No one intends to fall in love," Miles said sympathetically, shaking his friend's hand and sealing their deal. "But on Sanctuary Island? You won't have a choice."

Chapter One

Serena Lightfoot took a last, deep gulp of her coffee before regretfully tossing the rest in the big metal trash can by the front door. No food or drink in the library was a good rule. She'd implemented it herself when she took over as Head Librarian of the tiny Sanctuary Island Public Library two years ago.

But while she didn't miss the days of wiping down sticky reading tables or dabbing potato chip crumbs out of the spines of her precious books, Serena did occasionally regret the loss of the steady caffeine intake that had gotten her through grad school.

Better for your blood pressure anyway, she told herself firmly as she scuffed the bottoms of her high-heeled, lace-up Oxfords on the horsehair mat before unlocking the door and slipping into her domain, locking the door behind her. Inhaling the familiar comfort of paper, leather bindings, and book dust, Serena flicked on the overhead lights and dumped her crocheted bag on the reference desk.

This was one of her favorite parts of the day—the silence and solitude before the library was officially open. She could catch up on her cataloguing, work on the management system for the special collection of playwrights she was considering, check in the overnight returns. . . . Serena sighed happily, her fingers itching to get to work organizing things.

Although. She paused, biting her lip as her ancient PC booted up. If she were smart, she'd haul out the library budget and try, once again, to make the figures come out in the black instead of the red.

Agitatedly scraping her unruly blond curls into a loose topknot, Serena knew she now probably looked like the prototypical spinster librarian. But she couldn't be bothered to care about that with the incomplete budget hanging over her. She shrugged out of her navy blue cardigan and wiggled in her rolling desk chair to get comfy. Might as well settle in for an hour of wrestling with finances, she decided glumly. That sick feeling in her stomach wasn't going to disappear until she knew the Sanctuary Island Public Library would continue for another year.

But just as she clicked open her spreadsheet program, a loud knock banged on the locked library door.

Heart thudding quickly at the surprise, Serena stood up and walked slowly around the reference desk. She spared a fleeting thought for the fact that she was all alone in the library—but this was Sanctuary Island, the sleepiest little town full of the nicest people she'd ever met. There wasn't even a bridge or a causeway connecting it to the mainland;

the Virginia coastline was barely a gray smudge on the horizon, visible only from Honeysuckle Ridge, Wanderer's Point, and the lighthouse.

Another knock made her jump and roll her eyes at herself. She didn't have time for nonsense today. "The library is closed," she called firmly.

"I see." Even muffled, the voice through the door sent a strangely electric shiver down her spine. Brisk and British, but with a masculine, velvety warmth that made her want to wrap it around herself like a hand-knit blanket and rub her cheek all over it. The voice continued, "And what time will you be opening?"

Serena frowned. "The hours are clearly posted right beside the door," she replied. "Come back at nine."

There was an odd, awkward silence that lasted long enough for her to wonder if he'd gone away without another word. But then she heard a quiet, "Damn" before he raised his voice again. "Look, I'm sorry about this, but I'm not sure where else to go. I need your help. Won't you let me in, please?"

Catching her fingers twisting in the hem of her messily untucked button-down, Serena stilled her nervous fidgeting. "I don't think that's such a good idea."

The voice went low and silky with amusement. "I promise, I'm perfectly harmless."

Serena shivered again. That voice! He sure didn't sound harmless. He sounded like he'd be a danger to any woman's sanity—especially a woman who'd never had very good luck with men.

That was a decent point. After all, considering Serena's luck, Mr. Hot Voice would no doubt turn out to be a hundred and five, stooped and balding, and with typically terrible British teeth. Deciding she was probably safe, Serena laughed softly at herself and unlocked the door.

Standing on the library doorstep was an impeccably dressed, broad-shouldered man about seventy years younger than her projection. He stood straight and tall, easily topping six feet, and the amber glow of the early morning sun turned his dark hair into a thick halo of fiery auburn waves.

The man smiled urbanely, showing a mouth full of perfect white teeth, and Serena bit back a sigh.

Her first impression had been completely correct. Despite the perfectly tailored James-Bond-style trench coat, the glossy leather shoes, and the lazy way he leaned on the handle of his sturdy umbrella, there was absolutely nothing harmless about this man.

"Thank you so much," the man said, "I'm utterly in your debt. Miss—?"

"Serena," she said dumbly, then flushed. This man wasn't one of her pre-K storytime kids, who all called her Miss Serena in their little, piping voices. "Sorry, I mean, Lightfoot. Serena Lightfoot. Head Librarian of the Sanctuary Island Public Library."

He had the good manners to raise his brows as if impressed by the title she'd insisted on when the town council voted to hire her. Maybe it was meaningless in the grand scheme of things, but it meant something to Serena. That title was an achievement—it meant all her hard work, all the loneliness, betrayal and personal sacrifice, had been worth it.

A smile twitched at the corner of the British stranger's well-shaped lips, and Serena lifted her chin. Okay, so the

Sanctuary Island Public Library was tiny, a brick shoebox of a building that obviously didn't have room to house enough books to call for a fleet of librarians. But even if it was just Serena and her gaggle of part-time volunteers, she was still the Head Librarian!

"Miss Lightfoot," he said, tone full of grave respect even if his light gray eyes were dancing with laughter, "May I be so bold as to introduce myself?"

This wealthy-looking, extremely cultured stranger reminded Serena of how she used to feel in school when the popular kids would approach her solitary cafeteria lunch table and ask for help with their homework. Shrugging grumpily, Serena jammed her hands into the pockets of her faded corduroy slacks. "Knock yourself out."

Another slight, suave, glittering smile. "I'm Leo Strathairn, a visitor to your fair island, and I'm ever so pleased to meet you."

He held out his hand and, reluctantly, Serena took it. The touch of his smooth, strong fingers sent a jolt of heat up her arm, even in the chilly winter air.

A flicker of awareness glowed in the depths of Leo Strathairn's silvery blue eyes, and he held onto her hand as he said, "Thank you for opening your doors early—I understand what an imposition this is, but I simply didn't know where else to turn. I need a favor."

Unwilling to be charmed—in her experience, charming people always wanted something from her—Serena worked her fingers free of Leo's light grasp and stepped back over the threshold and onto her home turf. "Come on in and tell me what you need, then we'll see if I can help you."

Leo sauntered past her, idly swinging his umbrella, and

the moment the library door closed behind them, Serena knew she'd made a huge tactical blunder.

Enclosed within the musty silence of the old library, surrounded by the row upon row of books, the sheer, solid presence of Leo Strathairn was overwhelming. He seemed to suck all the air out of the room, simply by standing there and breathing as he glanced around the stacks with an odd, indecipherable expression tightening his chiseled features.

For the space of a heartbeat, Serena simply watched him take it all in, from the high, arched casement windows that were such a pain to clean, to the colorful crayon art lining the wall behind her desk. If he made fun of this place she'd poured her heart and soul into, Serena knew she wouldn't be granting him any favors.

But for the first time since she opened the door and laid eyes on him, all trace of a smile melted away from Leo's face. The sardonic glint in his eyes was overshadowed by something darker yet softer—something like yearning. Serena caught her breath at the man's odd wistfulness as he stared at her cherished books, but when he met her gaze again, it was gone.

"Lovely building," he said, neutral and polite enough to make Serena blink. Had she imagined that fleeting ache of emotion in his eyes? Maybe. Those light eyes were flat silver now, completely shuttered in the glare of the buzzing overhead fluorescents.

"Thanks," Serena said slowly. "It's on the historic register, but then, so is most of the island. Sanctuary is chockablock with old stuff."

"Americans have such a charming concept of age," Leo drawled, a little mocking but also fond. "Anything more than fifty years old gets slapped onto the historic registry, doesn't it? But I suppose it's all relative."

Serena stiffened. "So what brings you to our upstart little nation? I'm sure there are plenty of bigger, fancier libraries in your neck of the woods."

"I wouldn't know. I'm not much for libraries." He flicked an invisible speck of dust from the belted cuff of his immaculate trench coat.

Scowling, Serena crossed her arms over her chest. No matter how gorgeous he was, and how much that accent made her knees wobble, she couldn't be attracted to a man who didn't care about libraries, reading, and books. "And yet, here you are."

Leo smiled engagingly at her, and even the fact that Serena could tell he was exerting himself to be deliberately charming didn't completely negate the effect. "Because I'm in dire need of your expertise, Miss Lightfoot. I've been given an assignment, you see, and I haven't the foggiest idea how to go about it."

An assignment. Okay, that sounded like they were heading toward solid ground. Smoothing down her messy hair into something a little more businesslike, Serena stepped quickly around her desk and perched on her high chair. More comfortable with the width of the wooden research desk—and the metaphorical professional distance it provided—between them, she was able to return his engaging grin with a tight, cool smile of her own. "I'm glad to help. Is this an assignment for work or for school?"

His rust-colored brows arched up in surprise. "I'm a little old for a schoolboy, don't you think?"

He seemed to be a bit obsessed with age. Funny,

considering he couldn't be much older than thirty-five. "My Master's program was full of students of all ages," Serena told him. "There's no such thing as being too old to keep learning."

A spasm of darkness flickered across his handsome face. The way he'd tilted his head down threw shadows across his sharp cheekbones and elegant jawline, and the sweep of his lashes was like a fan of cinnamon against his fair English complexion. "What a pretty thought."

Trying not to bristle at his casual dismissal of one of the most deeply held convictions of her life, Serena kept her voice neutral. "I'm full of pretty thoughts. But I'm afraid we're too pressed for time for me to share more of them—I'll have to open the library soon, and my first appointment of the day is with a group of patrons who do not like to be kept waiting."

It was absolutely true—the five-year-olds who had storytime on Tuesdays hadn't learned patience yet. They were liable to stage a riot if she wasn't ready and waiting with the next chapter of *Charlotte's Web*.

"Forgive me." Leo inclined his head and leaned one insouciant elbow on her desk. "The assignment is neither for work nor study—it's for a wedding."

Serena blinked at her screen, fingers poised above her keyboard. "What?"

"A friend of mine is getting married on this island: Miles Harrington. Perhaps you know him?"

"Everyone knows the Harringtons," she said, mind racing. "The family has owned a big chunk of the island for generations."

And until recently, the three heirs to the Harrington fortune had never set foot on Sanctuary. Then, last summer they'd arrived one by one, each handsomer than the last, and set the town gossip machine to buzzing. Serena wasn't a big fan of gossip, and as a relative newcomer to the island, she didn't have a ton of friends, but even she'd heard all about how the Harrington brothers had swooped in and swept three lucky ladies off their feet and into the lap of luxury.

What she wouldn't give to have half an hour with a Harrington—any of them!—to tell them why they should pour just a tiny portion of their billions into sponsoring the local library.

"My friend, Miles, is the eldest," Leo explained. "And from what I've seen since I arrived, he's fallen arse over teakettle for his bride-to-be. He wants everything about their whirlwind wedding to be perfect, and of course, as his friend, I'm eager to oblige."

A tiny thrill of excitement rippled over Serena. Who didn't like a wedding? "I'm happy to help, if I can."

"Oh, you can." Leo smiled right into her eyes, his voice dropping into the thick tension between them like stones into a river. "You see, I've been tasked with choosing a love poem to read aloud during the ceremony. And I'm certain you'll be able to find me the perfect one."

A switch clicked in Serena's head, flipping through her mental files faster than her fingers could type in the search parameters for the card catalogue. "Absolutely, Mr. Strathairn. Let me just pull up a few anthologies and poetry collections, and you can start reading through them. Were you thinking modern poetry or classical? English or translations? Our poetry collection is small, but well curated."

Leo surprised her by reaching across the desk to still

her typing fingers with a touch. Freezing, Serena looked up into his gray eyes. "Actually, love, I had something else in mind."

She swallowed, vividly aware that the jump of her pulse was probably visible at the base of her neck. "Oh?"

Another brilliant smile. "I was thinking that you could go ahead and simply choose a poem for me."

Serena felt the flush of heat in her cheeks the moment before she consciously understood what he was asking.

It was like high school all over again, the hot jock flirting just to get her to do his homework for him. And it hadn't ended there.

Sick to her stomach at the memory of the last time she'd fallen for a persuasive man who only wanted to use her for her brain, Serena's voice shook with anger. "You want me to choose the poem you'll read at your friend's wedding for you. Why, because you're too busy and important and . . . and . . . *British* to do the work yourself?"

Surprise widened his eyes. Geez, when was the last time anyone had said "no" to this guy?

"I beg your pardon," Leo said stiffly. "I was under the impression that you're a research librarian at a public library. Isn't it your job to . . . well, research?"

"Research? Yes. Perform an incredibly personal and important service that ought to be between you and your friend, the groom, with zero help or input from you? You must be out of your mind."

Nobody was that charming or handsome without also being an entitled jerk. Serena had learned her lesson early and well.

But as Leo Strathairn drew himself up to his full, impressive height and stared at her with the morning sun streaming over his perfect, striking features, Serena felt a coil of heat tighten low in her abdomen.

If anybody was handsome and charming enough to make her forget the past, it was this gorgeous Englishman.

Chapter Two

Leo consciously relaxed his grip on the engraved mahogany handle of his umbrella and fought down a surge of panic. This wasn't going at all well.

The adorable librarian glared at him over the tops of her little black-rimmed spectacles, her pointed chin quivering in outrage, lush cupid's-bow lips parted to give him another dressing-down. And, God help him, Leo almost wanted to hear it. An enraged Serena Lightfoot, Head Librarian, was the most enticing thing he'd encountered in an age.

If the librarians at Westminster School had looked like her, Leo might not be in this mess.

But he *was* in this mess, for which he partly blamed that horrid public school that had educated countless generations of Earls of Rochester before him. If the headmaster hadn't been so intent on forcing his pupils to memorize Shakespeare and Johnson, Miles would never have gotten the wrong end of the stick about which of his friends would make the best reader for his wedding.

What was Leo meant to say? *I can recite* Twelfth Night *backwards and forwards, but if you want me to read books of poetry to choose the best piece for your wedding, it's going to have to be a very long engagement.*

Swallowing the acidic bile of shame with the ease of long practice, Leo stared down at the solution to all his problems. He'd made a hash of it thus far, and she'd need to be approached properly if he were to have any hope of success. If she wouldn't simply hand him an appropriate poem on a silver charger, he'd have to try another tack.

"You're quite right," he admitted readily. "Damned impertinent of me. I daresay it's too much to ask of anyone. But as I said before, I'm not much of one for libraries. The idea of being trapped here with all the old paper and dusty books, when the golden jewel box of this island is waiting to be opened . . . Damn. I'm sorry. I'm making a dog's breakfast out of this."

Leo grimaced and ran a hand through his hair, unable to resist peeking at Serena to see how she was taking the apology.

She wasn't swooning off her chair or anything, but he thought he detected a minute softening in the line of her mouth and at the corners of her extraordinary dark eyes. The contrast between the bright blond cloud of hair covering her head and the dark slashes of her brows over deep, velvety brown eyes was uncommonly arresting. By all that was holy, Serena Lightfoot was striking.

"Look, I know libraries seem boring and stuffy," she said, a hint of earnestness creeping into her tone. "But they don't have to be! Don't think of the books as two-dimensional pages of dry text—every book is a window to another time and place, a way to peer out at the world through someone else's eyes and to experience life in a way you never expected. The entire universe, and all of its wonders and mysteries, is contained in these pages!"

She swept her arms out to her sides, enthusiasm and passion reverberating through the empty stacks and echoing in Leo's chest. For a moment, a bare instant, he caught a glimpse of the endless possibilities Serena referred to, but as his gaze snagged on the brightly-colored banner hanging on the wall over her head, reality crashed over him once more.

He concentrated, suffused with a desperate longing he thought he'd conquered years ago, but the letters flipped and swam across the banner like a school of fish. The words flickered at the edge of his vision and darted away as soon as he focused on them, slippery and impossible.

Stop trying, he told himself viciously. *It's never going to happen.*

Struggling against the sucking quicksand of failure that wanted to drag him under, Leo grasped for the first conversational gambit that sprang to mind.

"You're right, of course. Libraries aren't boring."

"They're essential," she insisted, dark eyes glittering with fervent belief. "Public libraries provide a service to the community that can't be replicated any other way. People who can't afford to buy every book that interests them can come to the library and discover new authors, new genres, whole new worlds of information and opportunity that—"

Serena cut off the flow of her impassioned speech like turning off a tap, vibrant color flooding her cheeks.

"Go on," Leo encouraged, leaning over the desk and focusing intently on her. The way Serena lit up when talking about her library was entirely beguiling. She was nothing like the women of his set—neither the proper society ladies he'd left behind in London, nor the hard-partying models and actresses he'd casually dated in New York.

Serena Lightfoot cared, passionately, and she wasn't afraid to show it. He had to admire the inner core of strength inside a person who hadn't allowed life, with all its troubles and woes, to train her out of exposing her feelings.

"No." Her voice was subdued, her whole manner a shadow of the exuberant vitality she'd displayed moments ago. "I don't mean to go on and on. It's just that public funding for libraries is at an all-time low, and I'm primed for any chance to climb up on my soapbox to convince people that they need to support us."

Leo's mind sharpened, honing in on the solution. Simple, elegant, easy—he couldn't believe he hadn't picked up on it when Serena perked up at the mere mention of the wealthy Harrington family. He was usually more perceptive than that—but then, he wasn't usually faced with a woman as thoroughly distracting as Serena Lightfoot.

"You're quite eloquent in your arguments," he said slowly, shrugging out his coat and draping it over the research desk.

"What are you doing?" Serena gazed down at his discarded coat in alarm. "You're not staying. I didn't agree to help you shirk your responsibility to your friend!"

The grain of truth in that assessment stung, but Leo pressed on. There was no help for it. As much as he might wish to be the sort of man who could cull through hundreds of poems to find the very best one to suit the nuptials of one of his closest friends, it wasn't to be.

Pulling out his very best seductive, sideways glance, Leo dropped his voice to a purr. "Oh, I think we can help one another."

Serena's eyes narrowed. "How?"

"You help me choose a poem to read at Miles Harrington's wedding, and I'll guarantee you a donation for the library."

She swallowed audibly, her attention caught and held by his proposition. "How . . . how much are we talking?"

Leo shrugged. "Enough to cover the library's expenses for the next fiscal year."

"Do you have any idea how much money that is?" Serena pushed back from the desk so she could leap to her feet and pace. "It's a huge amount. I couldn't take that full amount from a single donor; there are rules, regulations, our tax status. . . ."

She was trying to talk herself out of this deal. Leo set his jaw as determination flooded him. "The money means nothing to me," Leo said impatiently. "Come along, surely you realize we can work out the details."

Serena paused, her arms wrapped around her midsection, and stared at him in bewilderment. "Why is this so important to you? I can't be the only person on earth who could help you figure out what love poem to read."

Set back on his heels, Leo considered the question. She was perfectly correct. He had friends he could ask for help, he had a valet and a personal assistant whose job it was to help him with whatever he required—and, indeed, they'd been his first strategy until he'd walked past the library and decided to try there on a whim.

But now that he'd met Serena? He wanted her, and no one else.

"Perhaps." Leo shrugged, enjoying the way her eyes darkened as her gaze swept over his chest. "But perhaps the wedding reading is only part of my goal now."

Her brow furrowed, the space between those dark slashes of eyebrows crinkling adorably. "What's the rest of it?"

Leo grinned at the suspicion in her voice. He sauntered around the desk, carefully so as not to startle her with sudden movements, but she stood her ground. Even when she had to tilt her head back to be able to meet his eyes, she didn't retreat.

Lifting one hand to the side of her fair, smooth neck, Leo touched a tender fingertip to the throb of her pulse in the hollow of her throat. Her breath fluttered out, hitching appealingly, and Leo went hard in an aching rush that left him light-headed.

"If I have to find a love poem," he murmured, "I want you to be the one who reads them to me. I'm sure I could find, hire, or coerce someone else into doing this—but I want to spend more time with you, Serena Lightfoot. That's why this matters so much to me."

She opened her mouth—to object or argue some more, Leo didn't know. He didn't wait to find out, either. Instead, he bent his head and closed the distance between them, covering her delectable mouth in a soft, nuzzling exploration of a kiss.

Fireworks burst through the darkness of Serena's closed eyelids. Her eyes had snapped shut instinctively the instant Leo Strathairn's lips touched hers, and for a long, breathless moment, she couldn't process anything but the heat of him, the fresh, spicy taste of his kiss, the lean strength of his body braced above her.

The kiss started soft, but from one heartbeat to the next, hunger roared over them both and turned the kiss greedy and desperate. Serena's senses whirled dizzily, every ounce of her focused on the man she clutched in her arms, until the sudden shift of the rolling chair's wheels jerked her from her sensual daze.

Gasping for air, Serena dropped her hands from Leo's shoulders to push at his chest. It was like pushing at a granite wall. He resisted for a heartbeat, fire blazing in the depths of his molten silver eyes, but then he blinked and stepped back smoothly.

"My apologies." He ran a hand through his hair, disordering the already wildly tousled waves of auburn. "That was more . . . intense than I'd imagined."

Serena, whose lips were still tingling, cleared her throat. "Intense. That's a word for it."

He still loomed over her, his wide shoulders blotting out the fluorescent lights. She'd had her hands on that chest, Serena remembered dazedly. She'd felt the hard slabs of muscle, barely hinted at by his buttoned-up attire, and her active imagination easily provided a picture of what those glorious sculpted planes would look like naked. Serena swayed toward him for an instant before she caught herself.

Humor tugged at Leo's handsome mouth. "Does that answer your question about why I'm working so hard to secure your assistance?"

Not exactly, since Serena wasn't a stranger to the kind of arrangement where a man thought he could use her feelings to get what he wanted out of her. But as she gazed up at Leo's ruffled curls and the mischief twinkling in his eyes, Serena knew she was going to give in anyway.

She'd just have to make darned sure all she gave up was her time and her help with his task—and that if she gave Leo anything else, it was something she could afford to lose.

"All right." Decisive as always when she'd made up her mind, Serena checked the clock high on the wall and cursed inwardly. "I'm in, but I have a few conditions. Number one, I need more than just one mammoth donation—I need community support, and since you don't have any connection to this island, you can't give me that. But you can help me get what I need."

Interest kindled in his expression. "How so?"

Deep breath in. "Your friends, the Harringtons. They have island connections, own property here, and their support for the library would mean a lot to the people of the town. So, in return for helping you with your poetry needs, I'd like an invitation to the wedding and a chance to convince the Harringtons to sponsor the library."

"Why bother?" Leo arched a brow questioningly. "Not that I'm refusing, mind you—I'd be honored to have you as my date to the wedding. But I already told you I'd give you the money the library needs."

Serena lifted her chin. "That's my other condition. If you're going to give me money, there can't be any more kissing. I'm not comfortable with what it would say about me if I got involved with you personally in return for a donation."

Dismay clouded Leo's bright eyes, and he went all stiff

and British again. "I certainly never intended to imply anything of the sort."

"I know that," Serena said, although the fact that he said it, and seemed to mean it, made her insides feel fluttery and warm. "And that's only part of it, anyway—"

She brought herself up short, appalled at what she'd been about to tell him.

Leo frowned. "What's the other part?"

"Um, nothing," Serena hedged, sidling around him and out from behind the reference desk to start getting ready to open the library. "I just meant to say, I'll spend time with you, if that's what you really want—but I'm not promising to sleep with you. So if any part of your proposition was based on that, we might as well get that out in the open up front."

A funny look came over Leo's face as he watched her bustle around setting up a circle of child-sized plastic chairs. Serena kept an eye on him as she worked, trying hard not to hold her breath for his response. She couldn't make any guesses based on his expression, which seemed to slide from stunned to stimulated.

"I'm not looking for a guaranteed bed partner," he finally said, all but purring the words in a sleek, low voice that sent shivers to raise the hairs on the back of Serena's neck. "If you'll agree to spend time with me, that's all I ask. That—and the opportunity to change your mind."

Serena gulped in a choked breath as Leo rounded the corner of the desk, scooping up his coat and umbrella as he passed, and strolled toward her. "Change my mind?" she squeaked.

Desire flared molten hot in Leo's smoldering gaze, and Serena tried to steel herself to withstand another of those drugging kisses, but all he did was reach out and tuck one of her longer curls behind her ear. His fingertips skimmed the shell of her ear, lighting the sensitive nerve endings on fire.

Serena only realized she'd closed her eyes when his dark, delicious voice startled her into snapping them open.

"I'll give you access to the Harrington family and the other wealthy wedding attendees, and in return, you'll help me with my ceremonial reading . . . and you'll give me the chance to seduce you." He smiled down at her. "Do we have a deal?"

For the first time in her life, Serena thought she could sympathize with Dr. Faustus, making his foolish deal with the devil. When the devil was this appealing, what mere mortal could resist him?

Telling herself she could keep her end of the bargain without giving up more than she could afford to lose, Serena opened her mouth and sealed her fate.

"We have a deal."

Chapter Three

Leo climbed out of his classic 1937 Jaguar convertible wondering if he'd found the right place. Miles's fiancée, Greta Hackley, had looked a little surprised when he'd dropped by her hardware store to ask how to get to Honeysuckle Ridge, but the directions she'd provided had seemed straightforward.

Now, as Leo pocketed his keys and stared out over the expanse of sunlit hilltop, all he saw was a lookout point covered in tall grass that waved in the cold, steady breeze off the ocean. Loud honking overhead tugged his attention skyward just as a flock of snow geese flew by. From where he stood, he could see most of Sanctuary Island laid out at his feet. The salt marshes and small lakes spread up to the north, bordered by shell beaches and protected coves.

Standing there alone at the top of the island, Leo had a

brief, disorienting sense of being the only human being in the world.

Certainly, Serena Lightfoot was nowhere in sight. Leo grimaced and jingled his keys in his pocket as he debated retracing his path down the winding gravel road to the inhabited heart of the island. He thought he'd followed Greta's directions, but he had to admit he'd spent part of the drive distracted, mulling over Miles's parting shot back at the hardware store.

As Leo had pulled away from the curb, his friend had come to the door to see him off. "Heading out to meet a beautiful, single woman at one of the most scenic spots on the island? I have a feeling I know which of you boys is going to lose the bet first. You'll be in love before nightfall. She's a lucky girl."

Miles hadn't quite hidden his smirk behind the coffee mug he'd raised to his lips, and Leo knew he was only joking. The knowledge that Miles wasn't purposely trying to mock him gave Leo the ability to smirk back and say, "Isn't there a quaint American colloquialism about counting chickens?"

Laughing, Miles had waved him off and gone back inside to watch his fiancée work. And Leo drove away thinking about exactly how he knew he'd be winning this bet. After all, no matter what happened with Serena Lightfoot, no matter how much her mixture of intelligence, sensuality, and ambition called to him—their connection could never be more than skin deep.

There was no chance of developing a real relationship with someone who could never know the deepest truth about him.

He didn't want to contemplate just why the knowledge of his imminent win filled him with nothing more than grim resignation. It wasn't as if he'd ever wanted more than a few nights of passion with a woman before. At least he'd have easy access to the Billionaire Club and a lovely custom helicopter to console him when this affair was ended.

Leo sighed and plucked his cell phone from his inner jacket pocket. But just as he was about to take his chances with the cell signal gods and try to GPS his way to the actual place where Serena had asked to meet him, he heard the crunch of footsteps behind him.

"You made it!" Serena beamed at him, a little out of breath but stunningly gorgeous in cargo pants, hiking boots, and a tight, fleecy long-sleeved shirt with a short zipper that exposed the delicate wings of her collar bones. Wisps of hair curled free of her messy braid and her skin glowed from the exertion of hiking up the hill.

Leo raised his brows. "If you needed a ride, I could have swung by the library to pick you up."

Laughing, Serena shrugged off the straps of a full, heavy-looking backpack. "We have to take advantage of these unseasonably warm winter days, and plus, I needed the exercise. Reading to kids and reshelving books all day doesn't burn as many calories as you might think."

Leo's gaze traveled down the length of her slim legs, heat that had nothing to do with the sun simmering under his skin. "You look to be in quite good shape, from what I can see."

He wished he could tell if the rosy flush in Serena's cheeks was the result of her hike up the hill or the sensation of his eyes on her body. "Thanks," she said, ducking her head a little. The sweep of her dark lashes against the pink of her cheeks made her look like a china doll—but there was nothing delicate or fragile about the frank female interest sparkling in her eyes when she glanced up at him.

Brimming with optimism for his seduction's prospects, Leo gave her a slow, suggestive smile. "Not that I don't appreciate the view, but may I ask why we're meeting up here rather than in your library?"

"You said you're not a library person," Serena reminded him, setting her bulging backpack on the grass and kneeling to unroll a blanket that had been tied below the straps. "I thought maybe you'd appreciate the chance to spend a little time out and about in this 'golden jewel box of an island,' as you put it."

Leo gazed out across the salt marshes and maritime pines dappling Sanctuary Island. Salt-laden air caressed his cheeks, and the dazzling sunlight struck blinding flashes off the undulating waves. "This golden jewel box of an island," he murmured, thinking about the cold, drizzly, gray skies and green pastures of the island of his birth.

"Yeah." Serena spread the blanket over the grass and anchored down one corner with the backpack. "That phrase stuck in my head for some reason, so I tried looking it up. I thought it must be a line from poetry, but I couldn't find it anywhere."

Caught in the chilly memories of the home he'd left behind, Leo shrugged and thrust his hands into his pockets. "Not that I know of."

Serena hummed thoughtfully, pulling Leo's attention back from the hazy smudge of the mainland in the distance.

She'd plopped down on one side of the blanket, legs stuck straight out like a little girl's, the backpack cradled between her spread thighs.

Lucky backpack. Noticing the way Serena's slim hands caressed the worn canvas, Leo felt a distinct tightness in his perfectly tailored trousers. But her next words cooled his ardor considerably.

"So it's just something you came up with. Which means, basically—you're a poet."

The words were a slap to the face. Rousing from his reverie on Serena's hands, Leo snapped, "Certainly not. Trust me when I tell you, I'm no poet."

"Hmm. If you say so." Serena unzipped the backpack and pulled a stack of books out of it, leaning to deposit one or two at each corner of the blanket to weigh it down against the lively breeze off the water.

Before Leo could insist that he *did* say so, Serena went on. "I've got some good romantic poetry here, but I tried to include a variety of different kinds of books. Wedding readings don't have to be goopy, sappy, and trite, you know."

"I'm glad to hear it," Leo said awkwardly, still a little off balance. The very idea of himself as a poet, someone who spun images into words. . . . His gut clenched and he stared sightlessly at Serena's selection of books of varying lengths and sizes, bound in every color of the rainbow.

She eyed him, concern shadowing her dark gaze, and Leo carefully arranged his expression to show nothing but bland amusement.

"Great. Have a seat." Serena nodded at the empty spot on the other side of the blanket, a safe distance away from the temptation of her curvy little body. Leo assessed the situation with a tactical eye and chose, instead, to throw himself down directly beside her. He needed the distraction.

And besides, Leo had no interest in avoiding temptation. He intended to indulge. And if that involved tempting Serena, so much the better. Especially if it allowed him to direct the flow of events here so that the only one doing any reading was her.

He thought he could manage to sit through a few love poems, as long as they were read aloud in Serena Lightfoot's clear, bell-like voice.

Leaning back on his elbows, Leo crossed his legs and ankles and savored every point of contact between them. He was close enough to feel the brief shiver that ran through her, and he tilted his face up into the thin warmth of the winter sun with a smile pulling at his lips. "Go ahead, I'm listening."

Serena, who'd frozen when he lay down perpendicular to her with his head practically in her lap, unthawed enough to clear her throat. "You want me to read you some options aloud?"

Humming in agreement, Leo let his tense back and shoulder muscles melt into the blanket. This was the most relaxed he'd felt since Miles issued his reading challenge. He opened his eyes and cocked his head to watch Serena dither sweetly over which book to choose first. She finally plucked a blue hardcover with gold gilt lettering engraved on the front and tucked her finger into the pages where she'd marked her spot with a pink sticky tab. All the books she'd brought were bristling with sticky tabs, Leo realized, glancing around at the portable library scattered across the blankets.

"How much time did you spend culling through all these tomes for wedding readings?" he asked, warmed by more than the sun.

"Not that long," Serena said defensively, pushing her tortoiseshell glasses up her nose. "I had some ideas right off the bat, and there are online resources, wedding forums where people suggest readings, that type of thing. It was all very interesting. From a research perspective, obviously."

"Obviously," Leo agreed, enjoying every moment with her. "What was the most popular reading on your Internet forum?"

"Well, the favorite Bible verse is probably that one from Corinthians I: 'Love is patient, love is kind . . .' It's mentioned frequently enough to make it number one."

"Love beareth all things, believeth all things, hopeth all things, endureth all things," Leo quoted dreamily, the final words of the verse rising out of his memory with ease.

Serena caught her breath. "Yes. It sounds like you're familiar with that one—although what is that? The King James version?"

Leo shrugged, the movement hitching his shoulders up enough to pillow his head on Serena's khaki-clad thigh. Oh, that was lovely. "Good old Church of England. I won a prize for Scripture knowledge at school once, you know."

There was a slight pause, then Leo felt Serena relax under his head. Settling in happily, he kept his eyes closed to better focus on soaking up the heat of her body.

"If you have Bible verses like that one already memorized, surely there's something in there that will work," Serena pointed out.

"Undoubtedly," Leo said agreeably, cracking one eye

open to peer up at her inquisitively arched brows. "If only—that would have solved a lot of problems. But Greta and Miles—well, more precisely, Greta and her mother, want to choose the Bible readings. My job was specifically defined as coming up with a secular reading."

"Okay, well, I have a lot of options for us to explore here. Where do you want to start?"

Hurriedly shutting both eyes once more, Leo nestled his head against the smooth, firm muscle of her leg and inhaled the salt-sweet floral of her scent. "You choose. Surprise me."

"Okay. This is kind of fun." Some of the same passion Leo had admired the day before crept into Serena's tone. "I've got quite the range here, from Plato's *Symposium*— the bit about how the twin souls split apart, trying to find their way back together—to an excerpt from a Miss Manners essay on marriage, which is actually wonderful. She makes the point that it's unrealistic to expect to find one other person endlessly fascinating, forever and ever, but that the world around us *is* endlessly fascinating. So marriage should be about finding that one other person to walk through life and experience the world with."

"I like that. Lord knows, my parents could have benefited from that advice early on."

With studied nonchalance, Serena said, "Oh, you mean your father, the Earl of Rochester?"

It took everything Leo had in him to stay loose and pliant, sprawled across the blanket, rather than bolting up out of Serena's lap. "How did you—?"

"Hello? Research librarian?" He could hear the eye roll in her tone. "I looked it up. It's not exactly a secret, is it?"

"I suppose not." Leo grimaced. "Although part of the reason I moved to New York was to be amongst people who neither knew nor cared about my illustrious parentage."

"Sorry. I guess I shouldn't have brought it up, but I've never met a real live lord before."

"I'm not actually a lord. It's a courtesy title for a younger son. My brother will inherit my father's title. It's meaningless, in every sense of the word."

"That can't be true." Serena's finger hesitantly brushed at the tense spot between Leo's brows, smoothing away the frown he hadn't been aware of. "If it meant nothing, you wouldn't have had to leave England to escape it."

Leo tensed for a heartbeat, then breathed it out on a huffed laugh. Opening his eyes, he studied her face from this strange angle. "Perceptive as well as beautiful? I believe I may be heading for trouble."

This time, he was sure the pink that rose to her cheeks was all his own doing. "You're not in trouble," she said stoutly. "Because we're not kissing again. Remember?"

"I remember exactly what I agreed to in this deal, and never kissing you again was not part of it."

Black lashes fluttered down, veiling those extraordinarily dark, velvety brown eyes. "You know, your title and ancestry aren't the only things I found when I looked you up."

Turning his head to nuzzle his cheek into her leg, Leo flirted up at her with a smile. "No?"

She gazed down at him narrowly. "Leaving England didn't save you from the limelight, it seems. *Vanity Fair*, *Page Six*, *Town & Country* . . . There are photos of you at a different party with a different woman on every society page."

Leo shrugged, obscurely uncomfortable with the knowledge that Serena had seen those stupid pictures. "One wants to keep busy."

"You're a very busy bee, apparently."

Trying to analyze her expression, Leo pondered her words for a long moment before finally decided to try an unusual tack. "You're right. I've been with a lot of women. And I could lie and say I'm trying to follow your Miss Manners' advice, searching for that one special person to share my life with so I don't end up like my parents, who are so bored by one another they can't come up with enough conversation to carry them through breakfast."

Serena's fingers fluttered through his hair in a caress as light as if a butterfly had landed on his head. "But you won't lie to me."

There was a certainty in her tone, combined with soft, pleased wonder that gave Leo the uncomfortable sensation of wishing deeply to be the man Serena thought he was.

He could never be that man—he'd been lying to her since he met her—but he could be honest about this, at least. "The truth is, I like women. I like the way you smell, the way you walk, the softness of your skin and the sweetness of your smiles, and the lithe, unexpected strength of you. Every woman has her own individual beauty, and I consider it my privilege to discover and appreciate it."

Serena gazed down at him, her fast, light breaths moving her stomach against his cheek. The look on her face was easier to read, this time: lips parted, cheeks red, pupils blown wide. "So when you say you want me . . ."

"It's because you're beautiful. Unique. Unlike any other woman—and I've known my share."

"I feel as if I should be put off by that," Serena breathed, cupping his face with one ink-stained hand. "But no one has ever honestly wanted me just for my body before. It makes for a surprisingly nice change."

Chapter Four

"Not only for your body," Leo protested, his big shoulders shifting restlessly against her. "That makes me sound awfully frivolous and shallow. Which I am, of course—but I'd rather you didn't realize it."

Serena grinned down at him, not fooled in the slightest. She felt giddy with the sense of having uncovered a secret about Lord Leo Strathairn; one she'd bet his bevy of socialites and aspiring actresses didn't know.

He wasn't nearly as frivolous and shallow as he liked to pretend.

I like the way you smell, the way you walk, the softness of your skin and the sweetness of your smiles, and the lithe, unexpected strength of you.

Liquid heat pooled low in her belly and between her thighs at the memory of those words. He'd been talking about all women, but Serena had felt every word like a dart to the heart, piercing and perfect. How was she supposed to resist this man?

She'd been drawn to him before she ever even saw his face, and her only defense had been her determination not to fall for yet another guy who only wanted to use her for her brain.

With a few short sentences, Leo had convinced her he wasn't playing at desire. He'd been completely up front about his motives. He'd asked for her research help, and he'd made it clear that his ulterior motive was getting her into bed.

For someone who'd only ever experienced the reverse—being led on by someone who had no real interest in her while he mined what he actually wanted from her brain—there was something devastatingly appealing about Leo's honest lust.

In fact, the phrase "devastatingly appealing" applied to pretty much everything about Leo Strathairn.

Striving to remember that she'd known this man for about twenty-four hours and that she wasn't the kind of woman who had meaningless affairs, Serena put on her best stern expression. It was the one she used when trying to get the four-year-old reading group to settle down and stay in their seats—and it was about as effective on Leo as it was on them. So basically, not at all.

His unrepentant grin and the mischief glinting in his bright eyes made him look boyish and carefree. Smothering the sudden urge to lean down and nibble that wide smile, Serena said, "We have a job to do, Mr. Frivolous. Unless you want to stand up there in front of all those wedding guests with nothing to read."

With a powerful twist of his broad shoulders, Leo settled more comfortably against her and closed his eyes once more. "I'm at your mercy. Do your worst."

Serena laughed. "Just for that, I should read you this passage I marked from *So Long, and Thanks for All the Fish*."

"Like the song in that movie about the hitchhiker and the galaxy?" he asked lazily.

Serena cocked her head and stared down at him, taken aback. "Like the Douglas Adams book the movie was partially based on," she said slowly. "One of the funniest science fiction writers of all time. Have you really never heard of him? He's British!"

Something flashed through Leo's eyes, gone so quickly Serena couldn't be sure she'd seen it at all. "I know the U.K. is smaller than the U.S., but it's a much larger island than this one. We don't actually all know one another."

"No, I realize that, I just . . ." Serena shook her head. "Not important. This passage is probably a little too out there for Miles and Greta anyway, but I do love it. There's a part at the end, where the hero, Arthur, has this long silence with a woman he barely knows, and instead of getting awkward and weird, they share a true, intimate moment. It always makes me think of how hard most people find it to be silent together."

He hummed thoughtfully. "I know what you mean. I'm quite guilty of that, I think—I have a tendency to want to break the silence, fill it up with noise."

"Well." Serena paused, unsure how personal to get. "It sounds to me like the silence you grew up with between your parents could easily have made you distrustful of what hides underneath the silence."

Leo's body turned to stone against her, his handsome

face cast in rigid lines like a marble statue. But before Serena's apology for her inappropriate presumption could rush out of her mouth, Leo shuddered and turned over to lie on his front.

Sliding one arm beneath Serena's thighs, he pressed his face to her stomach. His breath was hot and moist through the fleece of her sweatshirt, tickling the sensitive skin and stealing Serena's breath.

"You're a wonder," he mouthed against her belly, the words the barest whisper of sound. "How do you understand so much about me?"

Serena gave in to the impulse to thread her fingers into his tousled auburn curls and cup the nape of his neck, cradling him to her. "I got lost in the psychology section of the library last month. Couldn't help picking up a few things."

"It's not entirely comfortable for me," Leo admitted, his arms tightening minutely around her. "I'm not used to being seen through. Am I truly so transparent?"

The genuine worry in his tone had Serena frowning. "Why does it matter? I already know you want to sleep with me, and that you're not sticking around Sanctuary Island past the wedding. You've been totally up front that you want an island fling, and you want it with me. You're smart enough to realize I'm actually considering it. So what is there left to hide?"

Tension uncoiled from his shoulders in the instant before Leo got his knees under him and sat up, pulling Serena into his lap as if she weighed nothing. He gathered her in close to his chest and her arms went instinctively around his neck like a bride about to be carried over the threshold.

"You're considering it, are you?"

The deep rumbling purr of his voice shivered through her, that accent making her go all loose and trembly. His hard chest flexed against the taut, aching points of her breasts. Serena gasped and pressed tighter, blood pounding so heavily that each heartbeat shook her in the frame of his embrace.

Sucking in oxygen to try and clear her head, Serena struggled to pull back long enough to study his face. She wanted to try and read whatever secret he was holding back, but when her eyes met his, all she could see was the depth of his hunger.

Dark and fathomless as the ocean, Leo's need for her was real and undeniable. Whatever else she didn't know about this man, she knew that. And for Serena, whose experiences had taught her over and over that her only value was locked inside her brain, it was intoxicating to know that Leo Strathairn truly wanted her—all of her.

Yes, she was a smart, capable person, a dedicated librarian who valued intellectual work and lived a lot of her life between the pages of books. But when Leo looked at her like that, Serena felt her neglected body wake up and turn to him like a flower turning toward the sun—because she was more than her mind. She was flesh and blood, too.

Make that tingling flesh and hot, pounding blood.

As Serena's gaze dropped to Leo's mouth, she realized that this was her chance to find out what all those poets and playwrights and authors were writing about. With Leo, she could experience true passion, mutual and satisfying—even if fleeting.

If she passed up this chance, she'd never forgive herself.

"Actually," she said, unable to believe that husky, sexy voice was coming from her own throat, "I'm done considering."

Leo's large hands clenched in the cotton of the T-shirt covering her shoulder blades. "Oh?"

Serena nodded, their faces so close that their noses brushed, and she had to glance back and forth between his eyes to keep from going cross-eyed. "I'm ready to make a decision. And what I've decided is to not let you seduce me."

Disappointment tightened Leo's features, holding him rigid for a moment before he reluctantly began to release her. The moment he'd loosened his hold, Serena took a fortifying breath and shoved at his chest with all her might.

Leo went down on the blanket with a soft *oof*, and Serena scrambled up to straddle his trim waist. Clamping her thighs against abdominal muscles strung tight with surprise, Serena bent over him and smiled into his wide, shocked eyes.

Flushed warm with victory and anticipation, Serena squirmed against Leo's hardness and savored the pure pleasure that rocketed through her.

"I've decided to seduce you, instead," she told him. "It's my first seduction attempt. How'm I doing so far?"

Leo clasped his hands on the subtle roundness of Serena's hips and fought the urge to thrust against her softness. If this was truly her first seduction, he didn't want to do anything to startle her into drawing back.

"Very impressive," he told her, pleased that the strain he was under barely showed in his tone. "High degree of difficulty in executing your first maneuver. Full marks from the U.K. judge."

"But now that I have you where I want you, what am I going to do with you?"

Loving the playfulness, Leo grinned up at his amateur seductress and moved his hands from her hips to lace them behind his head. "Whatever you like, love. Consider me utterly and completely seduced."

Serena's smile went from naughty to uncertain, her hands on his chest lifting to hover tentatively above the fine Oxford cloth of his shirt. In protest, Leo curled his hips upward in an unmistakably suggestive move that stoked the heat of his passion to a burning flame.

He growled a little at the crush of his most sensitive bits against the yielding globes of her perfect backside, but Serena's loud moan drowned him out. Her thighs tightened as she rode back against his thrusts, and her hands clamped down on his shoulders for leverage.

She leaned to kiss him, her succulent mouth voracious and bold, without a hint of shyness or hesitance, and Leo understood. Serena would meet heat with heat, she would keep pace with his every passionate impulse, but she went cold at the first hint of his indifference.

As if he could ever truly be indifferent to Serena. But if even playing at it in order to let her take control made her feel unwanted, Leo had the perfect solution.

Tensing his abs, he surged upward to capture her pretty, elfin face between the palms of his hands. And because Leo had always appreciated knowing exactly where he stood, he said, "I want you."

The click of her throat as she swallowed was audible

even over the rush of the waves hitting the rocks below. She shuddered against him as if overcome by the simple statement of desire—or maybe by the incontrovertible evidence of Leo's desire, which she could now surely feel notched thick and heavy between her thighs.

"Take me, then," she whispered, her breath brushing sweetly at his lips before she tucked her face into his neck and locked her legs around his hips. "Show me what it's like to be wanted."

Leo crushed her close and bore her back onto the blanket, covering her with his body. But before the tide of hunger crashed over them both, he had just enough awareness for a flicker of curiosity: Was he truly the first man ever to make Serena Lightfoot feel desired?

Chapter Five

"Whew." Serena stared up at the blue brilliance of the afternoon sky through the stark, bare branches and savored every new ache and sore muscle. "So that's what all the fuss is about. I think I finally get it."

The warm rumble of Leo's laugh vibrated through her ribcage where they were still pressed together in a damp, sweaty, sated mess, wrapped cozily in the blanket. "Glad to be of service in your pursuit of knowledge."

Even though Serena knew he didn't mean anything by it, the comment hit a little too close to the tender bruise of her worst memories. She frowned and pulled away, shivering as the sea breeze chilled her overheated skin. "Don't say it like that. I wasn't just using you."

She could practically hear the way Leo's eyebrows shot upwards in surprise. "I certainly didn't mean to imply that. Nothing could be further from my mind, love."

"Of course." Serena could kick herself for saying any-thing. "Sorry, ignore me."

"Ah, but that's one thing I can never promise to do." Leo hitched himself over onto his side, and she felt his eyes on her while she patted around outside the blanket for her hastily discarded clothes. "What are you doing? Come back here."

Glancing over her shoulder, Serena caught her breath at the heady temptation of his perfect, leanly muscled form basking unashamedly in the dappled sunlight. She swal-lowed down the lump of emotion in her throat. "Don't you want to get back to the task at hand? We only have a few weeks to come up with your reading for the wedding."

"Sod the wedding," Leo growled, and Serena made an embarrassingly high-pitched noise as she was pounced from behind. The clothes she'd gathered went flying in all directions. "What's wrong?"

Apparently a single afternoon was enough to condition Serena's body to respond to Leo's. She arched under him instinctively, his bare chest searing into her back. Moan-ing low in her throat, Serena settled with Leo draped over her like a particularly hot, hard-muscled throw rug.

Even so soon after being turned inside out and left panting, Leo's closeness still had the power to shorten her breath. But the way his body bracketed hers also felt inti-mate and safe, almost protective. Somehow, it was easier to talk like this than face-to-face and fully clothed.

"Nothing is wrong," she promised him, hearing the thickness in her own voice. "Absolutely nothing, for once. You told me from the beginning that you wanted me, and I was able to believe you because why else would

you come up with such a flimsy pretext to spend time
with me?"

Pressed so tightly together, Serena felt the instant Leo
went stiff and wary, and she hastened to clarify. "I'm not
complaining! It's one of the sweetest things anyone has
ever done for me, actually. In my experience, it's usually
the exact opposite."

"I don't follow."

Serena cleared her throat. "Well, as it happens, I was at
the top of my class all through school. Let's just say there
was more than one football player who realized if he
smiled at me in the cafeteria, I'd fall all over myself to help
him with his homework—which usually translated to me
doing his homework for him. Until he passed that class and
dropped me like a bad habit."

She could hear the thunderous frown in Leo's voice.
"And this happened more than once?"

"For a supposedly smart person, it took me a ridicu-
lously long time to recognize the pattern."

There was a moment of heavy, charged silence broken
only by the cries of gulls circling overhead. Then Leo said,
very calmly, "I should like the name of every single callow
youth who used you that way. In alphabetical order, please,
to make it easier for me to track them down and destroy
them."

Serena laughed, even as Leo's staunch support warmed
her chest. "Oh, leave them alone. I console myself by imag-
ining them all pumping gas and collecting garbage for a
living. Staying stupid and ignorant forever is its own punishment, right?"

Leo hummed and stroked a contemplative hand down

her side, fingers pressing just firmly enough not to tickle. "You don't want revenge, even though these idiot boys clearly left you with an inability to believe in your obvious beauty and desirability."

"Well, they taught me the first lesson," Serena admitted, tilting her head until the blanket almost muffled her voice. "But grad school was where I earned my advance degree in romantic idiocy, as well as library science."

Pressing a kiss to the sensitive skin behind her ear, Leo murmured, "Tell me."

She couldn't resist the tender demand. Serena rolled her tense shoulders slightly, loving the way his arms tightened around her in response. As safe and secure as she'd ever felt in her life, she told him the story she hadn't told anyone in years.

"I didn't originally plan to be a librarian," she confessed. "It's funny how life turns out—I can't imagine being anything else, now. But when I started grad school, I thought I wanted to be a professor of library science. I did a ton of work and research developing a new reference system—it was an independent study I hoped to turn in as my dissertation."

"So what happened?"

This was the part that made Serena want to squirm with remembered humiliation. "The man I was dating advised me not to publish my work. He convinced me I'd be better off sticking it under my bed and refocusing my credits toward a degree in librarianship. Which is what I did."

"Why on earth did you listen to him?"

"Well, he was an expert in the field. In fact"—Serena squeezed her eyes right against the memory of Dr. Saul Obinger's kind, patient smile—"he was my dissertation advisor. So I sort of had to follow his advice. At least, he presented it that way when he explained why he needed to step down as my advisor before we could be together. At the time, I found it wildly romantic. It was intoxicating to imagine that this renowned, distinguished Ph.D. would want me enough to jeopardize his career by sleeping with me. Even after he stopped being my official advisor, he could've gotten in trouble for dating a student—although the rules are different for graduate students."

"But he wasn't jeopardizing his career," Leo guessed darkly. "Was he?"

Serena heaved in a deep breath, mostly to feel the comforting weight of Leo's torso anchoring her to the ground. "No. He was laying the groundwork to take my research and claim it as his own. He's the chair of the department now, well on his way to tenure . . . and I'm a librarian on an island so small it can barely support the public school, much less the library."

The world dipped and swayed around her as Leo curled his arms under her legs and shoulders to flip her up and into his lap. Serena's heart thundered against her ribs, dizziness forcing her to clutch at Leo's neck for balance. Even with all the brainless jocks who'd pretended to be interested in her in high school, she'd never been manhandled so casually before. Maybe it lost her some feminist cred, but she admitted privately that part of her loved knowing that Leo was strong enough to lift and cradle her effortlessly.

Cupping the nape of her neck in his large palm, Leo stared straight into her eyes. "You deserved better, Serena. I'm sorry."

The strain in his voice magically eased the strain

around Serena's heart from sharing such an embarrassing, emotionally scarring experience. "You don't have to apologize," she told him, framing his handsome, aristocratic face between her hands. "I'd given up on ever being truly desired until you came along."

If Leo were a better man, he'd probably have regrets about tumbling his sweet librarian—but luckily he was a scoundrel and always had been. With Serena warm and responsive in his arms, he couldn't find it in himself to regret a moment of their time together.

Regret, however, wasn't quite the same as guilt. And after hearing her tale of humiliation and betrayal at the hands of men who'd had ulterior motives for pursuing her, guilt burned at the lining of Leo's stomach. As much as he hated, instantly and unquestioningly, every man who had burned that shame into Serena's voice, Leo had to ask himself: Was he truly any different?

"You are perhaps the first woman I've met who wanted to be desired for her body rather than her mind," he observed lightly.

Serena laughed. "I know, it's kind of backwards. But it's not really about mind versus body. I'd hate it just as much if someone pretended to be interested in my research skills just so they could get in my pants. It's more about knowing that everything you want from me is on the table. Your ulterior motives are not ulterior! You told me from the first that you wanted to sleep with me. I like that. I've had enough of men hiding their true motives from me."

Leo suppressed a wince by running his fingers through the silky tendrils of her bright golden hair. "Ought we to think about getting dressed? I'm enjoying being the only man to get into your pants at the moment, and if someone else were to see you in the glorious altogether, I'd probably have to fight them off. Which I'm willing to do, obviously. But it seems a waste of time better spent in more pleasurable pursuits."

"I love the way you talk. Have you honestly never thought of writing your own poems?" Serena lifted herself off his lap, bracing herself on his shoulders for balance.

This again. Leo let her go reluctantly, his fingertips skimming the bare silk of her tanned skin and memorizing the texture in case he never got the chance to touch her again. "No," he said, more roughly than he intended. "I believe I can safely promise never to write a single line of verse."

Startled by his gruff vehemence, Serena glanced over at him as she rifled through the small pile of clothing. "What are you getting so mad about? It's hardly offensive to say you have a way with words."

She couldn't know how near she'd come to the scars at the center of Leo's psyche. Heart pounding, stomach roiling, he said, "It's not a compliment, either. At least, not one that I deserve."

Smiling uncertainly, Serena said, "Ah. Because everyone in England talks like you, right? Do they teach you that at Oxford?"

"Being an earl's son carries one quite far," Leo replied, glad of the topic change. His gaze snagged on the reverse strip tease happening before him as Serena shimmied her hips into her cargo pants. "But not all the way to Oxford, I'm afraid."

"Cambridge, then."

The way she cupped her breasts and jiggled to seat them properly inside the stretchy cotton of her bra made Leo's blood heat. "No, not Cambridge either."

She frowned. "Then where did you go to college? Or university, I guess y'all call it?"

Snapping to attention, Leo realized the danger too late. There was nothing for it but to tell the truth and try to brush it off. "I didn't. After I scraped through at boarding school, I never saw the point in further education."

"You never saw the point?" Serena's arms dropped before she could manage to get her shirt over her head. Standing above him half nude and wholly appealing, she blinked in dismay.

Leo reclined on the blanket, deliberately lazy, and shrugged. "My elder brother will inherit the earldom and all of its responsibilities. All that's left to me is to enjoy life and stay out of any terribly public trouble."

"Huh." Serena hid her expression by pulling on her shirt. "I don't mean to sound judgmental about your life choices, but that sounds a little . . . empty."

You have no idea, Leo thought bleakly, but when her tousled head popped out of the collar of her shirt, he made sure his expression reflected the sardonic amusement he used as armor. "Not at all. Life without expectations is very freeing."

"No one ever expected anything of you?" Serena's curious question was delivered gently, more of a tickle than a slap, but somehow it still stung Leo into sitting up and reaching for his pants.

"Perhaps, when I was quite young." He shrugged into his shirt and did up the buttons, idly noting the creases in the fine linen fabric. "But our mother died when I was only a little chap, and soon after that, my father gave up on me completely in favor of devoting all his time and attention to my elder brother, William."

Serena frowned sympathetically. "That's awful!"

"Not at all." Leo shook out his trousers and stepped into them, hitching the charcoal gray up his thighs. "Father was no fool. His every hope for the future of the family rests on William—it's only sensible that he should spend his parental efforts there, rather than wasting them on . . ."

A blinking idiot of a boy, too stupid even to learn to read.

Swallowing down the bitter memories, Leo flashed his most rakish grin and bowed from the waist with a flourish. "On a scoundrel and wastrel like me."

And that was true as well, because once Leo had gotten over being angry with his father, the world, and himself, he'd dedicated his life to not caring about anything. Which was harder than it sounded. Without meaning to, he'd made friends—Miles Harrington, Zane Bishop, and Cooper Haynes chief among them—and they had opened a tiny crack in the wall encircling Leo's heart.

Serena grinned, although there was a searching light in her black coffee eyes that made him nervous. "Come on, scoundrel. Let's get back to work. I'm determined to find the very best reading possible for Sanctuary Island's wedding of the century."

She curled up in the center of the blanket and immediately became absorbed in stacking her books in some sort of order that made sense only to her. When Leo sat next to her, though, she reached out at once to pull him closer.

Hooking his chin over her shoulder and curving his arms around her waist, Leo breathed in her scent of ink, paper, and book dust. Serena plucked the top book from her stack and started to read aloud, the gentle cadence of her voice washing over him like a song he could only hope would get stuck in his head.

And as they enjoyed the fading warmth of a bright winter's day and the freshness of a salty ocean breeze, Leo started to fear that the crack his friends had made in his armor was splitting open wider and wider . . . wide enough for pixie-like Serena Lightfoot and her passion for books to slip through.

Chapter Six

Over the next weeks, Leo spent his days exploring the island with Cooper, discussing the reception plans with Zane, and reassuring Miles and Greta that said reception wouldn't break any laws of God or man. And he spent his evenings, after the library closed, with Serena.

Not for the first time, he was glad he'd insisted on staying on at the Fireside Inn even when Cooper and Zane had succumbed to Greta's request that they move their things to the Harrington family home on Sanctuary Island.

After that first day up on Honeysuckle Ridge, Leo was determined to keep this affair dabbling happily in shallow waters. Leave the deep stuff to his friends; let them lose Miles's bet along with their hearts and their freedom. Leo had a good thing going with Serena, the perfect woman, who asked nothing of Leo except his desire.

Desire was something he could give her, freely and without hesitation. In fact, he was honest enough with himself to admit that he couldn't stop it now if he wanted to. His desire for Serena was almost a physical need. It was difficult to wait through the long hours of her work day at the library for the moment when she would emerge from the brick building and lock the heavy door behind her.

Leo made sure he was waiting at the foot of the library's front steps for her every day, with a smile and a kiss that communicated the hunger he'd stored up over their hours apart. And he was equally sure to resist her invitations back to her small cottage overlooking the beach.

Even though it meant a long, cold ferry ride back to Winter Harbor on the mainland, Leo preferred to conduct their liaisons at the picturesque Fireside Inn. Not only because it was shockingly romantic, with its comfortably appointed rooms and friendly, yet polished service, but because he had the sense that going to Serena's house would be too intimate. More like a real relationship—and that was a step he couldn't allow himself to take.

Besides, he reasoned as he stretched his long legs out toward the grate, Serena's beach cottage probably didn't have a rollicking huge fireplace like the one that dominated the Fireside Inn's main sitting room.

"Sitting here makes me glad the weather finally started turning wintry," Serena murmured drowsily, smudging the words against his shoulder as he cuddled her closer to his side. "A little chill in the air makes a roaring fire feel so good."

Pressing his lips to the golden curls crowning Serena's head, Leo darted a glance at the darkened front hallway. The innkeeper had gone up to bed an hour ago, dimming the lights with a knowing smile and silently leaving her guests to enjoy each other by the flickering firelight.

"What books did you bring for us tonight?" Leo asked, curious as ever about the bulging knapsack at Serena's feet. In between bouts of very pleasant distraction over the past days, they'd explored wedding benedictions, sonnets, quotes from defunct space cowboy TV shows, and nineteenth-century gothic romances.

"More poetry." Serena straightened, perking up at the mention of her beloved books.

Leo let her go without protest, even though the absence of her lithe, warm body against his side left him chilled. As much as he enjoyed discovering the abundant joys of Serena's sensually responsive body, he'd come to treasure these moments almost as much. Fully clothed, in no way improper—after all, reading aloud was a favorite drawing room activity of the staid Victorians—and yet he knew Serena more intimately through the passages and pieces she'd chosen to read him than he did through the careful removal of each article of clothing.

Serena Lightfoot was unlike any woman he'd ever known—unabashedly romantic, but in a quirky, offbeat way that made him smile rather than roll his eyes at the sentiment.

"More poetry, hmm? It's going to have to be quite something to compete with that one about how falling in love is like owning a dog."

Her eyes lit up, sparkling in the firelight. "I knew you'd like that poem! See, you always think I'm crazy at first, but I've got the goods. Admit it."

"Freely and unreservedly." Leo stretched his arms along the back of the sofa and crossed one ankle over the opposite knee. "I honestly never knew that expressions of sentiment—love—could be so . . ."

"What?"

He struggled to find the word he wanted. "Humorous. Playful?"

"Joyful," Serena suggested, voice low and happy.

Leo nodded, and Serena clasped the book in her hands to her chest in a paroxysm of unselfconscious pleasure. "You totally get it. I love that you get it!"

You get me, she didn't say. But Leo heard it all the same, and a pang shot through his chest like an arrow.

Uncomfortably aware that he hadn't been nearly as open with Serena as she'd been with him, Leo felt a deep-seated need to redress that imbalance in some small way. "In my house, growing up, 'love' was not a word one heard. Or spoke. I suppose I learned to think of it as a weakness."

"Your parents never told you they loved you?" Serena was aghast, eyes wide and dark.

Deeply uncomfortable, Leo stared into the glowing embers of the fire and shrugged. "Please. There's no need for the Oxfam eyes and trembling lips. I was hardly abused. In fact, I was given every advantage, everything I could possibly ask for."

"Exactly," Serena pointed out, pulling one leg up onto the sofa so she could face him directly. "Your parents gave you every *thing* you wanted—but not what you truly needed."

Leo pulled his well-worn mask of sardonic amusement over his face. "I assure you, what you call 'love' is not necessary for survival."

"Yes, it is."

The intensity in Serena's voice forced Leo to meet her laser-focused gaze. Still dazzled from staring into the fire for so long, Leo blinked away the dark stars exploding around Serena's head. She almost seemed to glow in the dimly lit room, a lantern to light his way.

Leo shook off the fanciful thought. "I don't even know what that means. How can you say that? How can you even believe in love, after everything that's happened to you?"

"First of all, because I've felt it."

Leo felt his upper lip curl into a snarl at the thought of Serena having real feelings of love for any of the men who'd used and discarded her, but she shook her head.

"There are lots of different kinds of love," she reminded him. "I love my parents, and they love me back—almost too much, sometimes! But I'd take my mother's nosiness into every aspect of my life and my father's constant offers to pay for plane tickets home over the alternative. At least I grew up knowing I was loved. Oh, I hope I never meet your father. I'd want to slap him silly for not telling you, every single day, how amazing and special and loveable you are."

Leo stared at the passion lighting Serena's elfin features. "I've only seen you like this when talking about your library and how important it is to the community. And your books."

A hot pink blush stained her cheeks, but Serena didn't back down. If anything, she became more impassioned. "And that's another thing! I know love is real because all those writers and poets can't be wrong. When I read about two people falling love, the truth of that resonates inside me—even if I haven't experienced that kind of romantic love personally. I know it exists. You have to know it, too. Haven't you been listening to the things we've read this week?"

Serena brandished the book she'd been holding, and it

fell open. She scanned a couple of lines quickly, her breath fast and light. "I mean, come on. Look at this."

Hooking her finger into the spine to hold the place, she turned the spread pages to face Leo. His gaze snapped from the incomprehensible jumble of black letters floating around the page to Serena's pleading expression. His heart jumped into his throat and expanded, choking him.

It was his worst nightmare, come to life. He couldn't move, couldn't make a sound. The silence stretched horribly.

"I'm serious," Serena insisted, shoving the book closer to him. "Read this line! Right here. How can you read this and not believe in love?"

Serena waited impatiently for Leo's silvery gray eyes to dart across the immortal e.e. cummings poem, already savoring the sound of his deep cultured tones smoothly telling her he carried her heart within his heart.

After knowing Leo for only a handful of days, it was ridiculous how much she longed to hear him say those words to her, even if he were only speaking the words of a long-dead poet, not making a declaration of his own. Everything inside Serena rebelled at the way Leo was dismissing the entire concept of love. She had to hear him take it back.

But he didn't. He didn't say anything. After a single, agonized glance, he didn't even look at the book in her hands. Frustrated, Serena shook the book until the pages rustled. "Hello? Anyone in there?"

When he finally spoke, his voice was as rusty as the inside of an antique watering can. "I don't know what you want from me."

I want to know I'm not alone with all these feelings and desires, Serena wanted to cry. *I want to know you're falling, too.*

Gathering her composure, she gently laid the open book in Leo's lap. "I want to hear you read that poem. Not even the whole thing, just the last stanza—and then tell me you don't have a clue what the poet is talking about."

If Leo could do that, if he could honestly look her in the eye and deny the existence of love when it stared him in the face, Serena might stand a chance at being cured of this doomed infatuation.

Leo flexed one strong, long-fingered hand before resting it on the open page. She heard the dry harsh rasp of his breath, even over the crackle and whoosh of the flames in the hearth. Bending over the book, Leo stared down at the poem for an endless moment, lips moving silently. Serena waited, pulse fluttering, for Leo to start reading.

Suspended in breathless anticipation, Serena wasn't prepared for the shock of Leo standing up from the couch in a rush of contained power. The book slid from his lap to the floor with a bang that made Serena wince for the state of the cover, but she couldn't take her eyes off Leo to check it.

He strode stiff-legged to the mantel and gripped it with white-knuckled hands. Every line of Leo's body thrummed with tension like a plucked violin string as he leaned forward to stare into the roaring fire. "I can't do what you want," he rasped, low and halting.

Disappointment lanced through her. "What? You can't tell me love exists because you still don't believe in it? Even after all the things we've read together, all the time we've spent together . . ."

Even after making me fall for you?

"No." Leo straightened and faced her with the posture of a man facing down a firing squad. "I mean, I can't read the poem aloud."

Still battling her own disappointment, Serena arched a mocking brow. "If you have such bad stage fright you can't read aloud to me in an empty room, how are you going to get up in front of a church full of people and do a wedding reading?"

"For God's sake," Leo burst out, stroking a hand through his hair and clenching until the muscles stood out in his forearm. "I don't have a problem with stage fright. I have a problem with reading. As in, I never learnt."

Despite herself, Serena's jaw dropped open. "What, at all? But you went to fancy British schools!"

"Fancy schools that owed a lot to my father's generous donations." Leo shrugged tightly, directing his stare to the side.

Unable to believe what she was hearing, Serena shook her head as she stumbled up from the couch. Her watery knees threatened not to hold her up under the tidal wave of realization crashing over her head.

Not again, was all she could think, but it *was* happening again.

"You lied to me," she said through numb lips, staring at the marble-cold profile of the man she'd come so close to giving her heart to.

"Because I was embarrassed," Leo said, still not even bothering to look at her. He shrugged, sending shadows dancing along the walls. "It's not the kind of thing a man likes to admit to. Being so thick, the best teachers in England couldn't knock reading into his skull."

"I don't understand. How did you memorize so many quotes?"

A pained expression tightened the corners of Leo's downturned eyes. "Ever notice I mostly quote from plays? I found recordings, watched videos, that kind of thing. For the rest . . ."

He paused, and a chill pooled in Serena's belly. She shook her head. "You couldn't have gotten through the English curriculum at your fancy English prep school without help."

A muscle ticked in Leo's jaw. "I did have help. I hid my problems from the masters, but some of the other pupils . . ."

Serena's heart froze. She knew the truth without needing to hear him say it. "You got girls to help you. Sweet, nerdy girls like me."

"I'm not proud of it," he growled. "But I couldn't go to the teachers, because they would have informed my parents. My father—"

But Serena could barely hear a word he said over the sound of betrayal wailing in her ears. "You're just like all the rest of them. Like every other man I've ever known."

He finally swiveled his head to pierce her with the silvery brilliance of his eyes. "No. That's not true," Leo said, taking an urgent step toward her.

Throwing up a hand between them, Serena halted his progress. She couldn't bear it if he touched her, that smooth, practiced, lying touch that had made her feel so beautiful and desired, when the whole time . . . "You said you wanted me. But all along, what you really wanted was—"

She broke off, heart hammering and mouth dry, unable

to believe that after all her caution, all the lessons she'd learned at such a painful cost, she had managed to fall into the same old trap.

Humiliation scorched up her neck and face, and abruptly, Serena needed to get out of the warm, cozy little room and away from the Fireside Inn. She needed the fresh, cold air against her cheeks as the ferry sped her back to Sanctuary Island. She needed to be alone.

Alone was safe. From now on, she'd remember that.

"Wait, Serena. I can explain. When I left school, I left all that behind me. But this wedding reading thing brought it all up again, like breaking open a wound that never really healed, and I couldn't stand to let Miles down. I couldn't stand to tell him the truth."

"You didn't want your friends to find out you can't read. So you used me."

"I didn't use you, love. I needed your help and I asked for it. I even offered to compensate you for it with a generous donation for that library which is so dear to you."

"I see," Serena said stiffly, wrapping her arms around herself. She felt chilled despite the roaring fireplace. "So what now? You'll pick out one of my selections, memorize it for the wedding, and then be off to New York again to take up with a new socialite?"

"Well . . ." He ran a hand through his hair, tousling it wildly. "Yes, I suppose that was the plan, though you make it sound awfully seedy. Please know that I truly appreciate the help you've given me, and the time we shared."

It shouldn't have changed anything. She'd known from the start that Leo Strathairn wasn't the kind of man she could keep, the kind of man who would stay by her side and experience the joys and sorrows of life with her. But now, on the heels of finding out he'd been lying—or at least omitting the truth—since she met him, Serena reached her limit.

Grabbing her coat and hat from the rack by the inn door, Serena wound her scarf around her neck without meeting Leo's gaze. "I have to go."

And then he was right next to her, his tightly muscled body crowding her against the door for a hot, thrilling moment before Serena could stomp down on her body's stupid, instinctive reaction. She shoved past him and out into the cold, ignoring the strain in his voice as he called her name again.

Running flat out in the direction of the marina, the pounding of her boots against the pavement echoed through the emptiness Leo's words left behind. Every gasp of frozen air was a knife in her lungs, but she hardly felt the pain.

All she felt was grief at the death of a dream she'd only dared to hold for such a short time. For the disappearance of the person she'd believed Leo to be. For the bright, happy, loving future she'd never get to taste.

That future was never yours to begin with, she reminded herself savagely as the lights of the harbor twinkled into view. *Love, passion, an honest relationship—those things aren't for you. How many times do you have to be slapped down before you stop trying to reach for them?*

Panting, thighs shaking and feet aching, Serena skidded down the dock toward the waiting ferry. All but throwing money at the surprised ferry operator's face, she hauled herself up the gangplank and headed for the spiral stairs to the top deck.

. "It'll be freezing up there," the grizzled old man warned. "You'll catch your death of darned foolishness."

Serena tuned him out and climbed the stairs. She needed to feel the wind on her cheeks—and at this temperature, it was a good bet she'd be the only passenger on the exposed deck. A quick glance around the empty bench seats showed she was right. Tossing herself down on a bench that faced out toward the open water—toward home—Serena finally let herself catch her breath.

Staring up at the matte velvet sky as snowflakes began to swirl down and dust the empty seats around her, Serena made herself a solemn promise.

This was the last time. Never again.

Chapter Seven

"You look like hell." Miles slid into the straight-backed chair across from Leo, his appraising stare never leaving the younger man's face.

Leo suppressed a grimace. He could well imagine the story his face was telling his perceptive, eagle-eyed friend. "Bad night."

"You Brits have such a way with understatement." The wry grin that touched Miles's mouth didn't hide the concern in his deep blue eyes. "What's up? How can I help?"

A lump of emotion knotted itself around Leo's vocal cords. The unconditional, unquestioning support he got from Miles and his other friends from the club was a wholly new experience for Leo. Just as when Miles had insisted on taking his new speedboat over to Winter Harbor when Leo called earlier, Leo wasn't entirely sure how to respond to the friendly consideration.

Unsticking his tongue from the roof of his mouth he said, "It's not a huge problem. At least, I don't think it is."

Surely if he told Miles the truth, Miles wouldn't shun him. Miles wouldn't jump up from the card table and run out of the Fireside Inn's sitting room as fast as his legs could carry him. Right?

"Whatever it is, we'll figure it out. I'm in problem solving mode," Miles said easily, hooking an elbow over the hard wooden chair back as comfortably as if it were one of the luxurious sofas in the Billionaire Club lounge. "Greta and her mother tend to spin each other up under the best of circumstances. Planning a wedding together? Not the best of circumstances. Thanks for giving me an excuse to get out of there for a breather."

Leo winced. He hated to add to the man's wedding-related troubles, but he had to come clean. He couldn't count on Serena's help to find the perfect reading any longer. Nerves coiled around Leo's midsection, squeezing like a boa constrictor. But he had to tell Miles, no matter how humiliating it was.

Even if he lost his friend, Leo simply couldn't let him down by pretending a miracle would occur between now and the wedding, mere days away. Serena had given him plenty to choose from, sure. But the thought of reciting one of the poems she loved most pierced his heart. Miles would simply have to choose his own reading, and if he still wanted Leo to deliver it, Leo would figure out how to memorize it, even if it meant having his poor, long-suffering valet read the damned thing aloud to him over and over until he had it.

This didn't have to be an insurmountable difficulty. So why couldn't he open his mouth?

Cold sweat prickled at his hairline and along his palms. For a moment, he wished he could curse Serena's name for consigning him to this hell—but he couldn't. He had only himself to blame for this situation. If he'd been honest with his friends—with her—from the start, he wouldn't be in this ridiculous, mortifying mess. Still, even though he knew it was impossible, he wished Serena were here with him. He'd never felt stronger or more of a man than when he was in her arms.

Not going to happen, he reminded himself ruthlessly. *You were never in her league, and now she knows it. What would a bright, clever woman like Serena want with a dullard like you?*

After all, the instant she found out how stupid Leo was, she'd been on her way out the door. Exactly as he'd feared. He could only pray one of his oldest friends would react differently—but Leo honestly didn't hold out much hope.

Wiping his hands against his trouser legs, Leo sat forward in the booth. He forced himself to meet Miles's worried gaze. "I have something to tell you. Something I'm not proud of."

The crinkle in Miles's brow hurt Leo's heart. "I'm listening."

Just do it, he thought desperately. *Quick and ruthless, like ripping off a sticking plaster.* Unwilling to watch for the moment when Miles's friendly concern would morph into derision, anger, or worse, pity, Leo directed his gaze and his words to the green felt-covered tabletop between them. "You see, Miles. When you asked me to do the wedding reading, I agreed. But there's a problem."

"What? For God's sake, spit it out, Strathairn."

Blowing out a breath, Leo nodded, but when he opened

his mouth to tell this man he admired and liked that he was a defective freak, too stupid to learn the simplest of life skills, another voice cut across the tense silence before he could speak.

"The problem," Serena said lightly, "is that there are so many wonderful readings out there!"

Leo's gaze flew to the petite woman standing in the sitting room doorway. Her beautiful blond curls were scraped back into a tight bun and her glasses were like a shield keeping him from analyzing the expression in her deep brown eyes, but she was here. She'd come back.

"That . . . doesn't seem like a huge problem," Miles said slowly, glancing between Leo and Serena with a bemused smile tugging at the corner of his mouth.

"It isn't." Serena shrugged, drawing attention to the backpack over her right shoulder. From experience, Leo knew it was likely filled to the brim with books. "I'm helping Leo narrow it down. We'll have something perfect chosen in time for the ceremony, don't worry."

Cocking his head, Miles studied Leo's frozen features for a heartbeat before a twinkle glinted from his eyes. "Well, it sounds like you've got your work cut out for you. I'll leave you to it, shall I?"

He stood before Leo could decide whether to stop him and tell him the truth, or instead be grateful for the reprieve. Part of him was thrilled to see Serena here, but part of him dreaded facing her alone once more—and hearing again the disillusionment and hurt in her voice.

But it was no more than he deserved, and Miles was already trading places with Serena, guiding her into the chair with a gentlemanly hand on her elbow. Nothing more than good manners, but Leo still experienced an extremely ungentlemanly urge to shove Miles away from her and publicly stake his claim on Serena in no uncertain terms. He stopped himself, but it was a close call.

I've been in America too long, he reflected with a ghost of his usual sardonic amusement. *I'm transforming into a rough and ready cowboy type, wanting to drag my woman off to have my way with her.*

If he thought it would work on Serena, Leo would happily cowboy it up.

"There you go," Miles said, surveying them with his hands on his hips. "Don't you two look cozy? And that reminds me, Leo, I mentioned you get a plus one for the wedding and reception, right?"

"Yes, of course." Leo darted a glance at Serena's still, impassive face. "I had planned to bring Serena, as a thanks for helping me with the reading . . ."

But he couldn't be sure she intended to take him up on it, now that she knew the truth about him.

However, he should never have underestimated Serena's drive to ensure the security of her library. Flashing Miles a brilliant smile, she said, "I'm honored! And very much looking forward to meeting your brothers and the rest of your friends and family."

"Wonderful," Miles said, rubbing his hands together in satisfaction. "It's a date."

And after delivering that embarrassing shot, along with a furtive wink in Leo's direction, Miles strode out of the inn.

Leaving Leo alone with the woman who'd run out into the cold of the night rather than spend another moment in this very same room with him.

"You didn't have to do that," Leo told her quietly. He

gripped his hands together in his lap while his gaze devoured every line and curve of her form. Every line and curve he could discern through the bulky cable-knit sweater she wore, at any rate. Luckily, Leo had been blessed with a vivid imagination and his memory of Serena's lithe, elfin beauty filled in the gaps.

She pressed her lush lips into a thin line, as if wanting to discourage him from remembering how it felt to kiss them. "Yes, I did. You were about to tell Miles your deepest secret, before you were ready and in a way you wouldn't have chosen, because I made you think there was no other choice."

Hope burst in Leo's chest like a star going supernova. "What you told Miles. That you intend to continue helping me—that was the truth?"

"Yes, I'll help you find the wedding reading. But that's all."

The exploding star of Leo's hope went dim. "You mean . . ."

Serena's shuttered gaze met his, straight and unflinching. "I'll stick to our original deal. The wedding reading help in return for a seat at the wedding and the chance to rub elbows with the Harringtons and the other potential library patrons. But it's a business transaction, nothing more."

"I was already planning to follow through with my pledge to the library," Leo told her, wanting to be clear that he wasn't a complete bounder.

She pressed her lips together and nodded grudgingly. "I appreciate that, but it's not necessary. Get me an intro to the right people, and we can call it even. I didn't sleep with you for the library donation."

"I never thought you did." Leo leaned in, his hands in tight fists on the table. "Not for a moment."

Serena's eyes softened slightly. "Thank you. As you said, I also very much enjoyed all that we shared, and I'd like to end it on a high note."

Even though he knew the truth of it already in the aching heaviness of his bones, Leo forced himself to ask, "So it's over then?"

"Yes" Serena said bluntly, without anger or accusation. "All of that is over."

The death of hope turned Leo's world black.

"You heard Miles—your invitation to the wedding is secure. You needn't bother going through the motions with the wedding reading now that you know how impossible it is."

Between one breath and the next, Leo had gone from a warm, living, breathing man to an icy, rigid marble statue. Serena's heart clenched. She'd done that to him, with her careless reaction to his revelation last night. Sure, maybe finding out he'd lied to her about his ulterior motives after all was a betrayal, and she'd been deeply disappointed that he had no intention of continuing their relationship after the wedding—but that didn't mean she was completely oblivious to how hard it was for Leo to tell her the truth. As she'd tossed and turned throughout the long, cold night, she'd dwelled less and less on her own bruised heart as the memory of Leo's self-disgust and long-held pain returned to her.

"It's not impossible," she told him firmly. She might not know him as well as she'd once imagined, but she knew enough to be sure he'd read any hint of coddling or sympathy as pity—and he'd despise her for it. "I have a plan."

She unzipped her backpack, but Leo stopped her from showing him what was inside by shaking his head. "Serena, stop. I'm telling you, you don't have to do this. I know you don't want to be here, so just go back to Sanctuary Island. I'll work something out on my own."

"No." Serena gripped the open edges of her backpack hard enough to imprint the teeth of the metal zipper into her palms. "I'm helping you. End of story."

"Why are you doing this?" he demanded, eyes suddenly flashing hot and alive with anger. "Now that you know what I am, have you come back to gloat over me? To point and laugh at the idiot?"

The sneer on his handsome face hit Serena like a slap. She could only imagine how the kids at school, maybe even the frustrated teachers, reacted to Leo's inability before he learned to hide it. She had a strong feeling he was dyslexic or suffered from a similar reading disability, which would explain how a man as intelligent as Leo couldn't keep pace with the rest of his class. And as much as she wanted to be indignant that he could ever think she'd behave like all the others in his life, how could she be? When she knew the way she'd reacted the night before had probably only reinforced years of shame and self-loathing.

That thought helped her stick stubbornly to her point. "Not at all. I'm here because I told you I'd help, and I keep my word. No matter what."

Leo crossed his arms over the width of his chest, straining the fine cotton of his button down and making his biceps bulge against the sleeves. "And I suppose what I want doesn't matter."

Serena clung to patience. "May I remind you that you seduced a woman you had no interest in, just to get help with this task? To me, that indicates a strong desire to find the perfect wedding reading for your friend's wedding."

A muscle ticked in Leo's hard jaw. "I never said I had no interest in you. In fact, as I tried to tell you last night, before you ran out of here as if your hair were on fire, you're completely wrong. I did want you. I still do."

The harsh, unyielding tone battered at the stone walls Serena had erected around her heart. Pulse leaping, she hastily shored up her defenses. "Well, as I've said, that part of the deal is off the table now. And listen, Leo—no matter what your real motivations were, no matter how big a lie you told or how . . . taken off guard I was by everything you said, I should have reacted better. You opened up to me with something that I can see causes you a lot of pain in your life, and all I thought about was how it made *me* feel. I'm sorry, I shouldn't have run out on you like that. No one deserves to be made to feel like a freak for something they have no control over."

"Bloody hell," Leo muttered. "Don't apologize to me. I can take a lot, but I can't take that."

Serena threw up her hands. "You shouldn't have to take anything! That's what I'm saying. You can't help being dyslexic."

Leaning across the table and barely moving his lips, Leo snapped, "What makes you think I'm dyslexic?"

This was obviously going to require some diplomacy. Picking her way delicately, Serena said, "Because that's the most common reading disorder. And despite what you may have been told, reading disorders have nothing to do with lack of intelligence. It's nothing to be ashamed of."

Old, remembered pain hardened Leo's eyes. "Of course. I should be proud of the fact that I'm thirty years old and it would take me an hour to struggle through a children's book."

"The people who should be ashamed are your teachers and your parents, who apparently never did more to identify the issue than blame you for it." Anger crisped the edges of her voice, and she tried to soften her tone, to keep her distance, but it just wasn't possible. "There are so many ways to tackle a reading disorder! Your parents should've gotten you into an intensive remedial education program the minute they noticed the symptoms."

Leo snorted, dropping his gaze. "My parents had far more important things to worry about than their second son's lackluster school performance. The start of hunting season, the next vote in the House of Lords, what hat to purchase for Derby Day. That sort of thing."

"I'm sorry." Serena spoke from the bottom of her heart. "You deserved better."

"So did you," Leo said, spearing her through with an intense stare. "I wish I'd told you the truth from the beginning. But I hope you can see why I never imagined you'd react like this."

"Like what?"

A small, humorless smile flickered across Leo's face. "Like someone who cares more about helping me than judging me. Even after the way I hurt you."

Hurriedly passing over that, Serena steered the conversation back to the point. "No one should be judging you," she told him firmly. "The fact that you have a reading disorder is not your fault. And it certainly doesn't mean you're stupid. Lots of famous and successful people have had reading disorders. American presidents, even!"

Dark amusement twisted his mouth briefly. "You Americans and your can-do spirit. I admit, I envy you that. Nothing defeats you."

Serena, who still felt pretty well defeated by the collapse of yet another relationship under the weight of lies, hidden motives, and unrealistic expectations, ignored the mocking lilt to his voice and forged ahead. "Being dyslexic doesn't have to defeat you either. Not unless you let it. There's always a way around a problem."

Before the stubborn ass could argue, Serena dumped the contents of her backpack onto the card table. Leo stared down at the scattering of bulky plastic audio tape and compact disc cases against the tabletop, his expression unreadable.

"I know you probably have whatever the latest, highest tech gadget is for listening to music, but the Sanctuary Island Public Library doesn't have the funds to transfer the old audiobook collection to digital files," Serena explained, unaccountably nervous. "I figured the inn might have an old-fashioned stereo you could use. If not, let me know, I'm sure I could dig up an old Walkman or something."

Leo fingered the edge of one of the CD cases, drawing her attention to the long-fingered elegance of his beautiful hands. She'd felt those hands sweetly caressing every inch of her body. Serena shivered, her skin feeling suddenly sensitive and too tight for her body.

"A way around the problem," Leo repeated quietly before looking up at her, banked fires burning like molten silver in his eyes. "I assume these are all poetry collections from the library?"

"Most of them." Serena hesitated a bare instant, then sifted through the pile until she found the CD in the plain, clear plastic case. "This one, though . . . I pulled together a compilation of recordings of my favorite pieces. Some of them we already went through together, and some are new."

A strange look flashed through his gaze, sad and resigned at the same time. But his voice was smooth and calm when he said, "I take it this is the help you spoke of earlier."

He wasn't accusing her of anything, but Serena stiffened defensively. "I never promised I'd sit beside you while you worked your way through the potential readings. If you can't find something that works in this collection of tapes and CDs . . ."

"I'm not complaining." Leo held up a placating hand. "I haven't the right. This is more than I deserve after the way I hurt you. I'm grateful, truly."

Serena struggled for a taut, silent moment. He had hurt her, but she could see in his shielded gaze, his downturned mouth, that he'd been hurt, too. "It's not more than you deserve," she finally said. "No one should be cut off from the world of literature and poetry, from books. If audiobooks are the best way for you to enter that world right now, I'm glad to be the person who unlocks the door for you."

"But you don't want to walk through it with me."

Fear drifted over her like a chilly draft over the back of her neck. He was far, far too tempting for a woman who'd never been very good at learning how to live in reality instead of dreams. Serena stood up and knotted her scarf tightly around her neck. "You don't need me."

Leo clenched his fists on the green tabletop, as if he were stopping himself from reaching out. "You're wrong about that, love."

The endearment was a shot through the heart. Bleeding slowly, Serena backed away from the table and the dangerously magnetic pull of the man. "I'll see you at the wedding. Whatever you choose will be great, I'm sure."

She walked to the door, heart pounding. But just as she was about to make her escape, some devil prompted her to take one, last look over her shoulder.

Leo had risen from the table to stand by the window. His tall, athletic form was a dark silhouette, outlined against the amber rays of the afternoon sun, his face cast in shadow. But his eyes glowed in the darkness.

Those stark silver eyes pierced her soul, hinting at a powerful storm of emotion Leo controlled with every ounce of his considerable strength.

"Please don't go," he said, his voice as harsh and deep as a distant growl of thunder over the open ocean.

If I don't go now, I'll never find the strength again.

Instead of that, Serena said, "Enjoy the books and the poems. I hope they help you believe in the possibilities of life. Because you can be anything you want, Leo. You can do anything you put your mind to. Don't let this reading. disorder, or your school experience, or your family's failings define you. I know there's more to you than a rich, idle aristocrat who doesn't believe in love."

With that, Serena forced herself to turn around and walk out of the Fireside Inn and leave Leo Strathairn behind yet again.

It hurt just as much the second time.

Chapter Eight

Serena glanced down at the wedding invitation, checking the time and place yet again. Pure nerves prompted it, since the line of parked cars edging the side of Shoreline Drive told her she'd arrived at the old yacht club where the wedding would take place in less than an hour.

She'd half planned to skip the ceremony and only attend the reception—she barely knew Greta Hackley, whose family owned and operated the hardware store on Main Street, and it was the reception where Serena was mostly likely to make the connections she need to keep the library running.

And the less time she spent as Leo Strathairn's "date," the better for her bruised heart.

But then this pretty, cream-colored invitation with the engraved outline of a starfish in the corner had arrived in her mailbox yesterday. Not only did the gold and ocean blue engraved lettering invite her to both the ceremony and the reception following, there was a handwritten note from the groom on the back.

Miles's dark, emphatic script looped across the card boldly, as straightforward as the man himself. When she read that he looked forward to seeing the woman who'd had such an impact on one of his best friends at his wedding ceremony . . . well, Serena didn't see how she could escape it.

And if a tiny, self-destructive part of her was anxious to find out which reading Leo had picked, Serena told herself curiosity wasn't a crime.

Wobbling a little on her wedge heels, Serena climbed out of her hatchback and remembered to snag her drawstring purse and navy cashmere shrug from the passenger seat. It was hard to know what to wear to a beach wedding after the weather had turned, but Serena was pretty sure the breeze off the ocean would be too cool for the sunny, orangey-red spaghetti-strapped dress she'd chosen, if the reception was indeed outdoors. At least the ceremony was inside, out of the cold.

Days and days since the last time she'd heard from or seen Leo Strathairn, "sunny" wasn't exactly how Serena would describe her feelings. But since local tradition held that it was bad luck to wear black to a wedding, she couldn't dress to match her mood.

Vowing to pretend to be happy, if only to keep from screwing up the wedding photos, Serena hurried across Shoreline Drive toward the quaint old yacht club overlooking the waves. A wooden boardwalk crossed the salt marsh and the sand, the island equivalent of a paved walkway from the road to the front steps of the building. Following a little family down the narrow walkway, all Serena

could see was the back of the tall father carrying his tod-
dler on his shoulders.

When the other guests stepped into the club and Serena finally glimpsed the way the room had been decorated
for the wedding, she gasped. She'd been inside the club
plenty of times—everyone on the island had used it as a
meeting space at one time or another, even though the local yacht club was long disbanded. But it had never looked
like this before.

The entire place was a fantasy of pale gold and ivory
satin, sprays of exotic orchids and dangling strands of clear
crystal beads turning the familiar room into a winter
dreamscape. Serena's stubbornly romantic heart thrilled to
the sight of it.

Rows of gilded straight-backed chairs had been set up
on either side of a wide, gold-carpeted aisle strewn with
white rose petals and tea lights in hurricane lamps. A
driftwood-posted arbor stood at the end of the aisle, draped
with filmy white and shimmering gold fabric that turned
translucent in the glow of the late afternoon sun through
the sparkling picture windows. The back wall of the yacht
club was entirely glass, so that the backdrop for the ex-
changing of vows would be nothing less than the majestic
Atlantic Ocean.

Picking her way to a chair in the back row, Serena had
no idea if she was on the bride's side or the groom's. She
didn't suppose it mattered. Feeling paper crinkling on the
seat, she retrieved the wedding program and smoothed it
with trembling fingers.

There was no sane, rational reason why which poem
Leo had chosen to honor his friend's marriage should matter so much to her. It had nothing to do with Serena, not

anymore. Still, her hands were shaking as she opened the program and skimmed until she found Leo's name.

All it said was "Reading by Leo Strathairn." Letting out a deflated breath, Serena sank back in her seat. Of course—the programs had probably been printed before he'd had a chance to choose.

The seats around her began to fill up with happy, chattering wedding guests in festive dresses in seasonal reds, deep evergreens, and lush purples. The men were all wearing the Virginia tuxedo: khakis and blue blazers. Serena knew she should be keeping an eye on what was clearly the groom's side, across the aisle. She should be scanning the crowd of New York socialites in navy and maroon silks and satins, the men in dark suits and ties—but it was all she could do to sit still in her chair without fidgeting while waiting for the wedding to begin.

A string quartet took up their instruments to the left of the arbor, and the first strains of Pachelbel's Canon in D floated over the air, the guests stilled into hushed anticipation. Reverend Davies, regally tall in her celebratory robes, took her place under the arbor as Miles Harrington, imposing and stern in his immaculate tuxedo, led his five groomsmen out from a side room to stand at the end of the aisle.

It was a handsome band of groomsmen, and Serena was aware of the ripple of delight that spread through the female guests, both single and married. The three Harrington brothers, each gorgeous in his own way, but with those intense blue eyes in common. And the three bachelor friends: Cooper, Zane . . . and Leo.

Smack in the center of the line of groomsmen, Leo stood proud and straight-shouldered, as comfortable in his perfectly tailored black dinner jacket and patent-leather shoes as most men would be in jeans and sneakers.

To the rest of the guests who looked at him up there, with his chestnut brown hair artfully tousled and a slight smile curling his lips, Leo would appear entirely calm and at ease. But Serena could see tension in the tilt of his head, the line between his eyes. He was nervous.

The bridesmaids walked down the aisle, three pretty women all radiant in deep blue silk, along with the bride's two brothers, who were standing up on her side. Serena recognized them from Hackley's Hardware on Main Street.

Licking her lips as the music swelled, Serena rose to her feet along with the rest of the guests as they prepared for the bride's entrance. A collective sigh went up when Greta Hackley entered the room, linked arm in arm with her mother.

Every head swiveled to watch them make the slow, stately journey down the aisle; every gaze darted to the bride swaying slender and beautiful in a gown of glowing ivory satin with long lace sleeves.

Everyone turned to watch—except Serena. After one quick glance at the bride, she always like to peek back at the groom, to catch the expression of stunned delight on his face at his first sight of the woman who would be his wife. Miles didn't disappoint her. Joy radiated from the man's pores, a sublime, certain happiness that wiped away any possibility of doubt in the power and truth of love.

Of course, that thought tempted her gaze to wander down the line of groomsmen to Leo. She thought she'd be safe, that he'd be staring at Greta along with everyone else—but when she turned to look at Leo, he was looking right back at her.

Their eyes connected with a sizzling snap of electricity that jolted through Serena's body like a lightning strike.

The moment lasted for barely a handful of heartbeats, but it felt like an hour. When Greta and her mother reached the end of the aisle and the guests retook their seats, Serena collapsed into her chair as if she were a puppet whose strings were cut. The wedding started, the familiar words achingly romantic, but it was all a blur to Serena.

All she could see were Leo's silvery gray eyes, burning into her across the distance that separated them. Even after she broke eye contact to pay attention to the ceremony, Serena still felt the heat and weight of his gaze.

And when the time came for his reading and he smoothed down his lapels before crossing to stand at the front of the arbor, Serena's heartbeat thundered louder than the surf outside the window.

Leo met her stare once more, dark and burning with purpose, and the moment he began to speak, he changed her life forever.

The week before the wedding had passed in a whirl of words, images, and imagination for Leo. He spent every waking—and some sleeping—moments plugged into the top-of-the-line headphones he'd had overnight-delivered to the inn.

He listened to every single audiobook Serena had left for him, but the one he came back to again and again was the homemade CD she'd burned and labeled in her neat copperplate script.

As unique and original as Serena herself, the selections

she'd chosen to highlight by carefully recording herself reading them aloud sifted through Leo's mind like snow falling on a lake. He loved the quote from a science fiction cult classic about how love is what keeps a spaceship in the air, almost as much as the e.e. cummings poem that Serena had tried to get him to read that terrible night. But it was while listening to a piece by a poet he'd never heard of, Rory Croft, that Leo realized what he had to do.

That poem crystallized a wordless thought that had been living in Leo's mind since almost the first moment he met Serena Lightfoot. Just as for the poet, Serena had changed Leo and brought happiness to his life, merely by being who she was. The mere fact of her existence made Leo want to be a better man.

And she deserved to know it.

Now, staring out across the sea of expectant wedding guests, Leo focused all his attention on Serena. He would speak each word he'd worked and slaved over for the endless days and nights they'd been apart, straight from his heart to hers.

"This is a poem I wrote," Leo said, tilting his chin up proudly and willing Serena to understand that she was the reason for all of this. "In honor of Miles and Greta's special day. Be kind—it's my first attempt at writing my own stuff. Don't worry, it's short. I call it 'Reading.'"

He cleared his throat as shock passed a blank pall over Serena's face. Ready or not, he had to begin. "Reading is the root of all love. When I met you, I read the loveliness of your soul in your lovely face. When you touched me, I read the generosity of your spirit in your generous touch. When I kissed you, I read the cleverness of your mind on your clever lips. When you spoke, I read the warmth of your passion in the warmth of your words."

Color flooded Serena's cheeks, and her lashes swept down, hiding her eyes from him. Leo's heart clenched, but he forced himself forward, the words beating in his chest like the wings of a trapped bird.

"You taught me to read the secret language of your heart," Leo said softly, spirits rising as Serena lifted her gaze to him once more. "And now, because of you, I can read the world of possibilities inscribed upon my own heart."

Her lips parted. Leo wanted to go to her, more than anything, to sweep her into his arms and whisper the final line of the poem directly into the delicate shell of her ear. But today wasn't about him. He anchored his feet to the floor and told Serena in front of God and everyone, "I learned to love when I learned to read . . . you."

The rest of the ceremony was an exercise in patience. Leo could only thank his parents and the boring society functions they'd dragged him to since he was a child; without that early training in feigning polite interest, there was no way he could have stood through thirty more minutes of vows, music, and wedding blessings—all while knowing that Serena was separated from him only by a dozen rows of chairs and sixty-odd wedding guests.

Schooling his features to show nothing but the genuine happiness he felt for his friend, Miles, and his sweet-faced, open-hearted bride, Leo gritted his teeth and smiled until his cheeks ached.

After the first kiss, the final triumphant music started playing the bridal party back down the aisle. From his position in the middle of the groom's side, Leo was third to walk, and because of the uneven number of men and women, he had no one to squire down the aisle. They'd planned that he and Zane would pair up and walk behind the bride's brothers. Instead, after a whisper in Zane's ear, Leo waited until Zane and the Hackley boys met in the middle and the wedding guests all started getting to their feet. Taking advantage of the jubilant chaos at the end of the ceremony, and the distraction caused by the Hackley brothers' well-timed hijinks as the two pranksters hammed it up for the crowd, Leo winked at a shell-shocked Cooper and slipped past him.

Circling around to the back row of chairs, searching the crowd for Serena's bright dress and vibrant blonde curls, Leo cursed under his breath while the rest of the guests broke into cheers as the new husband and wife paraded down the aisle.

The last seat in the last row was empty. Serena was gone.

Chapter Nine

A charmingly hand-lettered signpost stood in the sand at the foot of the porch stairs leading down from the yacht club, one driftwood arm pointing up toward the ceremony, the other pointing left, toward the reception. Heart in his throat, Leo jogged in the direction of the large glass-topped, clear-sided structure that had been erected on the flat sand farther back from the waterline.

He wanted to believe she'd be waiting for him on the dance floor, but it was deserted.

Desperately scanning the horizon, Leo's gaze landed on the getaway vehicle. Miles's beautiful, sleek, custom-built helicopter perched on a bluff overlooking the ocean, waiting for the bride and groom to climb aboard and fly away to the honeymoon Cooper had planned for them.

A hand landed on Leo's shoulder and he whirled, hoping it was Serena—but it was the groom himself, instead.

Dredging up a grin, Leo clasped Miles's hand in a

strong grip and shook it. "Congratulations, my friend! It was a gorgeous ceremony."

"And now for the party! Greta always imagined getting married on the beach. And even though it's a little too cold out for a true beach wedding, I couldn't disappoint my bride."

"This place looks amazing—and I see you even managed to order up a spectacular sunset for us to enjoy during cocktail hour. Not even God Himself would dare to disappoint you."

"Can't take credit." Miles shrugged. "Zane and the wedding planner, Felicity, did all the heavy lifting with the planning. Including timing things perfectly and coming up with a way to keep us all warm while still giving us this amazing view."

Leo stuck his hands in his pockets, feeling strangely awkward. "Anyway. Thank you again for allowing me to be a part of your wedding. It meant a lot to me."

Miles radiated love and joy as he glanced over to where his new wife was hugging her mother and shedding a tear or two. "Thank you for what you said. I knew you'd choose the perfect reading—but I never dreamed you'd be the one who wrote it."

A glow of pride warmed Leo's chest. "I'm glad you liked it. I wasn't sure—it's not the kind of thing anyone in my family has ever gone in for."

"You aren't your family." Miles's keen gaze, as always, saw more than Leo liked. Tongue in cheek, Miles clapped him on the back. "Anyway, the poem was great. You must have been inspired."

With a rueful laugh, Leo palmed the nape of his neck. "I was, yeah."

Miles arched a brow. "So. Can I take that to mean that you concede? I won the bet, as far as you're concerned?"

The terms of the bet came back to Leo in a rush.

I'm betting each of you will find the course of your life forever altered by your trip to Sanctuary Island. In fact, I'm willing to bet each of you will find love there.

"Well?" Miles blinked expectantly. "Did I call it, or did I call it?"

"The course of my life, forever altered," Leo murmured, his gaze sliding out to sea. The wide, open horizon, hinting at opportunities and possibilities the world had never held for him before. And all because of Serena. "You could say that."

"And what about the rest of the bet?" Miles pushed. "Did you find love?"

The crack in Leo's heart fissured and threatened to split apart completely, but he managed to smile. "I did, but then I lost it again."

Miles's blue eyes flickered, his stare darting over Leo's left shoulder. "I wouldn't be so sure of that."

With a sense of inevitability, Leo turned slowly and found Serena standing behind him with an uncertain smile on her glossy red mouth.

The groom winked at her before melting away into the night, presumably to collect his bride and get ready for their first dance as husband and wife.

Serena couldn't say for sure. She only had eyes for the groomsman.

Swallowing around the lump of emotion clogging her throat, Serena said, "Did I hear that right? You and Miles had a bet?"

Leo's eyes widened. "I'm not sure what you heard, but it's not what you may be thinking—it wasn't some sordid wager about getting a woman into bed or anything like that."

Serena laughed, the sound a little choked. "I know, don't worry. I heard . . . enough. I think. I have a few questions."

Stepping closer, Leo stared down at her. "Ask me anything, love, and I swear I'll tell you the truth."

Every part of Serena yearned toward him, her chest brushing his with every short, shallow breath. "That poem—you really wrote it."

"That doesn't sound like a question," Leo teased gently, his eyes roaming her face as if memorizing every line. "But yes. You told me you could see me as a poet. And when I listened to the wonderful words of the poems you recorded for me . . . suddenly, I began to see it, too."

"It was beautiful," she whispered, her heart so full she thought it might burst. "I loved every line of it. I'm so proud of you, Leo."

"Do you know, I'm proud of me, too." He smiled, a warm, confident grin without a trace of the brittle sarcasm he used as a shield. "But I never would have even attempted it without your encouragement. You were the mirror through which I glimpsed the man I want to be."

"See," Serena croaked, tears burning behind her eyes, "that's what I mean, that right there. Poet."

Instead of blushing or waving it away, Leo lifted one red-brown brow in a sultry arch. "What were your other questions?"

Nerves prickled along her palms, lifting every hair on her arms. Chickening out, she blurted, "Do you know what table we're sitting at?"

Some of the light dimmed from the bright stars of Leo's eyes. "The wedding party is at the two tables in front. Don't worry, though—if no suitable donors are at our table, I'll make sure to do the rounds with you, introduce you to some possible library sponsors."

Miserable with anxiety and kicking herself for her cowardice, Serena muttered, "Thanks. But I'm not so worried about that, since you didn't bother to listen to me when I said I didn't want your donation. The check arrived yesterday, so thank you for that. And I'm pretty sure the Harringtons want to sponsor the library. One of the brothers came by to see me a few days ago. Dylan, the one who married Penny Little."

"That's wonderful," Leo said, with genuine warmth. "I suppose I should be glad you decided to attend the wedding at all, after that."

"I wanted to." Serena dropped her gaze.

With a courtly bow, Leo offered her his arm and a smile that didn't quite reach his eyes. "Shall we go in to dinner?"

Serena wrapped her hand around the crook of his elbow, her fingers squeezing at the hot, solid strength of his muscles flexing under the suit coat. The moment she touched him, her courage came flooding back, and when he moved to guide them through the tables to find their seats, she dug in her heels and stopped him.

Leo turned back, an inquisitive expression on his face, and Serena said, "To hell with questions."

Stretching up on her tiptoes and curling her free hand around the back of his neck, Serena kissed him.

Desire roared to life, hardening Leo's body in a dizzying surge. He dragged Serena closer and plundered her mouth.

Drunk on the sweet taste of her, the taste he'd been sure was lost to him forever, Leo forgot their surroundings, forgot everything but the feel of her in his arms.

Until a loud wolf whistle and a round of applause jarred them apart, panting and staring into each other's eyes.

"Hey, that's the newlyweds' job!" someone shouted from the crowd of guests gathered at the edge of the temporary dance floor.

A blush darkened Serena's cheeks, but she laughed like bubbles popping in a glass of champagne, and Leo's heart exploded in a frothy shower of joy.

"Come on," he said into her ear. Grabbing her hand, he tugged her off the dance floor and out of the heated tent, away from the milling guests and the twinkling lights, across the sand and down to the cold water's edge.

The sun was slipping below the edge of the world in a golden orange explosion of beauty, coloring the surface of the ocean magical stained glass in constant, rhythmic motion. A chill breeze whipped off the waves, cooling Leo's heated blood enough that he could take Serena into his arms without immediately ripping off her clothes.

They'd get to that bit, he fervently hoped—but first, he had to make sure she understood.

"In case the poem wasn't clear enough," he told her, smoothing back the riotous, windblown mass of her curls, "and just so there are no questions about it later—I love you, Serena Lightfoot."

Her eyes were so wide and dark, he could drown in them if he didn't take care. "I love you, too. So much, Leo. I left that night partly because I couldn't take the thought of our time coming to an end."

"If you'd stayed, I would have told you that we can find

a way to make this work. Wherever you are, that's my home."

"I'm so sorry I ran."

"I understood," he assured her. "You'd been hurt too many times. The human heart is resilient, but if it's cracked too many times, it can't repair itself easily."

"My heart didn't fix itself." Serena smiled up at him, golden and perfect in the sunset. "You did that."

"Well, I want to keep it in good condition." Leo adopted a pragmatic tone. "After all, I intend to have use for it for a long while to come."

"Hmm," Serena purred, curling closer to his chest. "So I'm a possession now. Like your vintage Jag or your Saville Row suits. . . ."

"A prized possession," he corrected her. "Your heart is the greatest treasure of them all—and I promise to cherish it, for as long as you choose to leave it in my care."

"I don't know, that might be a very long time." Serena pressed tight to his body, fire heating her gaze. "My heart is pretty happy with you."

"Good. I'll take a lifetime warranty, then," Leo rasped out, then bent her back against his arm and dipped her over the sand to seal the deal with a kiss.

Bonfire Beach

Chapter One

Felicity Carlson bumped open the old yacht club's door with her hip and nearly sent her armful of binders, magazines, and note cards flying.

"This is why I need an assistant," she muttered, clutching her organizational supplies to her chest.

No one person could reasonably be expected to plan the biggest, most lavish wedding in the history of tiny Sanctuary Island on her own . . . but Felicity had never been very good at being reasonable when it came to setting goals for herself. And besides, it wasn't as if her fledgling company, of which she was President, CEO, and sole employee, could afford to hire anyone.

Yet, she amended the thought. She couldn't afford an assistant *yet*. But once she pulled off the wedding of billionaire Miles Harrington's dreams, Felicity would be set. Word of mouth would spread through the wealthy elite of New York, many of whom would have the chance to experience Felicity's work as wedding guests in four short weeks, and Dream Day Wedding Consultants would be set. She was prepared to hand out business cards right and left at the reception, so she could head home to Manhattan with a roster full of potential new clients. Rich ones.

That was worth pouring all her energy into the Harrington wedding, busting her butt and spending the last of her savings to outfit herself for this extended trip to Sanctuary Island, the bride's charmingly small and welcoming hometown.

Smiling at a brief but seductive daydream of paying off her maxed-out credit cards, Felicity dumped her load of three-ring binders and clipboards on the round entryway table. Intent on checking the progress of her decorations, her heartbeat quickened as she lifted the multi-colored curtain of beading between the front entryway and the main room.

Mental note: swap out the tacky disco beads for something more romantic.

But just as Felicity was mentally debating the virtues of a curtain of clear cut-crystal beads versus ivory satin swag, she realized she wasn't alone in the yacht club. Even though it was practically the crack of dawn, and her army of hired workers didn't usually show up a minute before nine.

And as she swiped the beads aside and peered into the room, Felicity realized with a shock that the tall, broad-shouldered man over by the picture window wasn't putting up any decorations . . . he was tearing them down!

Her jaw dropped but before she could march into the room and demand that he get his mitts off her dreamy, hand-picked ribbon bunting, he let out a salty curse and dragged the entire length of fabric off the wall.

"That's better," he muttered, the satisfaction in his low, rough voice reaching Felicity all the way across the empty space. He propped his big hands on his lean, denim-clad hips and glanced around, as if wondering what piece of wedding décor to desecrate next.

Jumping into action, Felicity let the bead curtain swing down with a clack and clatter. "Excuse me, but what do you think you're doing?"

The man turned to face her, and it was all Felicity could do not to suck in another shocked breath, because he was . . . in a word, gorgeous. Smooth bronze muscles flexed in his bare arms, below the short sleeves of his plain white cotton t-shirt. With his sinfully long legs encased in worn, frayed jeans and his lean jaw sporting several days of dark brown scruff, he should have looked completely out of place among the ethereal loveliness Felicity had been working to create for the wedding ceremony's back-drop.

Instead, backlit against the vibrant orange and pink of the sunrise visible through the huge picture window be-hind him, he was a monument to masculinity. He made the ribbons and lace of Felicity's decorations look silly and frivolous just by standing near them.

"I'm getting rid of all this girly crap," he said cheerfully. "I've got a wedding to plan in here."

She blinked. He sure didn't look like any of the male event planners Felicity knew back in New York. Those men were generally quite a bit more put together than this guy.

Felicity tore her gaze away from the wink of the dimple

in his unshaven cheek. Staring right into a pair of eyes so electric blue, they almost seemed to glow in the morning light, she shook her head. "There must be some mistake. I'm planning a wedding in this venue. I'm sure the owner understood that I'd blocked off the next few weeks for renovation and decoration."

He shrugged, as casual as if he hadn't just strolled in off the street and started tearing down all of Felicity's hard work. Reaching into his back pocket, he withdrew a battered brown leather wallet. "How much do you need to be convinced to take your wedding elsewhere?"

"I don't want your money!" Felicity stiffened. "This is outrageous. You can't waltz in here and throw a wad of cash in my face, and expect me to abandon the work I've put into this venue. It was a wreck when I found it, and I've already done extensive overhaul to make it perfect. My wedding is happening here in four weeks, end of story."

"Four weeks." He frowned, his sharp brows drawing together. "The wedding I'm supposed to be planning is in four weeks."

Felicity's stomach clenched, then sank like a rock tossed over a cliff. "My wedding is Miles Harrington and Greta Hackley. Who is yours?"

His keen gaze focused on her face. "Wait. You're not the bride."

She grabbed onto her patience with both hands. "No. I'm Felicity Carlson, wedding planner for the Harrington-Hackley nuptials. And you are?"

A slow, brilliant grin creased his tanned cheeks. Eyes glittering with mischief, he stepped forward and held out one long-fingered hand. "I'm one of Miles's groomsmen.

He asked me to help out with the wedding plans, so it looks like you and I will be working together."

On autopilot, Felicity let him clasp her hand. The slide of his warm fingers sent a shudder of entirely inconvenient feminine awareness all through her body. His grin widened as if he could read the quickening of her heartbeat and the melting of her bones in the dazed expression on her face.

"Zane Bishop," he said smoothly. "Lovely to meet you."

Every drop of moisture evaporated from Felicity's mouth. Swallowing around a tongue that felt twice its normal size, she said, "Zane Bishop. The C.E.O. of Whatever Entertainment?"

"And owner of three of the top five hottest nightclubs in Manhattan." Satisfaction glittered along the edges of his diamond-hard smile. "So don't worry, babe. I'm no amateur when it comes to throwing blowout bashes."

Not an amateur, no. A billionaire entertainment mogul couldn't be considered inexperienced at planning large-scale parties. Felicity racked her brain to remember the gossip mag articles she'd read about the legendary New Year's Eve bash at Houndstooth, Zane Bishop's impossible-to-get-into Meatpacking District club.

"Your last New Year's event got shut down by the police," she said with dawning horror. "For public indecency and disturbing the peace."

"It was burlesque themed. There may have been a little nudity, but nothing indecent. As my lawyers successfully argued." Zane shrugged, although the quirk of his lips told her he was enjoying her reaction. He liked shocking people, she realized.

Refusing to give him the satisfaction, Felicity pasted on

a polite smile. "Yes, I'm sure the strippers were all very tasteful."

"I'm not planning strippers for the wedding," Zane assured her. Felicity felt her eyes bug out as he continued, "I've already done burlesque, and I never repeat a theme. I was thinking more like Las Vegas Glitz."

She couldn't help it. She actually gasped aloud. If she'd been wearing pearls, she would have clutched them. Visions of sequins, feathers, and Elvis impersonators danced in her head. He had to be joking. "Glitz. At an intimate beachfront wedding on Sanctuary Island. Are you serious?"

"What I'm serious about is helping Miles."

For the first time since she'd walked in and seen him tearing down her pretty decorations, the line of his wide, expressive mouth went flat.

"One of my best friends asked for my help with this particular task, on one of the most important days of his life. Now, I might not believe in marriage or true love or any of that crap myself, but Miles obviously does. And I will not let him down."

Despite herself, Felicity was impressed by the determination hardening his jaw and darkening his eyes to flinty blue. For a moment, she felt a distinct throb of yearning for the loyalty and support Zane seemed to offer his friend so freely. As someone who'd been functionally on her own since she was a kid, part of Felicity was powerfully attracted to the whole idea of being able to lean on someone else.

But that was a dream, and she had to live in reality.

Calling up all her diplomacy, Felicity smiled at Zane

Bishop. "I get that you want to help out. I'm sure we can find something for you to do."

Something other than get in my way, interfere with my plans . . . and distract me with your perfectly chiseled jaw, rock-solid abs, and eyes the color of the morning sky, Felicity mused silently.

She'd dealt with plenty of difficult people in her day. With a combination of tact, patience, empathy, and practicality, she had dealt with everything from bridezillas to overwrought MOB's, from unreliable caterers to inconsistent florists.

But as Zane Bishop narrowed his eyes and crossed his arms over his wide chest, Felicity had a sinking feeling that she'd met her match.

"I'm not going to be shuffled off to the sidelines of this wedding." Zane liked to state his position up front, in no uncertain terms. "Call Miles if you want to hear it from him, but he's asked me to work with you. I can respect his wishes on that. Can you?"

Felicity Carlson gave him a determined smile, bland and shiny, with no hint of the fiery, passionate woman he'd glimpsed in her before she knew his name. "Of course."

Zane narrowed his gaze, taking in her prim little professional outfit. Nobody ought to be able to make a pencil skirt and blouse buttoned all the way up to the neck look so damn sexy. Although she'd been sexier before she found out who he was, when she was challenging him and generally acting like she'd be happy to personally kick his butt out of the yacht club.

It had been a while since Zane wasn't recognized on

sight, kowtowed to by everyone he came in contact with. Felicity Carlson was like a breath of fresh ocean air.

At least, she had been until she put on the Stepford Wedding Planner act and started holding back.

Looking for a way to get a rise out of her, Zane said, "Okay then. Are you ready to get to work? I'm thinking we start by jettisoning this ribbon and lace thing you've got going on in here."

To his disappointment, Felicity didn't take the bait. She pulled a pen from the sleek knot of honey brown hair coiled on top of her head, and picked up a red three-ring binder. "It's going to be wonderful to have some help with all this. But since I've got a good start on the ceremony itself, I suggest we focus our combined efforts on the reception. What do you say?"

Cheerful, business-like, boringly polite. Zane frowned, missing the crackle of electricity that had arced between them moments ago. Maybe if he poked at her, she'd ditch the mask and show him her true self again. "I bet you *are* glad to have some help—I checked out your company's website and it looked like this was your first wedding ever. How did you land a big billionaire fish like Miles?"

That determined chin tilted up, but she kept her voice even. "This is hardly my first time planning a major wedding, Mr. Bishop. Until a few months ago, I was the head event coordinator at Cadbury Estate."

Zane tucked his tongue in his cheek. The sprawling, well-preserved upstate New York mansion and property had hosted hundreds of lavish parties since the family started renting it out. If she'd been in charge there, she knew her stuff. Of course, the kind of event that usually happened at the Cadbury was exactly the kind of party Zane hated . . . stiff, fancy, upper crust, and dull.

"Let me guess." He flicked a trailing swath of lace in disgust. "Your vision for the reception is more of this."

She pressed her lips together briefly. "You mean classic elegance and romance?"

Zane snorted. "I mean deadly boring, unimaginative cliché."

He could practically hear the grinding of her teeth. "Look, Mr. Bishop. My vision of the reception doesn't matter. And neither does yours. The only thing that matters is what Greta and Miles want. All I care about is giving them the perfect wedding on their dream day."

"And using their 'dream day' to drum up business for your new company."

With a pragmatic shrug, Felicity pulled a chair up to the folding table shoved against the wall like an afterthought. "That's a byproduct. Happy clients equals good word of mouth. But the important thing is to make Greta and Miles happy. So let's get started."

Zane was unwillingly impressed. "You're hard to rattle, I'll give you that."

She paused in the act of shoving aside piles of fabric swatches, sample votive candle holders, and other assorted bits of décor. "Thanks? I think?"

"Most people fall into two categories," he told her. "People who like to have fun and enjoy life usually love me. But the other kind, all tightly wound and serious about everything—I drive most of them crazy inside of five minutes."

Felicity squared the corner of her binder with the edge of the table and gave him a look that raised his temperature by ten degrees. "If you want to make me crazy, you're going to have to work a lot harder."

Challenge accepted.

As Zane's mind raced through the options, Felicity cleared her throat. "This is the reception binder. I've got all the info in here—potential seating arrangements, table centerpieces, entertainment options . . . we'll need to work through it step by step and get Miles and Greta to decide on a direction to go in as soon as possible. Time is ticking down. Being able to throw around the Harrington name—and the Harrington budget—makes the impossible possible . . . but if we don't settle on a location soon, we're going to be in trouble."

Zane watched the way she moved, the graceful economy of her quick hands. No wasted energy, every part of her focused on the business of putting together a party. A woman as finely made as Felicity Carlson ought to be enjoying her life, not spending it making sure other people enjoyed theirs. It seemed all wrong to him, on a gut-deep level. This woman needed a good time more than anyone Zane had ever met.

Halting her recitation of the checklist they'd need to go through, Zane hitched one hip onto the table beside her binder. "I'm going to stop you right there. If I know anything about throwing a memorable party—and I think we can agree that the Houndstooth's waiting list packed full of A-list celebrities, sports stars, and socialites says I do—it's that the most important part of planning a party is to have fun."

Her sleek brows crinkled together in a way he did not want to find adorable. "I don't follow."

"If we have fun planning it," Zane explained, planting

a hand in the middle of the open binder and leaning over to catch her eyes, "the guests will have fun at it. Works every time. Come on."

Suspicion pulled the corners of Felicity's mouth down. "Where are we going?"

An unexpected throb of hunger beat through his blood. He wanted to kiss that tiny frown off her face, he realized. He wanted to sweep the binders and knick-knacks off the table and lay her down over it so he could unbutton all those stiff, pearly white buttons and see her bare and flushed with desire. He wanted her.

For an instant, the words of Miles's bet drifted through Zane's mind. His soon-to-be-shackled friend had marriage on the brain and an overabundance of confidence. Miles had bet each of his billionaire bachelor groomsmen that they'd find love on Sanctuary Island, or he'd give them his luxurious, custom-built helicopter.

Easiest bet Zane ever took, for sure. No matter how gorgeous Felicity Carlson was, or how much he planned to enjoy seducing her into having some fun over the next couple of weeks, Zane's heart was safe.

Reminding himself he had nothing to worry about and those helicopter keys were as good as his, Zane hopped off the table, grinning widely. He snagged Felicity's hand on his way out the door. "We're going to scope out the most awesome, exciting, coolest spot for the party."

"But I have a list of potential locations in my binder!"

Closing his fingers over hers, Zane said, "Leave the binder. We won't need it."

"But—"

He swept her through the entryway and out the yacht club's front door on a tide of enthusiasm and excitement.

Felicity kept up with him, her high heels clacking down the front steps. Until she stopped dead at the sight of Zane's beloved, hand-restored vintage bike, ripping her hand from his grasp.

"Besides," Zane concluded, triumphantly. "It would be hard to carry the binder on the bike."

"I'm not riding behind you on that thing," Felicity stated, crossing her arms definitively.

"Of course you aren't. This bike isn't made to take a rider pillion." He ran a loving hand over the khaki tan paint slicking the handlebars, then recaptured Felicity's arm to tug her around to the other side of the bike. "*This* is your ride, babe."

Reaching down, he pulled the gathered canvas cover off with a flourish, revealing the sidecar attached to his WWII-era BMW R75 motorcycle.

Chapter Two

"Is this thing even street legal?" Felicity yelled over the roar of the bike's engine. Her teeth clattered together every time they bumped over a crack in the road, and she clenched her jaw under the tight strap of the ridiculous black half helmet, complete with aviator goggles, Zane had plopped on her head before zooming the bike and sidecar away from the curb.

"Life is too short to worry about details like that," he shouted back, flashing her a blinding smile as they swerved to pass a slow-moving pick-up truck.

From her vantage point wedged into the sidecar, her tush mere inches from the surface of the road, Felicity could only squeeze her eyes shut and pray they weren't about to be flattened by oncoming traffic.

Dear Lord. Please don't let me die at the hands of the handsomest lunatic I've ever met.

Another bump in the paving jolted her eyes open to see

a long stretch of open road unfurling in front of their tires. They were racing away from the center of town, leaving its café and tiny library and all the cute little Main Street shops behind. Zane took another curve, just a hair too fast, and adrenaline flooded Felicity's blood in a tingling rush.

"How fast do you think I can get us all the way around the island?" Zane yelled, revving the engine. "The whole circumference—how long?"

"An hour."

"Pssh. Bet we can do it in forty minutes."

"This is your plan to scout for an event location?" Felicity almost shrieked. "To streak around the outside of the island at top speed?"

"How else will we know what Sanctuary Island has to offer?"

"Research! I've compiled extensive notes in the month since I arrived!"

The motorcycle chugged up a hill, cresting the top of it in with a shuddering growl that vibrated up through Felicity's bones to her back teeth. She could smell the salt of the ocean even over the petrol fumes.

Zane idled the engine for a precious, steadying moment, and Felicity took the opportunity to suck in a greedy breath of fresh, clear sea air. It should have been cold enough to freeze her lungs, but instead even the weather cooperated with Zane's insanity by providing unseasonably warm, lovely sunshine and clear, vibrant blue skies.

She glanced to her left and gasped at the beauty of the view over the rippling reed grass of the marshes, etched with sparkling narrow streams and dotted with a slow-grazing band of wild horses. The horses' tangled manes whipped in the breeze, their long tails swishing away flies as they picked their way through the marsh in search of tender shoots and sweet grass.

In the short weeks of her stay on the island, it was a sight she'd seen several times, but she couldn't imagine ever growing tired of it. "Beautiful," Felicity breathed, too soft to be heard over the grumbling purr of the engine, but Zane glanced down at her anyway. His electric blue eyes were hidden behind a pair of black wayfarers, making his expression difficult to parse.

Suddenly aware of the soft thrill of emotion she was probably broadcasting, after her silly girlish heart clenched at the sight of those horses, so wild and free—oh, dear. That wasn't how she wanted him to see her at all. Felicity hastily rearranged her features to show nothing but business-like interest and appraisal.

"This is a nice spot, although there's a stretch of beach that's even more convenient to the yacht club. We have to think about the logistics of transporting the guests from the ceremony to the reception." Pushing the aviator goggles up onto the helmet, Felicity shaded her eyes and tried to look at the idyllic view as she would any other potential event space.

The motorcycle engine cut out abruptly, with one curt jerk of Zane's hand over the ignition. Felicity shivered—she'd grown so used to the vibrations that without them, she felt weirdly light and empty.

"I must not have heard that right," Zane said flatly. "You want to have the reception on the beach. At night. It's not exactly summer, babe. You want the guests to freeze?"

Felicity nearly choked on her dismay. "I thought for sure the only thing we would be able to agree on was having the reception on the beach! We're on an island. What could be more perfect?"

A muscle ticked in Zane's rough-stubbled jaw. "And I thought I was crazy. It's too cold. Not to mention boring. No."

Felicity started trying to disentangle her legs from the sidecar in order to have this conversation properly. She couldn't deal with a man like Zane effectively while essentially squatting at his feet wearing a ridiculous helmet and bug-eye goggles.

Wrestling herself upright with as much grace as she could manage, Felicity ripped off the helmet and resisted the urge to do more than run a quick hand through her no-doubt hilarious hair. Her usual sleek, nicely highlighted, light brown bun must be squashed flat. "There are lots of ways around the weather. And we have to at least consider it, because I'm pretty sure it's what Greta wants in her heart of hearts."

"Her heart of hearts," Zane sneered. "Bull. You think it'll be impressive and win you a bunch of clients."

"That's not true!"

"Did Greta tell you she wanted a beach wedding?" Zane demanded.

Swallowing down the urge to prove him wrong at all costs, Felicity admitted, "Not in so many words. But I get the feeling, when we talk about options . . ."

"Feelings! Hearts!" Zane shook his head, obviously not buying into any of it, and Felicity blew out a steadying breath.

"Mr. Bishop, please. You don't get to just veto the beach as a location. I'm willing to look at other options, and I promise I'll keep an open mind. But you have to promise the same."

Those darn black sunglasses were an impenetrable shield, keeping Felicity from reading his expression.

"I don't want to have the reception on the beach."

What was his problem with the beach?

"Well, let's check out what else the island has to offer," she said, doing her best to be reasonable. "But it doesn't make sense to rule out the bride's first choice just because it's not what you want."

That got a quirk out of those handsome, chiseled lips. Not a true smile, but it gave Felicity hope. "I don't know. I'm pretty used to getting what I want."

"In your day-to-day life in New York, I have no doubt that whatever you say is the law. But we aren't in New York, and this wedding isn't business as usual for you.

"This is *my* day-to-day life, and I'm not used to sharing responsibility with anyone. My clients may make demands and have whims, but in the end, the buck stops with me. It's my job to take their wildest dreams and turn them into reality, and I'm used to doing it without any help."

Zane cocked his head. He looked incredibly dangerous, in a beautiful, masculine way—he could have stepped right out of an ad for aftershave or something. "You have help now."

A thrill surged through her like a wave on the shore. "Thank you. Does that mean you'll reconsider your veto?"

He nodded shortly. "Okay. The beach goes on the list as a possibility. But I want this wedding to be unique, special, as over the top and amazing as my friend, the groom. And for the record, I don't think the beach is special enough."

Struggling to understand his objections and see it from his perspective, Felicity said, "What if we go down there and check it out up close? I bet once your feet sink into the sand and you feel the salty breeze on your face, you'll change your mind."

A strange emotion flickered through his gaze, so swift and strong, Felicity was almost certain she must have imagined it.

"Not so fast." Zane grabbed her hand, the point of contact sending a jolt of heat up her arm. "If I agree to check out the beach, you agree to do it my way."

Right. The fun way. Steeling herself for a stomach-churning race across the wet, packed sand, Felicity fitted the helmet back over her hair and folded herself back down into the sidecar. "Agreed."

But, after revving the engine, Zane didn't point the motorcycle down the hill and pick up enough speed to make rattling along in the sidecar feel like a ride on a rickety wooden roller coaster. Instead, he executed a precise three-point turn and zoomed back in the direction they'd come from.

"Where are we going?" Felicity cried out, hastily buckling the chin strap on her helmet.

Zane held up a finger in an infuriating signal for silence. Felicity shut her mouth and narrowed her eyes, watching as Zane casually steered one-handed while pulling his cell phone from his jacket pocket and texting something with the other.

"It's illegal to text and drive," Felicity couldn't help pointing out, wondering what message was so urgent that Zane couldn't wait to send it. "If you need me to send a text for you, I can."

Glancing sideways at her, Zane grinned. "Unexpected advantage of the sidecar—hands free. Sure, catch."

He flipped the phone at her and Felicity grabbed for it, heart jumping into her throat. "Be careful!"

"Careful is boring. Live a little. What'd he say?"

The phone buzzed in her hand before Felicity could tear out her hair. Or his. Checking the screen, she read what had to be the response to Zane's text with a dawning sense of having stumbled into an upside down universe where nothing made sense. Her mouth dropped open.

"Tell me," Zane demanded.

"Miles says the helicopter and pilot will pick us up from the town square," Felicity reported dazedly, still skimming the rest of the text. She frowned. "And he also reminds you that you haven't won the bet yet. What bet? And what helicopter? What on earth are you planning?"

Zane roared around a curve, narrowly avoiding an oncoming car. The other driver honked and Felicity ducked her head, partly in order to assume the crash position and partly to keep from being recognized as crazy Zane's companion.

"That's a lot of questions," Zane replied, obviously unfazed. "Which do you want me to answer first?"

Another curve loomed, this one scoring a path around a hill with a sheer drop-off straight down to the ocean on the left. Heart hammering, Felicity squeaked, "Just concentrate on driving!"

She wasn't so terrified out of her mind that she missed the hint of a smirk that pulled at Zane's mouth as he shrugged and leaned into the turn. That was fine, she told herself as she squeezed her eyes shut and concentrated on breathing. Let him think he'd distracted her with fear for her life. When she got out of this ridiculous sidecar and back onto solid, blessedly motionless land, they'd have a little chat.

And Zane would answer every one of her questions, starting with fleeting look of panic she'd glimpsed on his face when she'd suggested taking a walk on the beach.

Zane whooped with pleasure, the rush of lift off making his entire body go light and weightless for a brief, heart-stoppingly awesome instant. "I love flying! Isn't this amazing?"

Her pretty red mouth set in a firm line, Felicity was balancing her camera on her knees and staring down at it as if imploring it to be interesting enough to distract her from having fun. "What's amazing is how fast you hustled us onto this helicopter. I would have appreciated a few moments on the ground to talk and plan without having to scream over a loud engine."

"We're not screaming," Zane pointed out, indicating the microphones built into their high-tech helmets. She'd made a face at swapping the motorcycle helmet for this one, but she'd been too busy trying to get him to answer her questions to argue about it.

Her sigh read loud and clear through the headset. Zane laughed, filled with the sheer exhilaration of soaring up and over the red, gold, and orange leaves rustling across Sanctuary Island's town square. The helicopter flight was exactly what he needed to shake off the lingering darkness that had shadowed him since they crested that hill and stared down over a pristinely beautiful stretch of sandy beach and the sparkling blue ocean beyond.

He knew most people would probably catch their breath at a view like that. They'd do their best to etch it on their memories so they could revisit the perfect serenity of the scene forever.

That wasn't an option for Zane. He'd locked a particular faraway beach into his brain a long time ago, and that memory was more powerful than any other. The instant he saw a pretty little postcard view like the one today, on the eastern coast of Sanctuary Island, his treacherous mind overlaid his sight with the memory of that other beach. That other day.

The day everything changed. The day Zane learned how precious and precarious life could be.

"Are you all right?"

Felicity's voice, slightly tinny through the helmet's speakers, was a welcome distraction from his thoughts. "Never better. Come on, close that binder and admit it— this is the best way to scout the whole island for the perfect party spot."

Her hand clenched around her ballpoint pen, her fist resolute on the open binder page. But Zane was sure he'd caught a hint of wistfulness in the widening of her amber eyes when she gazed past him out the giant open window. Turning her gaze determinedly back to the binder in her lap, she said, "We're short on time. I'll use this trip to take some notes and come up with a plan of attack. Let me know when we get there."

"Get where?"

"To the next potential location! I assume it's on the other side of the island? Although the whole island is tiny, I'm sure we could have driven it."

"We could've, but I thought this would be more fun."

She tore her gaze from her notes to give him a narrow look. Even with her hair whipping around her face and some color in her cheeks, Felicity Carlson gave off an air of competence and ambition that Zane had to admire.

"Is fun all you ever think about?" she demanded.

Sinking lower into the luxurious embrace of the custom Hermès leather seat, Zane squirmed his hips and let his legs fall open with a filthy smile. "No. Sometimes I think about sex."

"Of course you do." Felicity's cheeks had even more color in them than they'd had a minute ago.

"You don't think about sex?" Zane asked lazily, studying her face. The curve of her cheek and the fine-grained texture of her skin, the sweet bow of her mouth and the crinkles at the corners of her golden-brown eyes— somehow, those things were more interesting to look at than the whirling panorama view outside the helicopter's window.

She tensed slightly. "There's more to life than pleasure and self-gratification. I learned that the hard way. Think how much people could achieve if they channeled half the effort they put into getting laid, into something more productive, like their education or career."

"More productive, maybe. But not as much fun."

"There's that word again!" Felicity shook her head, but at least she was paying attention to him, not scribbling away in her binder. "Are you saying it's not fun to run a record label and a string of exclusive clubs and bars?"

"You're right, I did basically achieve the impossible— my job is about as fun as it's possible to be. And even then, sometimes it feels like work. Although I can always hire someone to take care of those parts of the business. Which I do. Drink?" Zane rifled through the well-stocked liquor cabinet between the passenger seats, and came up with half a bottle of gin and some tiny cans of tonic. "I bet there are even limes around here someplace. Want me to ask the pilot?"

But Felicity was like an extraordinarily lovely dog with a bone. "I'd think if anyone would understand the need to achieve, it would be a self-made man like you."

Zane gave her his best naughty wink. "You read the *Times* piece."

There, that was definitely a blush. But she didn't back down, and Zane had to admit, he liked her for it. Felicity "Fun Police" Carlson was turning out to be more interesting than he'd originally thought.

"Yes. I read. I research. I do my homework. It's what makes me good at my job." Crossing her legs with a silken swish, she arched a brow.

Okay. Zane was man enough to admit that his original thought about her had to do with the sinful length of her legs and the way she filled out that conservative suit. Riding a hot surge of lust, Zane leaned over the arm of his seat. "And let me guess. You're the best at what you do."

He liked the burn of determination in the depths of her brandy-colored eyes. Curiosity stirred in his chest. What drove a woman like Felicity Carlson? "Not yet. But I will be. And this wedding will propel me onto a whole new level."

"I knew it! You're just drumming up business for yourself."

She twisted to face him, pretty face alight. "Of course I want more business! I love my job. And the more I impress this guest list of New York's most powerful people, the better chance I have at being able to keep doing the job I love, for years to come."

"And then what? You can take over the world and be crowned Empress of All Wedding Planners?"

Some of the fire died out of her gaze and she sat back. "Mock me if you like. I'm sure my goals do seem small and petty compared with the number of lives and careers and people you control every day at your company. But they're *my* goals, and I intend to do whatever it takes to achieve them."

Regret was a fist pressing into Zane's sternum. He didn't like it. "Look, I'm sorry. I'm not trying to mock you. It's my automatic response whenever anyone gets going on how important their jobs are. I mean, outside of surgeons and emergency responders, how many truly important jobs are there? Take my entertainment company, for instance. I've made a lot of money at it, but I'd be the first to admit that no one lives or dies based on what I do all day long. It doesn't matter."

"Then why do you do it?" Felicity tilted her head to one side, as if she were puzzling through a conversation with someone speaking an entirely unfamiliar language. "I mean, I fell into wedding planning almost by accident, because I'd squandered all my other options—but now I love it. I truly can't imagine doing anything else. The look on a bride's face when she finds her perfect dress, the way the groom will try not to show how overwhelmed he is when he sees her walking down the aisle to him—I live for those moments. My work behind the scenes makes them happen smoothly. No, nobody lives or dies based on what I do, but I get to be a part of these couples' most important day. I get to make their dreams come true."

There was a look on her face, almost defiant, as if she expected him to make fun of her. But Zane couldn't. He couldn't do anything but stare at her as every word she spoke resonated through his entire body.

It was the second time she'd referenced mistakes in her past, hard lessons she'd learned. The realization struck a chord of recognition deep in his heart.

"Yeah," he said quietly, fisting his hands on his thighs. "I get that. And I can respect that."

The moment stretched between them, taut and thick with memories and hopes and unspoken words. Felicity broke it by glancing out the window. "So, where are we going? You never answered my question before."

He hadn't answered any of her questions, and he'd do his best not to. Zane never lied—life was too short to keep track of a complicated web of deceit—but he wasn't sure he could face telling the truth to Felicity. She was already burrowing under his skin, digging beneath bone and muscle to the living, vulnerable heart of him.

"Consider this a lesson in having fun," he said, glad the microphone masked the hoarseness of his voice. "Enjoy the flight."

Readying her camera, Felicity turned to gaze out her window, presumably searching for potential locations with single-minded focus. Zane breathed and tried his best to mimic the helicopter, hovering just above the island—never getting too close, never touching down, never getting caught.

Chapter Three

Planning the reception with Zane over the next two weeks proceeded, in many ways, exactly as Felicity had foreseen. They agreed on basically nothing.

She wanted a romantic beach reception; he wanted to rent a ginormous yacht. She wanted a classy jazz trio; he wanted to fly in one of his label's hottest rock bands. She wanted a dance floor for the guests; he wanted to bring in tumblers and acrobats. She wanted soft candlelight; he wanted a disco ball. Through it all, he'd managed to avoid ever stepping foot on the beach Felicity had earmarked as the perfect setting for a party.

And yet, in spite of their many frequent . . . okay, *constant* disagreements, something had shifted between them that afternoon on the helicopter.

"It's almost as if, before, I wasn't quite a real person to him," Felicity said, helping Greta Hackley do up the row of tiny seed pearl buttons on the back of her ivory duchesse satin bodice and the even smaller ones at the wrists of her hand-sewn lace sleeves.

"But now he's gotten to know you a little," Greta agreed. "So he can't treat you like one of his nameless, inter-changeable model-slash-socialite dates."

"We aren't dating!" Felicity met Greta's wide eyes in the mirror and saw her own cheeks and neck flush. "I mean, you know that. Obviously. I just felt like it needed to be said, since we're doing a lot of touring around this extremely romantic, picturesque island together, looking for the perfect place for your reception, and he's actually coming here to pick me up in a little while and oh my gosh, I'm going to stop talking now."

They were keeping the wedding dress under wraps in Greta's small apartment over the hardware store her family owned, so that Miles wouldn't see it and incur bad luck before the wedding day. But Zane had argued that it didn't matter if he saw the dress, so he should be allowed to come along. Felicity had managed to distract him with a list of caterers to contact to find out who was available for a prestigious, high-profile wedding on short notice. But he'd be over here before she knew it, ready and raring to go on another adventure around the island. All part of his quest to teach her how to have fun. She couldn't quite suppress a tiny smile at the thought.

"Please don't stop talking on my account! It seems like it's just about to get interesting." Greta winked in the mirror, reminding Felicity of the moment when Zane had winked at her on the helicopter.

Everything reminded her of Zane. This was not good.

"No," Felicity said firmly, buttoning the top button with steady fingers. "I'm here for your final fitting, not to discuss the reception. It'll be perfect. You don't need to worry about it."

"I'm not worried about it." Greta gave her a comfortable smile in the mirror, one work-roughened hand drifting down the fall of airy fabric draping her slim hips. "I mean, when I was a little girl I used to dream about a beach wedding, but the yacht club is almost as good. And I don't care what happens at the reception, honestly. At that point, I'll already be the happiest woman on the planet—I'll be married to the man I love. And nothing that happens or doesn't happen at some party will change that. For richer, for poorer, in sickness and in health, right?"

The familiar words tied an aching knot of emotion around Felicity's vocal cords. She'd been around a lot of brides, some more gushy and head over heels than others. But she'd never planned the wedding of any couple as clearly made for each other as Greta and Miles. These two would go the distance, Felicity was sure—although, from the spasm of sadness that crossed Greta's face, maybe the bride needed a little reminder.

Her hands stilling on Greta's lace-clad shoulders, Felicity smiled at the lovely bride in the mirror. "You and Miles are going to have a wonderful life together. Because you're not getting married to tick off a box on your list of life goals, or to have the excuse to throw a fabulous party. You actually want to spend your lives leaning on each other and supporting each other through whatever comes. Couples like that are rarer than you might think, but I know them when I see them. My parents are like you and Miles."

Lips trembling, Greta tried to return the smile but couldn't quite pull it off. She murmured, "In sickness and in health. Except most people who make that vow don't have a lifetime of sickness behind them, and the certainty of more in their future."

Felicity froze, recognition stinging through her like the crack of a whip. "You . . ."

"Kidney disease," Greta confirmed briefly, reaching for the box of tissues on the old-fashioned vanity. "I had a transplant when I was a teenager, but that won't keep me healthy forever. Miles swears he knows what he's getting into, but how could he?"

Everything about this conversation hit way too close to home. Scrambling for the composure and the sympathetic wisdom she'd been called on to offer many a bride or groom with cold feet, Felicity said, "No one knows exactly what they're getting into when they get married."

"I love him so much." Greta glared at herself in the mirror, dabbing at the corner of one eye and making a face that said she didn't like to cry. "And I know he loves me. But sometimes I worry that if I really loved him, I wouldn't let him tie himself to a woman who might turn into an invalid without warning."

"That's not your choice to make," Felicity pointed out. "It's his. He knows your history, he knows your prognosis— and, not to be crass about it, but he has the means to send you to the best specialists in the world, if you should ever need it."

"Exactly. Miles is an incredible man, brilliant, a hard worker who cares about the people who work for him . . . but he was born with money. On some level, I'm sure he believes that he can buy his way out of any problem. Including kidney failure."

"Money may not be able to solve every medical

problem," Felicity argued, driven by the memories and guilt Greta's situation had dug up. "But it certainly helps."

Greta went quiet for a long moment while Felicity busied herself twitching the fabric of the dress, checking the seams and the stitches holding the buttons. Anything to avoid the dawning realization on Greta's face.

"You sound as if you know something about living with a chronic condition," Greta finally said, breaking the silence tentatively.

This was not something Felicity wanted to talk about. Ever. It opened the door to too many other bad things, things she'd worked hard to put behind her and forget. But as she stood behind Greta Hackley, square-shouldered yet fragile in her ivory wedding gown, Felicity couldn't ignore her silent plea.

"Not me. My mother." Needing to sit, Felicity retreated from the mirror and perched on the hope chest at the foot of Greta's bed. Pulling one foot up and resting her chin on her raised knee, Felicity blew out a shaky breath.

Greta had swiveled the padded vanity stool to face her, and now she said, "We don't have to talk about it if it makes you uncomfortable. I didn't mean to pry."

"You weren't. It's fine." Felicity summoned up a smile, aware that it probably wasn't her most convincing effort. "If hearing a bit of my parents' story can help you feel more confident about marrying Miles, I'm happy to share it."

Happy was stretching it, maybe. But Felicity wanted to mean it. And sometimes that was good enough.

"Was your mother . . . I mean, is your mother—" Greta broke off awkwardly, unsure of what tense to use, and Felicity rushed to reassure her.

"No, no. She's still alive. Her condition is permanent, though. There's no cure for MS." Felicity heard her voice slip into the rote repetition of the many pamphlets and websites she'd studied when her mother was first diagnosed. "My mom's course of Multiple Sclerosis is the better kind, relapsing and remitting. It's possible to control some of the symptoms and to live close to a normal life span."

"Close to normal," Greta repeated softly, empathy brimming over in her bright eyes. "That's not quite the same as normal, is it?"

"Not quite," Felicity croaked. Clearing her throat, she forced herself to stay on point. "My mother was fine, a lot of the time. She got tired more quickly than other moms, and there were certain things she couldn't do. As I got older, and so did she, walking became more difficult. She started using a cane, then a walker, and finally a wheelchair. We had to move to a house that was all on one floor, so she could get around."

Felicity paused, struggling with how much to reveal. She didn't want this to turn into some kind of sob story, or to overwhelm Greta with negative images of the way her life could go, but . . . "I don't want to lie to you, Greta. It wasn't always easy, and we all made sacrifices, especially my father."

He'd given up a career he loved, teaching college math, to take a job with more flexible hours that would let him work from home on her mother's bad days. Money was always tight, and Felicity had worked for every penny she'd spent on clothes and a used car, when she wasn't helping out around the house.

Greta's face had crumpled a bit, like the tissue she still

clutched in one hand. "That's exactly what I don't want for Miles."

"I'm saying this badly." Felicity wrapped her arms around her raised knee and squeezed. Meeting Greta's anguished gaze head on, she said, "I asked my father once if he ever thought about how different his life would have been if he'd married someone else. We'd been up all night after an emergency trip to the hospital because Mom slipped and fell. She turned out to be fine, but we were all exhausted. I don't know what I expected him to say— something about being a tenured professor, maybe, or going out dancing because my parents used to love to dance, before Mom got sick—but I didn't expect him to laugh. He laughed for a solid five minutes, until he was almost crying. When he caught his breath, he wiped his eyes and— I'll never forget this. He said, 'Oh, honey. No. Why would I want to contemplate something so awful? Your mother is the one for me. The one and only. And I'd rather sit up all night in a hard plastic hospital chair at her side than dance a single dance with someone else.' "

Felicity's voice broke, her breath tearing hard at her chest, and when she looked up, Greta was crying openly. But she was smiling through her tears, and that gave Felicity the strength to smile back.

Ivory silk and chiffon whispered as Greta stood up and crossed the small bedroom to envelop Felicity in a crushing hug. "Thank you," Greta whispered, her tone thick with emotion. "I needed to hear that so much, and I know it was hard for you to talk about."

"But worth it, if it helps you believe that it's not up to you to decide what will make Miles happiest," Felicity said, pushing to her feet and holding her trembling bride at arms' length. "He's already made his choice—and he chose you, even if that means hospital beds someday, instead of dancing all night. We should all be so lucky to find someone who feels that way about us. Hold onto that, and hold onto him. Leave the rest to me—I'll make sure the day you commit your lives to each other is absolutely perfect."

Greta hugged her again, and Felicity returned the squeeze and repeated her vow silently.

Making this the wedding of the year wasn't simply about money and ambition—it was about helping this couple, who could almost be a younger, wealthier version of her parents, start their lives together the way they deserved. It was about making their dreams come true.

And maybe this time, if she was very lucky, some of the magic of their happiness would rub off on Felicity and let her start to dream again, too.

Backing away quietly, Zane leaned against the wall of the hallway beside Greta's bedroom door. He shouldn't have listened in, especially once it was clear how deeply personal that conversation was, but he couldn't help himself.

Done in by his need to know everything there was to know about Felicity Carlson. Who was unreasonably intriguing and unfairly tempting, for a woman who'd given up on fun.

But after what he'd overheard, knowing what she must have gone through when she was younger, maybe he could begin to understand her. The only trouble was . . . well, the same thing that always gave him trouble. He wanted more.

And he wanted to hear it directly from Felicity. He

wanted her to want to tell him whatever was left. Everything she hadn't said to Greta—because she'd been holding back. After only a few weeks together, Zane could tell when Felicity wasn't going all in. He wanted to know the parts of the story she'd left out.

So he'd ask. In a roundabout way, and already knowing the right buttons to push. Stomping on the tickle of guilt at the idea of using the knowledge he'd gained while eavesdropping, Zane rapped his knuckles lightly on the doorframe.

He'd made himself a promise a long time ago to never pass up an opportunity, to always go big or go home, and it had served him well. He'd go for it with Felicity and see what happened. Worst-case scenario, she'd shut him down and he'd lose all the progress he'd made in getting her to loosen up over days of motor biking and helicoptering.

Hmm. Actually, that worst-case scenario was unacceptable. He'd have to figure out a way around it.

"One minute," Greta called from inside the bedroom. There was the sound of a couple of noses being blown, and when Felicity pushed open the door to gesture him inside, her amber eyes were red-rimmed and her cheeks were blotchy.

Zane stared at her for the space of a heartbeat, trying to comprehend how he still found her so incredibly beautiful even with a pink nose and puffy eyelids.

Desperate to distract himself before he dragged Felicity in for a deep taste of those ripe, kissable lips, Zane glanced over to find Greta watching them with a smile dimpling her cheek. He pretended to stagger back, hand over his heart.

"Greta Hackley! Look at you. You're far too gorgeous to waste yourself on a stuffy old man like Miles Harrington. Let's hop on the helicopter and run away together."

Laughing and blushing, Greta swatted him on the arm. Actually, more of a punch than a swat—ouch—which made Zane remember she'd grown up surrounded by brothers. "Watch who you call stuffy and old! And do you really think that even if I ran away with you, I'd help you steal Miles's beloved helicopter?"

"It's practically mine," Zane scoffed. "Only a matter of time."

Greta only hummed thoughtfully, her gaze sliding to the little spindle-legged mirrored table where Felicity was busily packing up what looked like ten pounds of makeup into a black nylon case.

"Don't be too hasty. You haven't won that bet yet, mister." Greta wiggled her eyebrows playfully.

Felicity's head came up like a lion scenting prey. "The bet! I forgot about that. You never explained what it was all about."

"And I'm still not going to," Zane said, grabbing her elbow and steering her toward the door. "Because we don't have time. Bye, Greta! Thanks a million!"

"Anytime," Greta called back, laughing at him as he gently nudged Felicity into the hall.

"I'm starting to feel paranoid about this bet," Felicity complained, dragging her heels.

"Don't," Zane told her. "It has nothing to do with you."

Choosing not to examine why that felt like a lie, Zane hustled them down the exterior stairs into the narrow alleyway between the Hackleys' hardware store and the bakery. They had a schedule to keep, and no time for hashing out the details of Miles's lame, easy, in-the-bag bet.

"Then it shouldn't matter if you tell me what the bet is all about," Felicity argued.

"It's nothing," Zane insisted.

She snorted. "Nothing is exactly what I would have thought would make Miles Harrington part with that custom helicopter of his. He loves that thing. Is it really on the table?"

"It's not only on the table, it's as good as won." Zane clamped his mouth shut, wishing he hadn't said that. For some reason, those words felt like another lie. Her gaze sharpened on his face, almost as if she could sense it. Wanting to hide from that stare—and from whatever was going on in his mixed-up head—Zane whipped out the silk tie he'd snitched from Miles's room at the Harrington house.

Waggling his brows, he dangled it in front of Felicity like a piece of yarn in front of a kitten, hoping it would distract her.

"Oh no. What adventure have you devised for me this time?" Good-humored resignation warmed Felicity's voice, and Zane was relieved to see the twinkle of anticipation in her eyes. It had taken a little convincing, but Zane thought he'd done a decent job of introducing Felicity to the concept of fun. Despite the somewhat limited resources of such a tiny island. Still, Sanctuary Island had one unique feature they hadn't explored . . . until today.

Rather than answering in so many words, Zane moved to stand behind Felicity. Rubbing the smooth silk of the tie against her neck, he savored her shiver. "It's a secret. May I?"

She tensed a little when he covered her eyes with the tie, but she didn't pull away. Zane paused a moment, watching to make sure she was really okay. But when her shoulders lowered and she murmured, "I suppose I can trust you not to push me out in front of oncoming traffic," he grinned and tied a knot at the back of her head.

"You're as safe with me as you want to be," Zane promised, leaning down to whisper the words into her ear. She shivered again, and desire rippled hotly down the center of his body.

Felicity groped one hand out to steady herself against the red brick wall of the hardware store. Even to Zane's open, uncovered eyes, the light in the alleyway was dim and soft, with the walls of two shops sheltering them on both sides. Main Street was only a few paces away, but pedestrians strolled by on the wide, paved sidewalk and never glanced into the alleyway.

He and Felicity were almost impossible to see, Zane realized. Felicity's breath was coming fast and light, the wings of her shoulder blades fluttering against his chest, and Zane gave in to the irresistible urge to nuzzle at the satin length of her neck.

With a gasp he felt more than heard, Felicity melted into him, sealing their bodies together in a long, languid rush of heat. Zane went taut and hard, heavy with throbbing need. The rest of the world receded, the sounds of foot traffic and cars passing buried under the pounding waves of their combined heartbeats.

Zane's hands gripped Felicity's upper arms, the softness

of her skin hitting him like a shot of vodka. Her head fell back against his shoulder, her covered eyes turned up to the sky, and the slash of navy silk was midnight lush against the roses and cream of her cheeks. Her lips parted on a breath. Zane's control broke.

With a low sound that tore from his chest, he spun Felicity in his arms until her back was pressed to the brick wall, and kissed her.

Chapter Four

Felicity had never been kissed like this. Even in the Bad Year, the terrible year when she'd briefly lost her head—and almost everything else—in a misguided attempt to experience life, she'd never experienced this.

Hell, she'd had full-on sex that wasn't as hot, as consuming, as knee-weakening as Zane's kiss.

Black stars spangled the inside of her covered eyelids, and the lack of visual input made her extra aware of her other senses. The warm clasp of Zane's big hand where he palmed the back of her head to cushion it against the scratchy brick wall; the rush of blood throbbing in her ears; the slick slide of his velvet tongue mapping out the inside of her sensitive lips; the cinnamon-spiced sweetness of his mouth; the solid, muscular press of his thigh between her legs.

Felicity felt as if she'd been tipped sideways into an alternate reality, where pleasure and desire ruled her body, and her mind was a soft haze in the background. Her mind, which she'd cracked open like a walnut to share the tender pieces of her past with Greta, was happy to take a little break. And somehow, Zane's forceful, demanding kiss which could have overwhelmed her, instead seemed to fill her with strength. And a few demands of her own.

Clamping her thighs around Zane's, Felicity spared a brief moment to be sorry she'd worn pants today. Her hungry body wanted no barriers between them. But when Zane shoved in even closer, notching their pelvises together and making sensation explode in Felicity's core, she realized it was for the best. She might not survive this much pleasure if they were skin to skin.

An image of what Zane Bishop would look like naked flashed across her mind's eye, startlingly detailed, and Felicity moaned. The harsh noise Zane grated out in response only stoked the fire in her belly. She wrapped her arms around his neck and buried her fingers in the softness of his dark brown hair . . . and a shrill wolf whistle split the air.

Pulling back, Felicity heard laughter drifting from the open window of a passing car.

"Nobody we know. They're gone already, anyway," Zane said huskily, but the moment was broken.

Reality pressed down on Felicity's shoulders, a heavy burden she wasn't sure she wanted to pick back up. But she didn't have any choice. She'd sacrificed all her choices in one stunning year of poor decisions and self-indulgence.

She reached for the knot of the blindfold, which suddenly felt silly and pointless instead of sexy and freeing. Zane made an unhappy sound but he didn't stop her from tugging the silk tie off her head.

Blinking in the light, Felicity forced herself to meet Zane's clear blue eyes. "Well. I guess we've proved the old cliché true. Opposites do attract."

He eased his body away, obviously reluctant but reading her desire for space in the tightness of her smile. "We're not all that different, you and me."

Felicity licked her lips, the lingering trace of his warm spice flavor sending a tingle through her lower body. "Zane. Come off it. We couldn't be more different if we'd sat down and made a list of ways to be opposite. We don't agree on anything about the reception, which is supposed to be happening in two weeks, by the way, and meanwhile you and I are still arguing over where it should be held!"

Leaning one hand on the brick wall beside her head, Zane lowered his head to keep eye contact. They weren't touching, he wasn't caging her in with his arms, but she could see the taut muscles of his forearm. And she could feel the supernova heat of his big, hard-sculpted body. "We're more alike than you think," he contended.

The intensity in his expression sent a hook into Felicity's lungs, catching at her breath and forcing her to pay attention. "What do you mean?"

"We both learned our life lessons early and well." Zane pushed away from the wall, giving her his broad back and shoulders, tensing tight under the weight of whatever he struggled with.

"I don't . . ." Felicity shook her head, unable to follow, and Zane whirled to prop his hips against the white clapboard wall of the bakery.

"I heard you," he said. "All that stuff you told Greta, about your parents. I was outside the door, and I listened in. Because I was curious, and I wanted to know you."

Anger sizzled briefly in Felicity's belly, then died out. She tipped her head back against the rough bricks, unwillingly amused. "Lord. You really aren't used to having to ask for what you want."

"I'm fine with asking. But it's usually easier to simply take." Zane shrugged.

He'd heard everything she'd said about her past . . . and then he'd brought her outside, blindfolded her, and kissed her. Felicity wouldn't trade that kiss for any amount of politeness. "I might have told you all of those difficult, private things, if you'd asked. I might not. It would have been nice to have been given the choice . . . But I can't say I'm sorry you know."

The knowledge that he'd peeked into some of her worst memories and still wanted her made Felicity feel closer to him, more intimate even than that scorching kiss. Although . . . he didn't know all of it.

"Good," Zane said, relief bringing the sparkle back to his eyes for an instant before he narrowed them on her face. "So why are you frowning?"

Attempting to clear the thundercloud from over her head, Felicity sighed. "What I told Greta, about my parents and their unbreakable connection—I wish that were the only life lesson I learned, early on. But you don't know the worst of it."

"What could be worse than watching your parents deal with an incurable illness?"

Felicity eyed him, a sense of calm enveloping her. She could tell him the whole truth, and maybe it would help him to understand where she was coming from, the way she saw the world—but she wouldn't do it lightly. "Are you sure you want to know? This goes deeper than squabbling about reception details. Deeper than a kiss, and the attraction between us. This is real life, my life, and I don't share it with just anyone who happens to pass through it. If I tell you this story, it will mean something to me. Can you handle that?"

Zane stared, the serene resolve of her words flowing over him. He wanted to say that of course he could handle it. He wanted to demand how the hell she knew that it was hard for him to dive beneath the surface, that he preferred to live his life in the shallow end of the pool. He wanted to walk away.

But curiosity—the need to know this woman—stopped him.

Swallowing down the lump of emotion until it lodged in his chest like a stone, Zane kept his voice steady and sure. "Tell me."

She searched his face for a long, suspended moment during which Zane absolutely did not hold his breath. He had no idea what she was looking for, or what she saw in his expression, but eventually she said, "Okay. So you know my mom has MS. And you know my dad was her primary caregiver, from the time I was about eight years old, when she was first diagnosed."

Zane nodded, every particle of his being focused on the tall, polished beauty in front of him. Even after a kiss hot enough to burn down the world, even in the midst of revealing her darkest personal history, with her honey brown hair mussed and her makeup smudged, she still made everything in his body go tight with yearning.

"He worked so hard, my dad." Felicity's voice drifted a bit, her far-off gaze fixed on some memory. "My mom, too, when she could. But there was always more to do around the house. We couldn't afford help, and my mom's relatives would visit every now and then to pitch in, but they had their own lives, their own families, their own problems. My mother's illness was ours. Our family, our problem."

"Your life," Zane said, realization sinking in. "Your mother was the one who was sick, but it affected all three of you. You all had to live with it."

"I'm not complaining—obviously, it was worst for her. Some days, when the symptoms flared up, she'd be achy, unsteady on her feet." Felicity paused, and moisture welled along the dark line of her bottom lashes. "Sometimes she lost her words. She couldn't make herself understood, and it was like watching someone trapped in a prison, screaming to get out—but the prison was her own failing body. Her damaged brain, betraying her."

"That must have been tough to watch." Zane took a step toward her, not sure what to say, but damn sure he wanted to put his arms around her and shelter her from the memories that put that terrible, haunted pain in her pretty amber eyes.

But Felicity held up a hand to halt him, and Zane stayed put. There was a brittle courage to her stance that might shatter if he touched her.

"It was hard," she admitted. "But it was hardest on Mom and Dad. They were at home, dealing with it all the time. I could at least escape to school, but I felt guilty about it. To compensate, I worked hard in all my classes, I took on extra credit projects and joined any club that would have me—because I knew I had to get a scholarship. All our money, whatever my dad could piece together from the jobs he could do at home, it all went into my mother's care.

There was nothing left over for college. And I wanted to go to college, so badly I lived and breathed for that and nothing else."

Shame stole the color from her cheeks, leaving her pale as salt, her mouth a bitter twist of self-hatred. Zane got it. "College was your ultimate escape. Getting there would mean your life could finally start being about you."

Surprise flickered through her shadowed eyes. "Yes, exactly. And it was perfect, an escape I didn't need to feel bad about, because my parents wanted it for me. They were so proud when I got that scholarship, so pleased for me to have that chance. My mom cried. I think it had really weighed on her, that they couldn't set aside a college fund for me. She had to deal with that guilt, on top of everything else."

"Guilt is toxic," Zane said harshly, his own past threatening to rise up and swamp him.

Felicity frowned slightly. "Guilt can be paralyzing, but it can also be a good reminder. It can keep you from repeating bad choices and making the same terrible mistakes over and over."

Jerking his head out of his own memories, Zane shuddered all over like a dog shaking off water. Focus, he ordered himself. "So you fulfilled your family's dreams and went to college. Doesn't sound like a terrible mistake to me."

Felicity's shoulders hunched, and she propped herself against the brick wall as if she needed the support. "The mistake wasn't going to college. It was how I acted once I got to NYU. It was as if all the years I spent studying and working and helping out at home and making dinner every night . . . it all caught up to me. I didn't want to work.

All I wanted to do was party with these new friends who didn't know me as the serious, nerdy girl in the Latin club. They thought I was fun."

A faint, joyless smile tipped up the corner of her mouth as the shock of understanding zipped down Zane's spine. He had a bad feeling about what was coming next.

As if she could read it in his slack face, Felicity nodded. "Yep. I had so much fun that year, I forgot to go to class. I missed assignment after assignment, meetings with professors and emails from the dean. Almost as if I'd used up every ounce of self-control and responsibility when I was a kid, even once I understood how much trouble I was in, I couldn't stop partying. I was finally the fun girl, and people liked her so much more than who I used to be. I didn't want to give that up. But in the end, I didn't have a choice."

"You lost the scholarship."

It wasn't a guess, but she nodded in confirmation anyway. "Yep. I was too busy having fun to realize I was about to lose everything."

"What did you do? Did you move back home?"

"I was too ashamed." Felicity uncurled a bit, as if the lack of judgment in Zane's tone enabled her to stand a little taller. "My parents would have welcomed me, I know, but they would have been so disappointed. I couldn't face them. I got a low-paying, entry-level job as a receptionist at an event venue upstate to pay my portion of the rent on the student apartment I shared with three other girls, and I didn't tell my parents I'd failed out of college for three years. By that time, I had managed to work my way up from receptionist to event coordinator at Cadbury Estate, helping to schedule and plan parties, weddings, business retreats, what have you . . ."

"And you went from partying to planning other people's parties," Zane finished. His mind reeled, trying to take in everything she'd said—and everything she hadn't. He could easily imagine what her life at home was like, the constant stress and the shouldering of too much responsibility at too young an age. It was no wonder she'd gone wild at the first taste of freedom.

"So you see why I have a hard time letting go and enjoying myself?" Felicity stared at him as if willing him to understand.

"The last time you cut loose, it cost you your dreams. Of course I can see that," Zane said gently. This time when he moved to enfold her in his arms, she didn't stop him. Instead, she curled into his embrace with a breathy sigh that gusted warm and relieved against his shoulder. Running a soothing hand up her back, Zane said, "But that doesn't mean if you have fun, the world will come to an end."

She stiffened, but he held onto her, intent on saying this. "I'm not trying to minimize what happened to you, or say you learned the wrong lesson from it. I'm just saying . . . I don't know, balance. Moderation. I mean, haven't you had a good time, these past few weeks? And it's cost you nothing."

"Nothing except forward progress in picking out a reception location," she grumbled into his shirtfront, and Zane had to grin. That single-minded focus was what made Felicity a force to be reckoned with.

"Fair enough. But at least admit you've had fun, and the world didn't end."

Pulling back, Felicity tilted up her chin to gaze into Zane's eyes. "I suppose that's true," she said, a wondering tone creeping into her voice. "Although . . ."

"What?" Zane backed up a cautious step, wary of the look Felicity was giving him.

Flipping the crinkled silk tie back and forth between her fingers, Felicity said, "You know, I think I was able to let go with you because, for some strange reason, I trust you. I even let you blindfold me!"

Warmth suffused Zane's chest, along with a potent surge of possessiveness mingled with protectiveness. "You know I wouldn't let anything bad happen to you."

She glanced down, her cheeks going pink. "I think . . . I do know that. But what about you?"

Felicity peeked up at him through her lashes and sent Zane's heart rate pounding into overdrive. "What about me?"

"Do you trust me?" She lifted the tie, dangling it suggestively in front of Zane's face.

He swallowed hard as dark, sensual images crowding into his head, leaving no room for any thought beyond how desperately he wanted her. He would have agreed to anything, said anything, done anything, to keep Felicity staring at him with that heated, focused, connected gaze.

In answer, Zane took the tie from her and slipped it over his eyes, the silk warmed from Felicity's skin. He tied the knot securely, only the thinnest sliver of light entering the bottom of the blindfold.

"I trust you," he said, voice thick and hoarse with the passion and emotion she called out of him. "Do what you want with me."

Chapter Five

What Felicity wanted to do with Zane Bishop . . . the possibilities stopped her in her tracks for a good ten seconds. Oh, the things she wanted to do with him.

Remember the plan, she told herself sternly. *Fun in moderation is all well and good, but we still have a party to plan, and a ludicrously short amount of time to pull everything together. Do not get distracted by Zane's rough jaw and windblown dark hair and huge, flexing biceps . . . . shoot, maybe I'm the one who needs the blindfold.*

Laughing at herself, Felicity took Zane's big hand in hers and led him out of the alley and into the chilly autumn sunlight pouring down over Main Street. "Come with me. I want to show you something."

Felicity had to struggle not to be derailed by his contagious flirt of a smile. "Does this something start with you naked and end with us horizontal?"

Fighting back a blush, Felicity propelled the two of

them down the sidewalk. "No! And watch your step. I mean, don't watch, here just let me . . . oops!"

Zane righted himself from his stumble over a crack in the pavement, his fingers gripping tight around hers. "Let me guess. First time leading a blindfolded man around town?"

"You guessed right." Felicity kept her gaze trained on their path, trying to anticipate any rough or uneven spots that could trip Zane up. "It's a little nerve-wracking, if you want the truth."

He lifted a hand toward his face. "We can ditch this if you want."

"No!" Felicity paused, surprised and a touch embarrassed at her own vehemence. "I mean . . . not yet. I want to surprise you."

"Hmm." Those sinful lips curled into a naughty smirk. "And you like having me under your power."

Felicity couldn't deny it. There was something strangely satisfying about the way Zane was allowing himself to be led forward into a mysterious, uncertain future, with no guide in the darkness other than her hand and her voice. "What woman wouldn't enjoy having a wealthy, world-famous playboy in her control?" she replied lightly, but it was more than that. At least, on her end.

Zane, as always, seemed content with the easy banter, not looking for any deeper meaning. "Lead on, babe. I love surprises."

Felicity wasn't at all sure he was going to love this one, but she had to try. Time was running out.

Zane was no stranger to sexual games. Unlike his surprisingly innocent wedding planner, this wasn't his first round of blindfolded shenanigans.

But it was the first time he could remember feeling this charged and ready, this connected to the other person— especially when all their clothes were still on. For Zane, who'd started to find his constant merry-go-round of party hookups and short-term flings boring, this was a major breakthrough.

He knew he was jaded. How could he not be, when he'd spent his entire life making sure he experienced everything near-limitless wealth and power had to offer? But this—what he felt when he was around Felicity Carlson? This was something new. Zane laced their fingers together tightly, climbed into her car when she opened the door for him, and let her drive him over Sanctuary Island's winding, graveled roads to an unspecified location. He was entirely prepared to throw himself into whatever new adventure awaited him at the end of his blind journey.

But he could never have prepared for what Felicity had in mind. The car stopped and Felicity hurried around to help deal with the seatbelt and the door handle. Zane was pretty sure he could have managed it himself, but he wasn't going to turn down the opportunity to get Felicity's hands all over his lap.

Entirely focused on her nearness and the fresh apricot scent of her skin, it took Zane a minute to register the smell of salt on the brisk breeze. He froze for an instant, feeling the shifting grit of sand under his soles, and his chest tightened in lung-squeezing panic.

"Are you okay?" Felicity's alarmed voice pierced the ringing in his ears. "Wait, let me take off the blindfold. We're there."

Zane didn't need the blindfold off to know where she'd taken him. "The beach."

He blinked his eyes open against the dazzle of the sun off the waves, and stared out onto the scene of all his night-mares.

"I thought . . ." Felicity faltered, twisting the tie between nervous fingers. "It's the one potential party location we never really checked out. Not up close and personal."

Clenching down on the panic and despair that wanted to suffocate him, even when he stood merely at the edge of the road running along the beach, Zane squared his shoulders. "It's fine. You're right, we should check it out."

She was never going to give up on the beach, which even Zane could admit was the most obvious location for the reception. Not unless he could convince her it really wouldn't work. So that's what he'd do. He'd step out onto the sand, walk down to the foamy white edge of the water, stare out over the dark, treacherous waves . . .

"Are you coming?" Felicity asked, raising a hesitant brow at him over her shoulder.

Zane couldn't move.

He stared down at his feet, willing them to carry him forward, but they were rooted to the gravel shoulder of the road as if he were a centuries-old tree. "You go ahead. I'll be there in a minute."

Felicity's eyes widened, and Zane controlled a wince. Even he could hear the raw edge to his voice. "What's going on? You really don't want to go down to the beach with me."

Zane closed his eyes. He couldn't hide it. And since he couldn't hide it, maybe the only thing to do was to tell her about it. Maybe then she'd see why the beach was the worst setting in the world for a wedding reception.

"I don't go to the beach." He crossed his arms over his chest and leaned against the hood of Felicity's sensible blue sedan, stretching his legs out in front of him. "I haven't since I was a little kid."

That was the easy part. He'd said that much before, with a shrug and an easy change of subject, distracting whoever had asked with an invitation to do something more fun, exciting, exotic, and decadent.

The hard part was glancing up into Felicity's soft, watchful eyes as she studied his face as if she'd be quizzed on it later. "What happened when you were a little kid, Zane?"

There it was. The question he tried never to think about, the memory he'd do anything to erase. But sitting on the hood of Felicity's car and staring out over the merciless vastness of the ocean, Zane felt the memory swirl up to the surface of his mind, unchangeable and undeniable as the tide.

"I grew up in Pennsylvania, in farm country. My parents used to have a vacation condo, though, on the coast. We went there every summer, my parents and me, and my older brother, Michael."

Felicity perched next to him on the car, the sweet line of her body warm even against the chill of the wind coming off the water. "You have an older brother?"

"Had," Zane said tightly, around the ache in his throat and the burning behind his eyes. "Past tense. Michael died when I was ten, and he was thirteen."

"Oh, Zane." Felicity reached out to him, anguish in her voice and sympathy in her gaze.

It was a fight to let her touch him, not to jerk away from

the softness of her curves leaning into him, the steady support of her arm around his shoulders. Part of Zane didn't want the comfort, didn't want to think he needed it—and maybe didn't think he deserved it. But through sheer force of will, he stayed still and let Felicity tug him close.

"I'd say we don't have to talk about this," she murmured, pressing her forehead into the space between his neck and his shoulder. "But honestly, I think we do. Or at least, you need to talk about it with someone. And I'm here."

"Do you think I'd discuss this with just anyone?" Zane grated out, every muscle tense and straining. "I don't talk about Michael. Ever."

"Why not?"

"Because." The words ripped out of his chest, cracking him open. "It's my fault he died."

"No, it wasn't." Felicity gripped his shoulder more tightly, pulling back to stare seriously up at him.

Startled, Zane jerked away from her. "You don't know that. You don't know anything about it."

"I know you were ten years old," she said firmly, with no hesitation. "You were a child. No matter what happened, no matter how you feel about it now, it wasn't your fault."

Zane smiled, bleak and wintry enough to hurt his cheeks. "Ah, Felicity. You, more than most people, know how much responsibility a child's shoulders can carry."

"And, as someone recently pointed out to me, that's not exactly healthy. But go on—you were about to tell me what happened."

Striving for the light, easy storytelling tone that had never eluded him before, Zane said, "I'm sure you can fill in the blanks. We were at the beach, and I swam out too far. The waves were bigger than I thought, rougher. I couldn't keep my feet."

Without warning, the flat words gained depth and dimension in Zane's head, sucking him down into the stinging cold blackness of the waves closing over him, picking him up and throwing him down onto the scraping ocean floor. He gulped for air, gasping in shock when he breathed easily.

He wasn't that kid anymore. He was safe. And Michael wasn't. "You know, it's strange. In movies and on TV, when they show a person drowning he's always waving his arms and calling for help—but that's not what it's really like. I just sank. I kept trying to get upright, to push down on the water with my arms, but I couldn't get them above the surface. And I definitely didn't have the breath to shout or scream. To this day, I don't know how Michael even realized I was in trouble. But he did."

Felicity remained silent, but her slender hand found his much larger one and squeezed. Zane didn't understand how such a small thing could give him the guts to go on, but it did.

Staring out over the empty, calm ocean, Zane said, "Michael swam out to me and got me turned right side up. He pulled my head above water just as another wave crashed over us, and he . . ."

For the first time, Zane's voice broke. Humiliating tears burned like acid behind his eyes, but he clenched his back teeth and got through it. "My brother got his hands under my arms and lifted me up, over his head, and somehow I got on top of the wave and rode it in toward shore a little ways. Enough that I could touch down. I turned to try and find Michael, to grab him and pull him in with me. But he was gone."

Felicity's fingers spasmed in his hold. "Zane, oh. Oh my God."

It was a prayer, more than anything else—a prayer for mercy, for help, for something to ease the pain. But there was nothing. "My brother saved me. And in doing so, he lost his own life."

Zane dashed the tears from his cheeks and scrubbed his hand over his face. In a choked voice, Felicity said, "Don't. It's okay to cry."

Exploding off the car in a fierce rush, Zane stalked a few paces down the road before whirling to stare at her. "I'm not ashamed of crying. But my brother earned more than a few pointless tears from me. That's not how he would have wanted to be remembered, and it's not what he would have wanted for my life. He always wanted the best for me—he was an amazing older brother. I was damn lucky to have him for ten years. And for all the years I out-live him, I have his memory, and what he taught me."

Felicity slid off the hood, her cheeks paler than the sand stretching down to the water. "What did he teach you?"

"Life is short." The truth of Zane's existence was a coal burning in his chest, lodged against his heart and impossible to remove. "No one can say how short, so you'd better *live* while you can. Every moment, every breath, could be your last. Never let an opportunity pass you by. And have fun. Because Michael will never get to do any of the things he dreamed about, the things we talked about late at night after lights out. So I do them for him. For both of us. That's how I moved on."

Something flickered in Felicity's eyes, then she blinked and it was gone. "It's strange, when you think about it. We both grew up under a cloud, overshadowed by dark events beyond our control. I responded by holding myself in check and trying to keep as much control as I can . . . and you let yourself go. You let yourself experience things to the fullest. You wring every drop of happiness you can out of life. I wish I could be more like that."

"You can," he promised her, meaning it with everything in him.

"I think . . . I'm ready to try. If you'll help me."

"Anything." So many promises, when Zane had managed to make it through his entire life without ever promising anyone anything. But he couldn't regret it when a slow, tremulous smile bloomed across Felicity's face.

She leaned back on her elbows against the hood of the car, like a classic pinup girl in a fifties magazine. Crooking one slim finger, she tilted her chin up in invitation. Only the rapid rise and fall of her chest gave away her nerves.

"Come here," Felicity said, all throaty and husky. "And help me experience life to the fullest."

In three long strides, Zane was at her side. Her eyes were hot enough to sear his skin, and when he reached for her, she gasped at the hungry slide of his hands up the outsides of her silken thighs.

Clasping her slender waist, he marveled at the feel of her—delicate, fragile, yet somehow totally in control of her own power as a beautiful and desirable woman. It was addictive. Zane's body throbbed, thick and heavy with the molten beat of his blood.

When Felicity boldly leaned up to grab hold of his collar and pulled him down to cover her, Zane grinned, wild and free. There was nothing on earth like watching Felicity Carlson come apart in his arms. Nothing he'd experienced before in his life of decadent pleasures even compared.

Zane sank into the moment, lost and found in Felicity's tight embrace.

Chapter Six

"I can't believe we did that." Felicity hitched her shoulders against the rear bumper of the car and leaned into Zane. "I can't believe *I* did that."

"No regrets?"

The light ease of his tone was at odds with tension she could feel in his strong, hard-muscled body. The body she'd felt every inch of, pressed against her and moving with her to create sensations she'd never even imagined possible . . .

Felicity smiled up at him and tried to find the energy to rearrange their rucked up clothing into something passably respectable. "None. Except maybe the fact that we didn't take the time to get somewhere private where we could undress each other—and maybe find a flat surface."

At one point, too caught up in each other to notice insignificant details like gravity, they'd slid right off the hood of the car and onto the ground. Cursing fluently, Zane had

twisted them at the last second so he landed first and cushioned her fall. Felicity couldn't help but laugh, even knowing it might piss Zane off. From what she remembered
of her Bad Year of college hook-ups, boys did not enjoy it
when girls got the giggles during sex.

Well, maybe that was the difference between boys and
men, she reflected now as she watched answering humor
lighten Zane's incredible blue eyes. Because Zane had
thrown his head back and laughed right along with her,
then growled and lifted her above him and made her
gasp. She'd never realized sex could be both intimate and
playful, intense and silly at the same time.

"Flat surfaces are overrated," Zane told her, with the air
of a wise old man imparting deeply serious advice. "You
get more points for style and high degree of difficulty if
you go for slanted, bouncy, or otherwise unstable surfaces."

"*You're* unstable," Felicity retorted nonsensically, lifting
her mouth for a kiss.

"But you love that about me." The words hummed
against her swollen, sensitive lips, and Felicity told herself
the shiver that shot down her spine was from the sensation . . . not from the sound of the "L" word in Zane's rich,
deep voice.

She didn't want to move. All her muscles and bones felt
weighted to the ground with spent pleasure and exhaustion. But the ever-present timer in her head kept relentlessly
ticking, reminding her that time was running out.

"What I would love," Felicity said, disentangling herself and struggling to her feet, "would be to nail down a
reception location. I've planned everything I can without
that last piece of the puzzle in place."

Zane glanced at his wafer thin sports watch. "So. The most amazing sex of your life distracted you for all of . . . eighty-seven minutes. I must be slipping."

"Who said it was the most amazing sex of my life?" Felicity responded tartly, hands on hips.

The smoldering look Zane directed up at her from his boneless sprawl on the ground made Felicity's thighs tremble and her cheeks heat. There was something unbelievably sexy about Zane's confidence, especially now that she'd peeked behind the curtain and glimpsed the reasons behind everything Zane did.

His brother's death had scarred him. Zane might think he was over it, that he'd moved on by living his life a certain way—but Felicity could see that there was still healing to be done. For instance, even now, Zane avoided looking past her and out across the beach to the sea.

Holding out a hand to help brace him, Felicity felt a thrill when he clasped her fingers and let her tug him up. They were in this together.

"You're right," she said, quiet and simple and to the point. "It was the best sex of my life, because for the first time in a long time, I let go and allowed myself to enjoy it. And you're the one who showed me how. So thank you for that."

His eyes heated to the color of the blue flames at the heart of a fire. "It was my pleasure, I assure you."

"Let me show you something in return." Felicity tried not to beg, but his answer mattered so much.

Zane zipped up his jeans, leaving the top button undone in a way that played havoc with Felicity's hormones. Shrugging back into his waffle-print cotton Henley shirt, he gave her a wary glance. "The beach?"

She nodded, doing her best to project calm emotional support. "You wanted me to admit that the world wouldn't stop turning if I let go and had fun. We proved that together. Now let me prove to you that you're strong enough to stand at the edge of the ocean."

Fair was fair, Zane supposed, swallowing as a chill sweat broke out along his hairline. Ignoring the clenching of his gut, he said, "Sure. What the hell."

Relief and happiness turned Felicity's smile up to eleven. She clasped his hand, apparently not minding that his palms were a little clammy, and walked backwards onto the edge of the sand.

With Felicity holding his hands and pulling him forward, Zane managed to take that first step out onto the sand. The shift and scratch of it under his shoes tightened his stomach, bringing up memories, but Zane held them at bay by staring into Felicity's soft amber eyes.

He inhaled salt sweet air and the sound of gulls calling to each other as they rode the breeze overhead. Sharp, dry cord grass brushed and caught at his jeans as they tramped through the dunes to the wide expanse of flat beach. The sound of the waves rushing in filled Zane's ears, and for a disorienting heartbeat, the crying gulls sounded like humans shrieking for help. Zane tensed, but Felicity linked her arm through his elbow and stood shoulder to shoulder with him. As if it were the two of them against the world . . . or at least, the two of them against Zane's darkest nightmares.

The Atlantic Ocean rolled out before them like a vast, endless blue void. White-capped waves surged and danced, hiding untold dangers in the depths below. Zane forced himself to confront it—not just the view of the ocean but the undertow of his memories. "This is the same ocean that killed my brother."

Felicity's arm tightened around his, but her voice was calm. "It's never the same ocean. The water ebbs and flows, the tides go in and out, and everything changes. What happened to you and your family was horrible, Zane. But the ocean is as beautiful as it is terrible. And it has a lot of meaning, for a lot of people. I'm sure Miles and Greta would love to celebrate their vows right over there." Felicity pointed a little ways down the beach to a protected inlet, small and intimate looking.

Heart pounding, Zane pictured it. He pictured himself in a suit, after standing up with Miles, who reminded him of Michael so much that at times, it was hard to be around him. Could he do it? Could he dance at Miles's wedding reception, on the sandy beach he'd avoided for so long, and be happy for his friend?

Surprise washed through him. Instead of dread, the image felt good—right. It was what Miles wanted, and Miles should get to live his dream of the perfect wedding. Zane wanted that for him, and since he could never give it to Michael, he'd do his damnedest to make sure Miles got everything he wanted.

Which, for some reason, included Zane working together with Felicity Carlson to plan the reception. Maybe Zane owed Miles a thank you.

Drawing in a deep, cleansing breath, Zane cracked his neck and dropped Felicity's arm so he could turn to face her. She stared up at him with hope and compassion brightening her eyes to the color of ancient gold coins, and Zane couldn't resist dipping his head to steal a kiss from her berry-pink lips.

His next breath came straight from Felicity's lungs, and it gave him strength. "It's going to be a beautiful wedding," he murmured, nuzzling against the silk of her cheek. "And it's going to be a beautiful reception, too—right down there in that cove."

Felicity breathed in sharply, pulling back to search his face. "You mean it? We can go ahead with the reception on the beach?"

The words didn't want to come, choked up behind the knot of emotion in his throat, so he nodded instead. It was all worth it, the pain of reliving the past and the vulnerability of being here with Felicity, for the way her face lit up with happiness and excitement.

As she burst into explanations and plans for what she envisioned the reception to be like, Zane let his eyes drift to half-mast and listened with only half an ear while he kept one arm around her shoulders and concentrated on the feel of her at his side. She fit there so perfectly, as if there had been an invisible space carved out of the universe just for her, and he'd been carrying it around with him all his life.

Breaking off in the middle of an estimate for how long it would take to build a temporary wooden walkway across the cord grass marsh to help guests get from the yacht club to the reception site, Felicity met Zane's gaze. "Thank you. I know this isn't your first choice, and that it's not completely comfortable for you, but it means a lot to me. And I know it will mean a lot to Miles and Greta."

Zane shrugged it off, uncomfortable with her gratitude.

"No big deal. It's not like we'd found another alternative for the reception location anyway. And this will be convenient to the ceremony, no transporting the guests someplace else. It's the practical solution."

"I agree, but I know . . ." Felicity paused, worry shadowing her gaze. "I know it costs you something to be here, and to plan to spend even more time here. I just want you to know that I appreciate it, and I think we're doing the right thing. For several reasons."

Zane wasn't sure what those reasons were, but as Felicity went back to lamenting the fact that she'd left her binder in the car and she couldn't make notes on all her ideas, Zane hugged her in close to his side once more. And even as he pressed a kiss to the honey brown hair crowning her head, he realized he'd do a lot more than stand on a beach to keep from losing this.

Chapter Seven

Felicity wasn't a child. She understood that the fact that she and Zane were now sleeping together—sneaking down the hallway at Harrington House, avoiding the creaky floorboard and laughing breathlessly when they slipped into each other's beds—did not mean they'd never fight again.

Of course, the fact that both of them were guests at the Harringtons' huge, rambling Victorian house on Island Road eliminated several of the major obstacles to continuing their affair. For the last few days, they'd taken shameless advantage of their proximity, and every time they came together, Felicity felt herself unbend a little more. Under Zane's tender hands and hungry gaze, her heart opened like a flower. No matter how often she reminded herself that this was only a fling, Felicity's stubbornly hopeful heart never quite got the message.

But amazing compatibility in the bedroom—and in the

back of her car, against a tree, and once, memorably, in the bathroom at the Firefly Café—did not necessarily equal compatibility anywhere else. Once they'd agreed to hold the reception on the beach, she'd sort of assumed the party planning would be relatively simple from there on.

Not so much.

"I don't get it. Why wouldn't you want me to fly in Dash and the Danger Boys? They're the top music act on my label. They sell out stadium concerts. Women throw their panties on the stage and men rock out to their badass sound." Zane kicked his booted feet up on the porch railing and slouched down in his cushioned wicker chair. "What I'm saying is, they're the new hotness. And I can get them here, on zero notice, to play a freaking hundred-person wedding. That's the coolest thing I can think of."

"It's the flashiest thing you can think of," Felicity corrected, snapping her binder closed. She ran a hand through her hair, grimacing at the tangles, and wished she had a rubber band to tie it back the way she did for her kickboxing classes at the gym. This conversation was every bit as much of a fight.

Zane shrugged. "So? People like a spectacle."

"At a wedding, people like romance," she argued. "And a hard-drinking, hard-living hard rock band doesn't scream romance."

"Romance." Zane's upper lip curled. "The best thing we could do for Miles is help his wedding transcend the usual tired clichés. Let's give them all something to remember! A unique wedding experience they'll never forget."

Felicity kicked her bare toes against the white-painted floorboards to set the porch swing into furious motion. "I don't know how to explain this to you, but Miles and Greta don't care about unique. They don't want to make a spectacle of themselves. They just want to dedicate their lives to each other, and to share that precious occasion with their friends and family in one intimate, special, *romantic* evening."

"And you think some jazz quartet is going to be special enough."

"It would allow people to dance, at least," Felicity pointed out.

"No one can dance to that boring, dusty old music." Pulling out his phone, Zane quickly thumbed through it and turned it to face Felicity. "This is what gets people to dance. Trust me. I didn't make as much money as I have by playing Sinatra in my clubs."

Felicity leaned over to take the phone, her gaze drawn to the splashy homepage for the most popular and exclusive of Zane's nightclubs, Mystique. Live music, hot bands, good cocktails, and a throng of scantily clad, model-beautiful people heaved and writhed across the screen. And yes, they certainly did all look as if they were having a wonderful time.

"But we're not talking about one of your clubs, Zane." Impatient, she tossed the phone back to him and crossed her arms over her chest. "This is a wedding, and weddings are supposed to reflect the personalities of the couple tying the knot. Not the personality of an overgrown teenager who's made a fortune by catering to people's desire to forget their troubles on the dance floor."

Zane's boots hit the porch floor with a thud as he sat up straight. "In other words, you think I'm making this all about me."

"A little bit?" Felicity bit her lip, torn between pushing

the argument further and doing whatever it took to erase the flat, hurt look from Zane's eyes. "Look, I know your intentions are good. I get that you want to give Miles the most amazing wedding reception in the history of the world, because he reminds you of your brother and this is a milestone you'll never get to share with Michael. I understand."

"You understand nothing." Zane threw himself out of his seat and paced the length of the wraparound porch.

Studying the V of his broad-shouldered, lean-hipped back in his tight gray sweater, Felicity's heart ached for him. She understood more than he wanted to admit. She knew this man, deep down, in a way that scared her because it shouldn't be possible between two people who'd only met a little over three weeks ago.

But Felicity was used to facing facts. And the fact here was that she was in big trouble with Zane Bishop. Because the temptation to bring a smile back to his face almost outweighed her longstanding need to present perfection on the professional level.

Almost.

"Okay." She blew out a breath that stirred her bangs on her forehead. "Let's table the entertainment question for now and go back to the décor. We agreed on enclosed, heated structures to protect guests from the ocean breeze. The clear roof and sides will allow guests to enjoy the sunset over the water during cocktail hour, then they can dance under the stars! The company I work with will deal with setup, floor leveling, additional heaters if we want them, and of course, lighting."

Resting his hands on the porch railing, Zane slanted her a look. "Let me guess. No disco ball and colored lights."

"Not at all." Felicity smiled encouragingly. "I'm happy to talk color. I'm thinking a wash of pink or coral, something warm and flattering. And of course we'll want luminarias like tea candles in paper bags or hurricane lamps along the boardwalk and any other walkways between venues. We could carry that theme through into the tents, with strands of paper lanterns."

"Sounds lame."

"It sounds romantic," Felicity gritted out. "Honestly, have you ever even been to a wedding before?"

"Romantic, romantic, romantic." Zane shifted his weight, thrusting his hips back and dropping his head between his bent arms. He groaned. "I hate that stupid word."

A pang shot through Felicity's chest, but she tipped up her chin. "Intimate, then."

"Even worse." Zane straightened abruptly, casting a smoldering look in Felicity's direction. "Unless you mean it in the sexy fun times way. Because I'm always up for that."

Liquid heat pooled in Felicity's belly, temptation thick and tangible in the very air between them. Reading the desire in her face, Zane strode toward her and curled his big hands around her back. He set one knee on the porch swing bench to steady it, looming over her like some ancient god come to life to seduce a poor mortal woman into giving up everything for the joy of his touch.

When he kissed her, Felicity's well-trained body responded instantly. A shiver lifted the hairs at the back of her neck and tightened her nipples to taut, hard knots. As if he were attuned to every pulse of her heart, every inch of her sensitized skin, Zane slid one palm around to cup her breast. Her nipple nestled into the hot center of his hand, which assuaged the ache there while stoking the fire in her center even higher.

It was the middle of the day, and they were in full view of anyone who happened to walk down Island Road, or anyone who looked out the front window of Harrington House. But none of that was enough to pierce the cloud of sensual desire that surrounded Felicity along with Zane's strong arms and huge, overwhelming body. Her brain shuddered to a stop, her thoughts drowned out by the pleasure flooding her system.

Until Zane nipped at her bottom lip and nuzzled down her jaw to her neck, whispering, "This is the kind of intimacy I can get behind."

It was as if he'd dashed a bucket of cold water into her face.

Spluttering, Felicity hauled herself upright and hitched her shirt back into place. The sudden move rocked the swing, knocking Zane off balance and sending him back a step. Concern darkened his face. "What's wrong?"

Heart stuttering, Felicity was terrified she'd never be okay again. "Sex is all you're ever going to be able to give a woman, isn't it?"

Zane's expression shut down so fast, Felicity wondered if she'd imagined the stark flash of fear. "I haven't heard any complaints."

"That's why you veto everything I suggest for the wedding reception, anything that hints at something deeper than the surface, where you like to live . . ."

"Hey." His jaw jutted aggressively even as he retreated a pace. "I live my life to the fullest. That's what I'm all about."

Shaking her head in despair, Felicity said, "No. You

wade through the shallows and avoid the depths. You want spectacle, excitement . . . fun."

"Well, yeah." Zane shrugged one shoulder. "I thought you were on board with that now. Didn't we prove you can have fun and not lose everything?"

The genuine bewilderment in his voice tore at Felicity's heart. "Moderation, right? That was your word. The same way I needed to remember not to be all business and control all the time, you need to know that life can't be nothing but fun. At least, not for me. I need more."

Zane turned on her like a cornered animal, face lined with anger. "Then you're a fool. Asking for more is asking for pain. Yeah, I live on the surface—that's where all the air is. Why would I want to get sucked down below the water? So I can drown?"

He choked off his words when Felicity reached for him, unable to help herself. "Zane, no. Don't you see, I can't keep going like this with you. I can't pretend I can be with you every night, fight and laugh with you every day, and keep from . . ."

"From what? Enjoying yourself?" Zane sneered, painfully handsome in the fading afternoon light.

Felicity took a long look, filling her heart to the brim with the image of this damaged, vibrant, exciting, totally unavailable man. "Sure. Let's call it that," she said quietly as she let the truth crash over her.

Zane Bishop was never going to fall in love with her. He wouldn't allow himself to feel anything that real, that permanent, that deep. And Felicity?

She had to get out while she still had a hope of halting her headlong plummet into a lonely, unrequited forever.

Bending down, she gathered up the binders, papers, and

colored pens and sticky notes that had slid off the swing in all the commotion. "You win, Zane. The reception is all yours."

He recoiled as if she'd struck him. "What are you talking about," he demanded harshly.

Keeping her head down, Felicity was proud of the steadiness of her voice. "I'll work with Miles and Greta on the wedding ceremony at the yacht club, but I'm done planning the reception. Decorate it however you want, bring in your rock stars and acrobats—hell, light the beach up with fireworks and stadium lights. Whatever you want, but leave me out of it."

"You're talking crazy. What about putting on the perfect wedding to impress Miles Harrington and all his fancy friends?"

Zane leaned one shoulder against the white column that supported the porch roof, a deliberately amused smirk twisting his mouth. That smirk faded quickly when Felicity finally met his eyes.

She didn't know what he saw in her expression, but whatever it was, it convinced him she was serious when she said, "Congratulations. Goal achieved. You taught me that perfection isn't the be all, end all of life. So plan the party on your own, and email or text me if you need help finding vendors. I'll see you at the wedding."

Felicity slipped by him, intent on heading upstairs to pack her bags. She'd see if her bride minded if she moved her things over to Greta's old apartment. Forcing her numb brain to go through the motions of making a plan and executing it, Felicity was startled by the hand that landed on her shoulder.

For a brief, ecstatic moment, her heart jumped into her

throat. Had she gotten through to him? Would he stop her from leaving? But one glance at Zane's closed, granite-jawed face dropped Felicity's heart down into the pit of her stomach.

Only a single flex of the muscle in Zane's jaw betrayed his tension. With an easy, empty smile that nothing to warm his ice-blue eyes, he said, "I didn't picture you as someone who gave up and walked away from something good. Guess you're not the person I thought you were."

The words cut deeply, but Felicity refused to let him see her bleed. "It's always a mistake to try to change someone else into who you want them to be. I guess we both learned a valuable lesson here."

Before he could retaliate and push her into saying something she might regret, Felicity turned and walked away.

Chapter Eight

"You know what this island needs? A bar. With alcohol. And cool people." Zane bent over and rested his hands on his knees, trying to catch his breath.

Cooper Haynes paused a few steps ahead of him, further up the hill and not winded at all, the jerk. "A hike clears your head. Alcohol only dulls it."

"Maybe I want to be dull," Zane grumbled, straightening and glaring up at the sharp sunlight filtering through the maritime forest canopy.

"What you want is a distraction," Cooper pointed out. "And since Leo is holed up at the Fireside Inn listening to poetry or something, and Miles is busy trying to relate to Greta's brothers, and you struck out with your wedding planner, you're out of options. It's explore the island with me, or drink in Miles's kitchen alone, like a sad bastard."

Zane didn't want to admit that the idea of drinking himself under the kitchen table sounded kind of appealing.

Maybe he was a sad bastard. Digging deep, he pasted on a who-cares grin and said, "Where are we going, anyway? Tell me this isn't one of those hikes that goes around in circles and is a lame-ass metaphor for how the journey is the point, not the destination."

Casting him a look of mock annoyance, Cooper pointed up the trail to the crest of the hill where it flattened out into what looked like a rocky cliff. "Don't be a dick, or your destination is going to be the choppy water at the base of that cliff, when I push you off it. If you ever make it to the top of this hill."

Zane tamped down the instinctive shudder at the sense memory of cold waves closing over his head and strode determinedly forward. "Keep your shirt on, I'm coming."

They finished the hike in silence, emerging from the trees onto a flat rock that looked out over the horizon. The ocean stretched out endlessly, like gray-blue paint smudged across a canvas, and for the first time since he was a kid, Zane could admit that it was beautiful.

Felicity had given him that. And then she'd walked out of his life like it all meant nothing.

"What's eating you?" Cooper squinted at him through the bright winter light, his flannel shirt, dark jeans, three-day beard growth making him look like a lumberjack. "You usually can't hold onto a bad mood for two minutes, much less two days."

Anger pulsed, hot and bright, under Zane's breastbone. "I'm fine."

Plopping down on a rock shaped almost like an arm-chair, Cooper pulled the stopper out of his canteen and took a long glug of water. "Right. Because moping around with a scowl is totally normal for you."

"So I'm not ever allowed to have an off day." Zane crossed his arms, and turned his back on the view. "You saying you're only friends with me because I'm a good time—and if I stop being fun, you're out?"

Real irritation crinkled Cooper's dark blonde brows. "Don't be a moron."

Coop's scowl reassured Zane like nothing else could have. He could actually feel his shoulders drop two inches when the muscles uncoiled from battle-ready tension.

"Sorry, man." Zane blew out a breath. "It's been a long week. And I've still got a ton to do if I want to pull it out for Miles's party."

"The wedding planner is supposed to be helping, right? If she's not towing her weight, sic Greta on her. That woman is fierce when it comes to people taking advantage of her fiancé."

They smirked at each other, seriously amused at the idea of anyone daring to take advantage of Miles Harrington, the most powerful, controlled, masterful businessman any of them knew. But the man did turn into a pussycat around the woman he loved, so maybe it was a good thing Greta had claws of her own.

Zane ran his fingers through his hair. "Nah, I don't want to ask Felicity for help."

Looking uncomfortable, Cooper said, "Look, I don't want to pry. And I definitely don't want to set myself up to give you relationship advice because, dude, I'm the least qualified guy in the world, on that front. But it seemed like things were going okay with that chick."

"They were." Zane tipped his head back into the breeze, letting the sun dazzle his eyes. "At least, I thought they were. I guess she felt differently."

Cooper made an unimpressed noise. "I saw you two together. Trust me, bro, if she felt anything different from you, it was that she wanted to get married and have your babies immediately, if not sooner."

Zane's heart rate, which had finally slowed down after the workout of an uphill climb, revved back into overdrive. "Shut up. You think so?"

Wriggling his shoulders against the rock as if he were scratching an itch, Cooper made a face. "I'm not an expert on lady facial expressions and body language. But yeah, man. She was seriously into you."

"Then why did she walk away?"

The raw pain in the words vibrated through the air between them, making Zane wish he could swallow them back. Feeling his neck and ears heat with embarrassment and discomfort, he sauntered over to the edge of the rock to peer down at the roiling waters churning against the cliff face below.

When Cooper's response finally came, he was using a tone Zane had never heard from him before. "You really like this girl, don't you?"

Zane wanted to deny it. More than anything, he wanted to be able to laugh it off, to snap back that Felicity Carlson was nothing special, just one in a long line of good time girls whose names he could barely remember a week later. But the lies stuck in his throat.

"Yeah," he said hoarsely, the low words nearly lost in the crash of waves below. "But I don't know what to do about it."

The scrape of fabric against rock told him Cooper was standing up. In a moment, Zane's friend was at his side, staring down into the abyss with him. "Take it from me,"

Cooper said, a grim light entering his pale eyes, focused on something Zane couldn't see. "When you find her—the one woman, the special one—don't screw it up. Don't let her go. Fight for her. Because if you lose her now, you'll regret it for the rest of your life."

Felicity consulted her clipboard and went through her checklist one final time.

"But everyone isn't here," Greta fretted, fingers twisting in the hem of her sweater. "Should we wait for them?"

"We always knew the entire bridal party wouldn't be able to make it for the rehearsal." Miles was so good at soothing his bride—the instant Greta heard his voice, her fidgeting fingers stilled and color came back to her cheeks. "The ones who are here can fill them in."

"Who are we missing?" Felicity asked, stepping around the cluster of bridal party under the flower-bedecked arch to peer into the holding room off to the side of the main yacht club space. That was where the groom and his men would wait tomorrow while the guests arrived, but it was empty now.

She should have done a head count earlier, but she'd been reluctant to run into a certain groomsman.

"Zane can't make it," Miles announced, looking up from his phone. "He just texted to confirm. He's got too much to do on the reception, last-minute stuff."

Guilt twisted Felicity's belly. She should be helping him—it was her job, she was being paid for it. But since that day on the porch, she hadn't heard a word from him. She could only assume he was using his own staff to sort out the myriad problems and inevitable issues that arose with event planning.

Clearing her throat, Felicity raised her voice to command attention. "All right ladies and gentlemen, we're going to get started."

But even as she issued directions to the assembled family members and friends, consulted with the officiant about the order of things, and kept track of everything in her binder, Felicity was aware of a yawning emptiness inside her. Even the gorgeous fairy tale she'd brought to life inside the bare bones of the old yacht club couldn't comfort her. Zane wasn't coming.

This was stupid. She had walked away from the reception and Zane in order to protect herself from having to be around him. So why was she dismayed and deeply disappointed not to see him here tonight?

It was only that she'd worked herself into a tizzy about it, she decided, smiling a little as Greta and her mother sashayed down the aisle. Felicity had done her best to prepare herself for the expected shock to her system of coming face-to-face with the man she'd been on the brink of tumbling head over heels for. But she'd braced for a blow that didn't come, and now she was having a hard time unclenching her muscles.

It had nothing to do with missing him. That would be ridiculous, since they barely knew each other.

Ignoring the tiny voice inside that protested whenever she tried to lie to herself, Felicity nodded to the matron of honor to go through the motions of taking the bride's bouquet so Greta and Miles could join hands under the arbor.

The bridesmaids and the bride's brothers stood silhouetted against the backdrop of the ocean view, which would be even more magical tomorrow, with late afternoon sunshine pouring in and sparkling through the dozens of cut-glass prisms Felicity had strung from the ceiling. Even now, in the violet gloom of twilight, the yacht club almost glowed. The walls, covered in shimmery pale gold fabric, reflected the dancing light of the candles they'd lit to get a sense of how it would look on the day of.

Objectively, Felicity knew she'd achieved her goal. Stepping into the ceremony space was like stepping into a dream of joy and love. She'd poured every ounce of romance in her soul into this room, and it showed.

Maybe that was why she felt so hollowed out as she gazed around at the results of her work. But her job wasn't done yet.

Once the officiant took over, describing what would happen during her part of the ceremony, Felicity finally did a quick head count. With the two younger Harrington brothers as co-best men, and the two billionaire bachelors from New York as Miles's groomsmen, plus the absent Zane, there would be six on the groom's side. They'd planned for even numbers, so there should be six on the bride's side . . . but with the bride, her two future sisters-in-law, and her two brothers standing up with her, there were only five. Which meant they were even at the moment, missing one person from each side. Huh.

Felicity consulted her notes and breathed a sigh of relief. They were still on track—the last bridesmaid wasn't scheduled to arrive until late that night. A quick check of the flight tracker app on Felicity's phone showed that Vivian Banks's flight from New York was running on time. Everything was going according to plan.

Felicity should be happy. She usually loved the wedding rehearsal. High spirits and nerves combined for wedding parties that made jokes, laughed, and buzzed with excitement through all the last-minute organization and instructions. Felicity loved to watch the way family members teared up when they first saw the bride and groom staring into each other's eyes in the very spot where they would become husband and wife. She also appreciated the chance to keep an eye out for any potential problems on the horizon—disgruntled guests, groomsmen too intent on partying it up, that sort of thing. She'd confiscated more than one flask from a groomsman's pants pocket in her day. No groom was showing up late and hungover for his wedding on Felicity's watch.

Forcing her attention back to the action, Felicity tuned in just as the officiant said, "And then I'll tell you to kiss the bride."

From her spot off to the side of the gold-carpeted aisle, Felicity had a perfect view of Miles Harrington's face. He arched a brow at Greta and reached for her with both hands. "We should probably rehearse that too."

"It's the only responsible thing to do," Greta replied with a slightly breathless laugh.

Miles never took his eyes off her face. And when he cupped her cheeks in his big hands, his mischievous grin melted into something softer, deeper, and intensely private. Miles leaned in and brushed their noses together, making Greta laugh, and in the instant before he kissed her, he whispered, "Thank you for taking a chance on love."

Felicity caught her breath. She was the only person standing close enough to overhear, and every word shot through her like a dart.

Then the entire wedding party broke into applause and cheers as Miles swung Greta around and dipped her low over his arm in a wild parody of a movie kiss. It was a big, dramatic moment that called for swelling music and fireworks, but all the fireworks were exploding in Felicity's head.

Taking a chance on love.

Wasn't that what she'd had the opportunity to do? And she'd thrown it away, too afraid to take that risk and put herself out there. But if love wasn't worth risking it all, then what was?

And as the bride's mother cried and the bride's bothers rushed the laughing, kissing couple to pretend to beat up the groom for smooching their little sister in front of them, Felicity stood motionless amidst the happy chaos and wondered . . .

Was it already too late for her and Zane?

Chapter Nine

The first time Felicity caught sight of Zane again, it was ten minutes before the start of the wedding. All morning, as she'd raced around the yacht club pinning hems, directing photographers, corralling bridesmaids, and finding the music stands the string quartet needed for the ceremony, Felicity had shoved her burning need to speak to Zane down into the bottom of her chest. It was all she wanted, but it was likely to be one of the most important conversations of her life—if he'd even speak to her at all, which she wasn't sure of—and she couldn't have that conversation in the middle of the final countdown to the vows.

Impatience chafed at her like a wet swimsuit, but she'd made a commitment to Miles and Greta, and their happily ever after had to come first. There would be time later to sort things out with Zane . . . she hoped.

It all came down to how he reacted when they were finally face to face for the first time since she broke up with him. Felicity held onto the idea that she'd be able to tell from one glance into his eyes whether she still had a chance with him or not. That notion was all that got her through the inevitable semi-disasters that accompanied any wedding, from the underskirt of the wedding gown tearing and needing to be patched and filled out with the plastic bags the bridesmaid dresses had arrived in, to applying adhesive sandpaper to the yacht club steps to make sure no lady guests slipped in their delicate high heels.

Felicity narrowed her focus and bulled her way through the morning and afternoon, the entire day of preparation passing in a whirl of flash photographs, laughing bridesmaids—the last one arrived in time and perfectly prepared, thank goodness—makeup, hair styling, and tearful moments of excitement and anticipation. Everything was going smoothly, and Felicity had the satisfaction of knowing that whatever insane spectacle Zane had made out of the reception, at least the wedding ceremony itself would be exactly what Greta and Miles had envisioned.

And then, at last, it was time. The guests had arrived, oohed and aahed over the sprays of white hothouse orchids that turned the cozy old room into an exotic, otherworldly bower, sparkling with rainbows from the crystal prisms overhead. They'd settled into their gilded ladderback chairs and watched the string quartet set up off to the side of the arbor, which was made of two gracefully twisted pillars of driftwood that had been hand painted in shades of gold and silver.

The officiate entered from the holding room door, concealed behind the shimmery bunting swagged diagonally from the top of the arbor, and smiled at the assembled guests. With a wave of her white-and-gold robed arm, the groom and his groomsmen walked out, single file, to stand in front of the arbor.

Six tall men in impeccable black tuxedoes, each incredibly handsome in his own, unique way with the vast glory of the sunlit ocean visible through the picture window behind them. A ripple of feminine appreciation sighed through the wedding guests, but Felicity had eyes for only one man.

Standing second to last, between Leo and Cooper, Zane Bishop outshone even the groom to Felicity's hungry gaze. His dark brown hair waved back from his chiseled cheekbones and high, broad forehead. The flash of his bright, sky-blue eyes was visible even across the rows of seated guests that separated them.

Felicity was so caught up in the breathless anticipation of when he would first glance her way, the moment she'd be able to read his feelings in the set of his expressive mouth and the glitter of his gaze, she nearly missed the officiant's cue to get the bridesmaids walking. With a start, she hurriedly pushed open the door at the back of the room and smiled as Vivian Banks stepped out to begin the procession.

Zane still hadn't looked at her.

In fact, even once all the bridesmaids and the two bridesmen had made their slow, stately way down the aisle to take their places at the arbor, and every eye in the congregation had turned back to watch as the bride finally entered the room . . . Zane kept his gaze straight ahead.

His handsome face was perfectly composed, almost stern in its stillness as he listened seriously to the officiant's greeting. Felicity was supposed to be sneaking around to the side of the ceremony to keep an eye on things and be on hand, just in case . . . but she couldn't make herself move. She stood at the back of the room and stared at Zane, willing him to glance her way. But he never did.

And as despair gripped her heart in an iron fist, Felicity realized she had her answer.

The rest of the wedding passed in a haze. Felicity, who cried at every wedding she planned, was too numb inside to shed a single tear. Not during the intensely moving reading by Leo Strathairn, not during Greta and Miles's vows, and not even at their first kiss as husband and wife. It was a much sweeter, more romantic and less showy kiss than the huge dip they'd rehearsed, but Felicity gritted her teeth through it. She had a terrible feeling that if she started to cry, she wouldn't be able to stop.

The only hiccup in the proceedings came from Miles's other groomsman, Cooper Haynes. Felicity hadn't seen much of him during the wedding prep—he'd been off exploring the island, and mostly strong and silent when he did appear for a fitting or the wedding rehearsal. She'd made a note of him as completely reliable and unflappable, not someone she needed to worry about. She'd been wrong.

He was a statue through the entire ceremony, like a sculpture carved out of ice. And when the moment finally came for him to move, to follow Zane and the other groomsmen up the aisle, Cooper hadn't taken a step. For a long, awkward pause that hopefully went unnoticed by anyone else in the general festivity of the recession back up the aisle—the hilarity of the bride's loud, funny brothers mincing up the aisle on Zane's arm, simpering and cooing and pretending to be bridesmaids instead of bridesmen. But Felicity, who'd averted her eyes from Zane's laughing face, caught the frozen paralysis of Cooper Haynes facing down the woman he was supposed to squire up the aisle.

The last bridesmaid, the one who hadn't been at the rehearsal the night before. Vivian Banks. She was pale beneath her glossy waves of black hair, smiling in a brittle way that looked as if it might shatter at any moment. More cracks appeared in her calm facade every second that Cooper stared at her, motionless.

It took a hissed word from Greta and a glower from Miles to knock Cooper out of his trance. He jerked as if he were coming awake after being in a coma for ten years, and even from the back of the room, Felicity could clearly see the shock and dawning anger on his face. She held her breath and prepared to step in—although she had no idea what she thought she'd do. Run around behind Cooper and push him up the aisle by force? But luckily it didn't come to that. With a clench of his jaw and a thunderous brow, Cooper held out a rigid arm to Vivian Banks.

She laid her hand on his arm, barely touching him, and the two marched up the aisle in stony silence as the music crested and the crowd erupted into cheers for the bride and groom. Miles looked at Greta and, in an unrehearsed move, stepped close and swept her up into his arms. Then he carried her down the aisle while she threw her head back and laughed up at the swaying, dancing glass ornaments hanging like stars from the ceiling.

It was over. Felicity's part was done, and it had gone off without a major hitch. Relief filtered through the haze of exhaustion and numb regret for the choices she'd made.

Moving on autopilot, Felicity hustled out of the yacht

club to make sure the driftwood sign pointed the way down the makeshift boardwalk to the reception site. If she hurried, she could beat most of the guests to the beach. She'd find Zane and—well. Felicity's throat closed. It would be hard to talk to him, knowing he could barely stand the sight of her, but she could offer her help with the reception, if he still needed any. It was the least she could do.

The hand-painted signpost she'd stuck in the ground was exactly where it should be, indicating which way to turn to get to the reception. The narrowness of the walkway meant they had to file along two or so at a time, which would give the wedding party, who'd gotten up the aisle first and fastest, a few moments to regroup before the rest of the guests arrived at the tents. But instead of following the well-lit walkway she'd had created, Felicity hurried up to the graveled road and took the back way into the reception. Crossing through the patch of gravel they were using as a parking lot and staging area, she passed black-jacketed servers running between the truck and the buffet tables set up in the tents down on the beach.

The clear-sided structure they'd agreed on was set in the sand like a diamond nestled in a jewel box, gleaming and beckoning with the promise of warmth against the cold wind. Felicity was so captivated by the radiant, magical effect of the glass tent, she almost missed the black touring bus parked off to the side, partially obscured by a tall sand dune. Moving closer and squinting through the gloom, she saw the words "Dash and the Danger Boys" scrawled across the side of the bus.

So he'd brought in his rock stars after all.

Felicity tried not to be disappointed since she'd expected nothing less when she'd walked out on the planning a week ago. But it was hard. It felt like the final nail in the coffin of her hopes that Zane might come to see that there was more to life than flash and fun.

There was love. But only if you were brave enough to try for it.

Mouth turning down in an unhappy curve, Felicity released a shuddering breath and told herself to get a grip. She still had a job to do. If nothing else, maybe she could salvage some career prospects from the mess she'd made of her personal life. She'd just head down to the reception, make sure Greta and Miles were fine and didn't need anything, and maybe schmooze with a few potential clients among the guests.

She sighed. What once had lured her with the shiny potential of more work and higher profile events now seemed like an unbearably exhausting chore. All she wanted was to slink back to Greta's old apartment, run a bath in the enormous cast-iron, claw-footed tub, and steam away her aches and pains.

But since the worst, most persistent ache was buried deep in her chest, where warm water couldn't soothe it, Felicity pulled herself up and walked down the sandy hill to enter the glass tent.

The change from the moment when she opened the sturdy door and stepped from the frozen night and into the dazzling heat and twinkling light of the party tent was magical. Felicity's heart stuttered as she gazed up and around, taking in the lavish crystal chandeliers throwing glittering sparks across the white walls and providing a soft ambient glow over the dance floor and banks of round tables.

Every table sported luxurious ocean blue brocade table-cloths, gleaming gold plates and silver cutlery, and a gorgeous centerpiece of shells, sand dollars, starfish interspersed with sweet forget-me-nots and spiky fringed sea lilies. Felicity turned a slow circle, feeling a smile spread across her face as she realized she would never have to be ashamed or embarrassed to have her name associated with this wedding.

No matter how crazy Zane's rock band or possible circus performers turned out to be, everything looked lovely. Every single detail lifted Felicity's spirits, from the polished parquet dance floor to the complete lack of disco balls, to the incredible view of the sun about to slip below the horizon so the guests could enjoy the sunset during cocktail hour. She spied a passing waitress with a tray full of classic martini glasses brimming with what looked like chocolate liqueur drizzled with something white and creamy.

"Excuse me, what are those?" Felicity asked, unable to restrain her curiosity.

"The wedding's signature cocktail," the waitress replied, offering Felicity the tray. "The Winter Beach, a dark chocolate and peppermint martini with sea salt foam. Would you like one?"

"No thanks." Felicity smiled as she waved the waitress away. She didn't need alcohol to rev her up right now. Buzzing with a sudden surge of energy, she looked around the tent for someplace to pitch in, but everything looked extremely well organized.

Her gaze landed on the knot of bridesmaids and family members by the entrance, and Felicity squared her shoulders. Here was something she could do—corral the wedding party into a receiving line to say hello to each guest and welcome them to the reception.

Heart beginning to thump, Felicity set off across the tent, her eyes seeking through the small group of laughing, hugging, twirling people for that one, certain tall figure—a man with dark brown hair, killer cheekbones, and eyes the color of the deepest part of the ocean.

"What do you think of my party?"

Zane's deep, velvety voice stopped her in her tracks just as she reached the center of the dance floor. Whirling to face him, Felicity teetered in her sensible wedges and instinctively reached out to Zane in the instant before she realized how awkward it would be if he stepped back.

But he didn't. With one smooth step forward, he caught her arm and steadied her, his blue eyes intent and focused on her face.

Tingles of sensation coursed up her arm from their single point of contact, and Felicity could only be glad she was wearing a dove gray pantsuit, complete with long-sleeved jacket. If he'd touched her bare forearm, she might well have swooned—and then she'd have to retire forever from public life to escape the humiliation.

"Okay there?" No amusement curled his lips or lightened his serious expression.

Felicity nodded and made herself stand up straight. "I'm fine. Just a little tired."

She hadn't slept well since she'd walked out on Zane, a few hours of light dozing every night, if she was lucky.

Gaze sharpening, Zane said, "Me too."

For a giddy moment, Felicity thought he was telling her that he, also, had been having trouble sleeping without her.

She shook her head to try and snap herself back into reality. "Right, of course. You must be exhausted, after pulling all of this together. It looks beautiful, Zane."

"You like it." It didn't sound like a question, but Zane's grave gaze scanned her face as if searching for an answer.

Felicity nodded. "It's amazing. You did a wonderful job, and I know Miles is going to be so touched at all the work you put in. You're a really good friend."

A slight frown gathered Zane's straight dark brows, as if that wasn't the answer he'd been hoping for. "Let me show you around."

Every inch of her skin yearned toward him. It was all Felicity could do not to sway into his arms. But this was exactly what she'd wanted to avoid when she walked away the first time. Except that had been a mistake. Hadn't it?

Confused and heartsore, she fell back on what she knew. "I should really check in with Miles and Greta, make sure they're all set up for the receiving line."

"Miles and Greta are fine," Zane said firmly, taking her elbow and steering her off the dance floor toward the back of the tent. "They're solidly encased in an ecstatically happy bubble that nothing is going to pop, since we gave Greta the beach wedding of her dreams . . . and ensured that Miles didn't have to wait until summer to have her. I promise, they can handle the receiving line on their own. What do you think of the chandeliers?"

Distracted from her instinctive protest, Felicity glanced up again. The two large fixtures hung suspended from the slim white beam that peaked at the top of the glass roof, curving gracefully out and sending beams of warm light over the whole enclosed space. "They're lovely. Really nice choice. Better than a disco ball."

She tried to smile, to make a joke out of it, but Zane never cracked a grin. "Would you say they're romantic?" he demanded.

Floundering, unsure of what was going on with him—she'd never seen Zane go this long without laughing—Felicity stammered, "Uh, sure. Yes, of course. Classic romance."

Zane relaxed a little, satisfaction settling around his shoulders like a cape. "That's just for during cocktail hour and dinner, though. Wait till you see what I have planned for the beach outside, once the sun goes down and the party really gets started."

"Fireworks?" Felicity guessed, bracing herself for a rousing round of did-you-get-the-right-permits and did-you-check-the-sound-ordinances.

"Nope." Zane lifted one mysterious brow as he steered her toward a door in the clear tent wall facing the water-front. But before Felicity could be ask if she needed to run back to the yacht club to grab the coat she'd forgotten in her hurry to find him, a quick drum lick and screech of guitar behind them announced that Dash and the Danger Boys had taken the stage.

"You got your band down here," Felicity observed, glancing over her shoulder to where the four hot rock-stars who currently topped the Billboard chart were setting up, checking their amps and slinging the straps of their instruments over their brawny shoulders. They weren't dressed as provocatively as Felicity expected—yeah, tight leather pants and dark denim prevailed, but they were all wearing silky blue button-down shirts over them.

The color matched the table linens perfectly, and

Felicity shot Zane a surprised glance just as the front man stepped forward, tapped the mic, and flicked a lock of his long hair out of his lean, handsome face.

"We're going to warm up," he said quietly in the faint Cockney accent that had conquered a nation of squealing teenage girls. "This one is a special request from our boss, who brung us out here to play for you all. Oh, and cheers to the happy couple."

With no further showmanship, the lead singer struck a low, sweet chord on his guitar and leaned in to croon "At last . . . . my love has come along."

The rest of the band picked up the lyrical melody, lifting the strains of music up to a glorious crescendo. The lyrics filled Felicity's head, every note plucking an answering string deep in her body, and she gasped as the lead singer went on to belt out how glad he was that his lonely days were over.

"Dash and the guys are going to play jazz standards all night long," Zane murmured into her ear. "They were excited about it, actually. I made sure they've got some Sinatra in their play list."

Zane's heart was kicking harder than the drum beat from the stage. He couldn't tell what Felicity was thinking from the wide, shocked look on her fine-featured face. And she wasn't giving him much to work with verbally either. Apparently, the shock of Zane Bishop being romantic had struck her dumb.

"Come on," he urged, deciding if he was going in, he might as well go all in. "I've got one more thing to show you."

"Out in the cold? As you pointed out, it's kind of nuts

to throw an outdoor party on a beach in the wintertime, much less to walk down to the shoreline."

But Felicity didn't resist the tug on her hand, her cold fingers barely twitching in Zane's grasp. He clasped the slender digits tighter and brought their joined hands to his mouth, breathing on them to warm them up. His mind raced ahead, down the beach to his last big surprise. That would chase away the chill of the night air.

He led her away from the heated tent and across the sand to a mammoth pile of driftwood a few safe feet back from the high tide mark. The line of luminarias along the boardwalk flickered in the distance, lighting the path from the yacht club to the glass-sided reception hall, but all the guests had already found their way to the party. It was only the two of them shivering out in the gusty salt breeze off the waves.

Keeping tight hold of Felicity, Zane reached his free hand into his pocket and withdrew his favorite silver Zippo lighter. "This was my brother's," he told her, not even trying to hide the husk of emotion in his voice. "I thought it was so cool, the way he'd flip it open. He showed me how to light it one-handed, by catching the lid on my pants leg and striking the flint at the same time. Let's see if I still have the touch."

"Zane, what is all this?" Felicity sounded overwhelmed, near tears herself, and Zane's heart swelled until it felt as if it would burst out of his chest.

Flipping the Zippo down in one swift move, he breathed a sigh of relief when the spark struck on the first try. A tiny flame flickered up from the lighter, dancing in the wind, and Zane bent to hold it to one of the tinder sticks he'd placed strategically around the bottom of the drift-wood pile.

The flame smoked, then caught, racing down the stick to the center of the pile. Zane smiled at the crackle of fire and pulled Felicity with him as he lit the other tinder sticks around the base, one by one, then stood back to watch it smolder into life.

"It'll take a while to really get going," Zane explained, looking for the right words to say what he felt. He'd never been speechless in his life, but words were harder when the feeling behind them was real.

"Zane." Felicity stopped there, just his name, and he didn't know what that meant. Maybe she didn't understand yet what all of this meant.

"You didn't want a disco ball or fireworks, so I built a bonfire on the beach instead," he said, watching the val-iant flames struggle to catch and grow. He didn't want to look at her, in case she had actually gotten it but thought all of this, his last ditch effort to show her his heart, was unbearably lame.

"I wanted candlelight, you wanted a disco ball—so your compromise was crystal chandeliers followed by a bonfire on the beach?"

Her voice sounded strange. He couldn't read the tone. "You wanted jazz and I wanted rock stars," Zane clarified doggedly, still staring at the struggling fire.

"So you gave me rock stars singing jazz," Felicity finished. "On the beach. Oh, Zane!"

When he finally mustered up the courage to glance down at her, an entire constellation of stars shone from her eyes. Cheeks flushed pink, sleek fancy braid torn to pieces by the wind, eyes shining and chest heaving, Felicity had never looked more beautiful to him than she did in that moment. Because she got it. And she didn't think it was lame.

All of that made it easy for Zane to say, "You wanted romance. And I wanted to give it to you. Because you deserve it, and because I love you."

Twin tears made silvery tracks down her cheeks, but Felicity was laughing, too, as she threw her arms around his neck and all but climbed him like a ladder. "I love you, too! I was going to tell you as soon as I saw you today, but then you wouldn't even look at me at the wedding, and I thought . . ."

Zane clutched her to him greedily, hands molding her beloved curves and lifting the wonderful, wriggling weight of her in his arms. Felicity wound her legs around his waist and buried her face in his neck while he told her, "I couldn't look at you. I knew if I did, I'd knock down the bride and her elderly mother to get to you."

She gave a watery gurgle. "I'm glad you restrained yourself. And I'm so glad I left this party in your hands. It's like something out of a dream."

Nuzzling the hair at her temple and glorying in the clasp of her thighs and the strong arms twining around his shoulders, Zane smiled. "I thought you don't believe in dreams."

Drawing back to meet his gaze, Felicity said, "You make me feel brave enough to believe anything. But in my wildest dreams, I couldn't have imagined the party as a perfect blend of you and me. I love it."

Zane had to kiss her for that. He delved into the deep sweetness of her mouth, almost lightheaded with relief that this incredible woman was able to read the love letter he'd crafted especially for her. A love letter written not in words on a page, but in the notes of a love song and the flicker of firelight.

They kissed under the stars, suspended between the infinity of the night sky and the vastness of the ocean, and for the first time since Zane was a child, he wasn't afraid of forever. Not with Felicity in his arms.

Lantern Lake

Prologue

Miles Harrington stood beneath the driftwood arbor in the cozy old yacht club with the winter ocean churning on the other side of the plate glass window. He gazed across the assembled wedding guests—Sanctuary Island's warm, friendly, quirky residents on the bride's side . . . New York's wealthy elite on the groom's.

In the heart-thumping anticipation of these last few moments before his bride appeared, Miles could barely focus on anything other than the insistent, possessive drive to make Greta Hackley his, now and forever. But since it would probably be bad form to stride up the aisle, tear open the door at the back of the room where she was waiting to make her entrance, and carry her off, Miles forced himself to stand still.

Casting about for a distraction, Miles registered the swell of the music as the string quartet began to play the processional piece and the first bridesmaid appeared. His

attention snapped to her as recognition and memory filtered through the wedding haze.

Ah, yes. Vivian Banks. This should be interesting.

It took all of Miles's control not to turn his head far
enough to sneak a glance at the final groomsman standing arrayed behind him. He was more than curious about
Cooper Hayes's reaction to coming face to face with the
One That Got Away, after all these years—in fact, Miles
had a lot riding on this moment.

Specifically, his beloved custom-designed luxury helicopter.

It all started with a bet, that each of Miles's three young
billionaire bachelor friends would find their hearts and
their lives irrevocably altered by spending time on Sanctuary Island. After all, it worked for the Harrington
brothers! Miles's other two groomsmen, Leo Strathairn
and Zane Bishop had already fallen, and fallen hard. But
this was the moment when Miles would discover whether
his final bachelor buddy would succumb to the magic of
the island.

Okay, so in Cooper's case, there was less "island magic"
involved, and more straight-up manipulation and strategy. Miles's fiancée had made fun of him for being a
matchmaker, but Miles had a long history of putting together incredibly successful business deals. He didn't see
why pairing off his friends with the loves of their lives
should be any more difficult.

So far, it hadn't been. And from the beginning of this
bet, Miles had been counting on Cooper to be the easiest
of them all.

But as Vivian Banks glided gracefully down the aisle
toward them and Miles caught a glimpse of her ex's reac-

tion out of the corner of his eye, Miles started to wonder if his matchmaking skill would finally be put to the test.

Because Cooper Hayes didn't look like a man who'd just set eyes on his long-lost love for the first time in a decade. He looked pissed. Like he wanted to make someone pay.

And in the instant before the Wedding March struck up and Greta finally appeared, capturing every scrap of Miles's mind and heart and attention for herself, he realized—Cooper wasn't only angry at Miles for bringing her here. The true target of Cooper's slow-burning fury was the only woman he'd ever loved. The woman Miles had been sure his friend *still* loved.

Sorry, Viv, Miles apologized silently to his childhood friend. *I may have miscalculated this one. But you two are going to have to sort it out on your own, because I have a wedding to complete . . . and a wedding night to enjoy.*

Chapter One

For the first time in a long time, Cooper Hayes felt his itchy, wandering feet grow heavy and immovable. He was anchored to the yacht club's weathered hardwood floor, the weight of past and present colliding to root him to the spot.

She was here. Against all odds and decency, the woman who broke his heart ten years ago was a bridesmaid in the same wedding Cooper was standing up in.

The groomsman on Cooper's right, his friend Zane Bishop, muttered out of the corner of his mouth, "Dude. Isn't that—?"

"Vivian Banks," Cooper confirmed. The feel of the name in his mouth was like chocolate—sweet, dark, and bitter. Something he'd loved when he was a kid . . . before he became allergic to it on a trip to the Ivory Coast.

"What the hell is she doing here?" The outrage in Zane's hissed whisper made Cooper feel better.

Despite the fact that he'd been asking himself the same

question, Cooper shrugged minutely. "She and Miles go way back. Family friends. Guess she and Greta got close."

Cooper ground down the need to walk out on the whole damn thing. Miles couldn't have realized what he'd done.

Despite the man's ruthless willingness to do whatever it took to win their bet, he'd been a good friend to Cooper for a long time. Eleven years, in fact, and he'd stuck by Cooper when other people had given up on him.

People like Vivian Banks, for example.

So Cooper gritted his teeth through the ceremony, the love songs and poetry and vows of eternal devotion no more than static in his ears. He got through the whole thing cloaked in a cloud of anger and hurt—the kind of pain that didn't fade over time—until the crowd of guests erupted into loud cheers and applause.

Startled, Cooper looked up to see Miles and Greta locked into their first kiss as husband and wife. That was the cue to the rest of the wedding party to start the recessional back up the blue-carpeted aisle. And that was the moment when Cooper realized exactly which bridesmaid he'd be escorting.

Without meaning to, he locked eyes with Vivian on the other side of the flowers and shimmery-fabric-draped altar. She'd missed the rehearsal the night before, but she seemed to know what to do. She stepped forward, her lovely, unforgettable features set in a blank mask of pleasantness.

And Cooper stalled out.

His feet—usually so ready to move, to carry him forward on whatever adventure beckoned—remained planted under him. All he could do was stare at her.

The woman staring back at him with dawning panic behind her indigo eyes looked almost the same as the girl who'd ground her designer heel into Cooper's heart a decade ago. The same wavy black hair, same porcelain skin that showed the stain of a blush so well, same perfect bow-shaped lips. But her eyes . . .

Still the same rich blue, so dark they were almost purple, but instead of the carefree laughter and mischief he remembered, this woman's eyes were shadowed with loss . . . and an echo of the pain Cooper carried like an extra weight in his trusty shoulder pack.

Stomping down his instinctive reaction, which was to find out who'd made Vivian hurt and make them hurt worse, Cooper shook his head at himself. She was probably just embarrassed that he'd left her hanging for thirty seconds, standing alone at the front of the congregation waiting for him to escort her up the aisle.

Cooper stepped forward, refusing to rush or show any discomfort with the situation. He hadn't done anything wrong. He had nothing to be ashamed of.

When he was close enough, he offered her his arm. Cooper willed her to meet his eyes, silently daring her to look him in the face after what she'd done to him, but she didn't. Instead, she ducked her head slightly in a gesture he could never remember seeing before, and let her hand settle gently on his arm. The barely-there weight of her touch reminded him of the time he'd been hiking in Michoacan and stumbled upon a swarm of migrating monarch butterflies.

He'd stood like a statue as the delicate insects alit along his arms and shoulders, even on top of his head. He hadn't felt their landings; if he'd closed his eyes, he wouldn't have known they were touching him. But he would have heard them. More butterflies had swooped and fluttered around him, the light whisper of their wings filling his ears exactly the way the thickened throb of his heartbeat pounded in his ears now.

He and Vivian walked sedately up the aisle through the parted sea of smiling faces, but none of it registered in Cooper's brain. All he could see, all he could hear, all he could feel was Vivian Banks.

"I didn't realize you were part of the wedding party," he muttered, low enough that only she could hear him.

The slender fingers on his arm tightened minutely, only for a second, then relaxed. "I'm sorry," she said, her voice softer and more tentative than his memories. "I don't know why they didn't tell you. I asked Miles to make sure it was all right with you—I would've been happy to attend as just a guest. Or I would have stayed away, if you told Miles it would bother you to see me. But I guess he didn't ask."

Cooper clenched his jaw, forcing his voice to smooth disinterest. "It doesn't bother me to see you. Why should it?"

Her head ducked further, as if she wished she could hide. "After the way things ended between us . . ."

"Ancient history. I moved on a long time ago. In fact," Cooper said as they reached the end of the aisle and pushed their way out of the yacht club and into the fading afternoon sunlight, "I should probably take this opportunity to thank you."

"To thank me?" Vivian removed her hand in order to wrap her arms around herself. The unseasonably warm Sanctuary Island winter seemed to have finally turned, and the wind blowing in off the ocean snapped with cold. The dark blue satin of her bridesmaid dress may have matched her eyes, but it wasn't doing much to keep her warm.

Without a second thought, Cooper shrugged out of his tuxedo jacket and swirled it over Vivian's shoulders. Smoothing the lapels over her crossed arms, Cooper stared down at her and willed himself to feel nothing.

But none of the meditation techniques he'd learned in India or the exotic herbal remedies he'd sampled in China would be enough to keep Cooper blissfully calm and detached. Not when he stood mere inches from the woman who'd changed his life forever. Not when he was close enough to smell the light vanilla scent of her perfume and see the fine-grained texture of her silky skin.

Vivian Banks was within his grasp for the first time in ten years. And Cooper would be damned before he let her slip away again.

At least, not before he punished her for the sins of her past.

Vivian shivered, but with the body-warmed folds of Cooper's dinner jacket enfolding her, she couldn't blame it on the cold ocean breeze.

After her divorce, she thought she'd be only too glad never to be close to another man again. And for the last two years, she'd been right. She could glimpse a hot guy across the grocery store parking lot or down at the hardware store and feel nothing—not even a flicker of interest. She'd congratulated herself on being done with desire forever.

Apparently, she'd celebrated that victory over her body a little too soon. Because it turned out that her body had only been in hibernation . . . just waiting for the moment when it sensed Cooper Hayes's huge, overwhelming, electrifying presence once more.

Tough poop, Vivian told herself. She'd had her chance with Cooper, and she did worse than blow it—she obliterated it.

Staring out over the sand dunes with their lopsided fencing and hardy scrub grass, Vivian felt her eyes burn a little. She blinked hard. "What on earth could you possibly want to thank me for?"

Cooper's big, warm hands settled on her shoulders like the weight of all her mistakes, pressing her down into the sand. "Well, if you hadn't left me standing at the courthouse with a marriage license in one hand and my dick in the other, I probably wouldn't ever have left Brooklyn and traveled the world."

And become a billionaire. He didn't say it, but Vivian couldn't help thinking it. As someone who had just spent her last scrap of savings on a dilapidated lake cabin a fraction of the size of the immaculate house she grew up in, Vivian was keenly aware of how low the mighty had fallen . . . and how high Cooper had risen since they last knew each other.

Fate might be fickle, Vivian reflected, but you could always count on her to have a sense of humor.

"If what happened between us helped push you to reach your true potential, then I can only be glad," she said, her throat tight, but her voice steady.

His hazel gaze sharpened. "You kept up with all that? I would've thought once you washed your hands of me, you'd stop caring about my 'potential.'"

I never stopped caring, Vivian wanted to say. The words trembled on her tongue, but she'd learned something about caution and self-preservation in the last ten years. She held the words back with an effort. "I heard you designed a cell phone app that streamlined the process of getting prescription medicines to patients. And that you licensed it to the American Medical Association for big bucks."

Cooper shrugged, digging his hands into his trouser pockets. He'd always been uncomfortable with praise, uneasy in the spotlight. She'd been the head cheerleader . . . he'd been the scholarship kid who nearly got kicked out of their Calculus class for arguing with the professor.

"I didn't do it for the money," he said stiffly, stabbing a pang of sympathy through Vivian's heart. She knew exactly what had motivated him to use his God-given smarts to create that particular bit of software.

"You helped a lot of people. Maybe even saved some lives."

If Vivian hadn't been searching his face so diligently, she might have missed the flash of grief buried deep in his green-gold eyes. "I didn't do it for the money," he repeated, with a smile that seemed only slightly forced. "But it sure has been nice to be able to fund my travels around the world. I've been to Bangkok, Jerusalem, Tokyo, Rome— all the places we used to talk about, and a lot more in between. But I guess you've been around the world a time or two yourself, by now."

Vivian glanced away, afraid of what he might see in her expression. "No. I never have."

Cooper's voice roughened, gruff with some unnamed emotion. "That husband of yours turned out to be a homebody, huh?"

Her gaze flew back to him. "You know I got married?" What else had he heard? Did he know the extremely public and humiliating reasons why she was no longer married?

Cooper squinted into the distance, taking on a bored tone. "Miles mentioned it a while back. So how's married life treating you?"

Relief was a sour tang at the back of her throat. He didn't know. But it wouldn't take more than quick Google search for him to find out. It was only a matter of time.

"I'm divorced," she told him quickly, watching for his reaction. "A couple of years ago."

But if she'd expected him to light up like a kid on Christmas, she was doomed to disappointment. Cooper only cocked his head, his face a mask of indifference. "Too bad. I guess nothing lasts forever."

The doors to the yacht club opened behind them and the bride and groom spilled out on a tide of cheers, laughter, and applause. The joyful noise covered Vivian's involuntary gasp at the sharp pain that speared her at Cooper's cold words.

"What are you two still doing standing here?" Greta cried from her perch in Miles's arms. She looped an arm around his strong neck, waved her bouquet of deep blue hydrangeas and kicked her feet in a froth of ivory satin. "It's time to kick up our heels and dance the night away!"

"One dance," Miles growled into her ear, a smile tugging at his mouth. "That's all I can promise before I drag you home."

Vivian watched the way Greta blushed and smiled, a complicated mix of emotions whirling like a blender in her stomach. Memories of her own joyless wedding butted up against the dreams she'd had about the man at her side, but she couldn't be bitter as she gazed on her friends' utter happiness. No one deserved it more than these two, who had been so good to her, even including her in their most special day.

Reminded of her bridesmaid duties, Vivian looked up the stairs at the happy couple. "Is there anything you need, before the reception? Anything I can do?"

"You've done so much already," Greta protested. "But I guess, if you wouldn't mind hanging onto my bouquet?"

"Of course!" Vivian smiled, pleased to make herself useful, but her eyes widened when Greta exchanged a quick, mischievous glance with her new husband and lifted the bouquet.

"Here, Viv, catch!"

Greta tossed the bouquet down the yacht club stairs to land unerringly in Vivian's outstretched arms. She blinked down at the cluster of exuberant blue and purple blossoms, the stems wrapped in white ribbon and secured with pearl-tipped pins.

"You caught it," Greta said, delighted.

"I think that counts, don't you?" Miles winked at his wife.

She nodded. "Oh, absolutely. It's settled."

Don't say it, Vivian begged silently as a flaming blush scorched up her neck and into her cheeks. *Please don't.*

Miles grinned his corporate shark smile. "Looks like you're up next, Viv. Wonder where we can find a groom for you."

The fact that she would never be able to repay Miles Harrington's loyalty and generosity to her over the years was all that kept her from trying to kill him with her brain.

Unable to stop herself, Vivian risked a glance at Cooper. The look on his face made her suck in a breath. She'd always been able to read him. No matter what happened, no matter how silent he got, Vivian had always known exactly what he was thinking.

Not anymore.

Cooper was smiling, but his eyes were dark and hot, hinting at an inner turmoil Vivian could only guess at. With an ironic quirk of one golden-brown eyebrow, he offered his arm to her once more, as impeccable and graceful as any of the wealthy, privileged boys they'd gone to school with.

"Let's get to the reception," Cooper said smoothly. "Who knows? Maybe Prince Charming will appear. Most people meet their future spouses at weddings, after all."

Chapter Two

Cooper had once been invited to a Hindu wedding while he'd been in Bangladesh, a spur-of-the-moment invitation that had resulted in him getting to participate in a raucous, colorful three-day-long celebration that involved clouds of incense, beautiful women in bright saris, and a pair of elephants. Cooper was no stranger to weddings.

But this reception on a small, pristine stretch of beach on Sanctuary Island was like nothing he'd ever seen.

Beside him, Vivian gasped. He glanced down at her, transported back in time by the giddy appreciation on her beautiful features as she took in the splendor of the glass-sided, clear-roofed structure. The dark blue carpet beneath their feet echoed the color of the ocean spread out under the darkening sky beyond the glass tent. From the tables to the crystal chandeliers to the bandstand set up by the gleaming parquet dance floor, Miles and Greta had created a wedding wonderland.

It was the perfect setting for what Cooper had in mind.

Miles and Greta were swarmed by the guests and family members trickling into the tent. Keeping a firm hold of Vivian's hand, Cooper went in search of the table that would give them their seat assignments for dinner. He wasn't disappointed.

"Looks like we're both at Table Two," Vivian said faintly, casting a sidelong glance at him.

Cooper smiled in dark satisfaction as he scanned the room for the table with the number two engraved on a note-card sticking out of the beach-themed centerpiece of starfish, sand dollars, and blue flowers. If Miles had known what Cooper intended to do with Vivian Banks, he probably wouldn't have been quite so helpful about setting them up for a romantic evening together.

Let the punishment fit the crime. It was a sentiment Cooper had seen played out in countless cultures, all over the world. And even though in this case there was no proportional response to the way Vivian had betrayed everything they'd had together with no explanation, Cooper wasn't one to pass up an opportunity.

He had tonight. One night. A single night of seduction, sensual pleasures, and temptations. A night to exorcise his demons and lay his memories of this woman to rest once and for all.

And in the morning, he'd walk away from Vivian without a backward glance. Poetic justice. All he had to do now was sweep her off her feet.

Putting his plan into effect without delay, Cooper deftly snagged the bouquet from her grasp and set it on one of the gilded place settings at table two. Then he plucked his tuxedo jacket from her shoulders and draped it over the back of the chair at the next place setting. "Now our seats are saved. Come on, let's get this party started."

"The band is still setting up," Vivian protested. "And aren't we supposed to wait until after the bride and groom have their first dance?"

"You snooze, you lose." Cooper took her hand and pulled her across the dance floor to the bandstand. Waving the band's front man over, Cooper leaned up to mutter his request in the guy's ear. He didn't totally get the amused smirk the punk-haired Englishman gave him when Cooper slipped a fifty-dollar bill into the pocket of his silky blue shirt, but a moment later, the familiar strains of the song he'd requested picked up.

Whirling Vivian onto the dance floor, Cooper took her into his arms and spun them both into a languid waltz as the guy he'd tipped crooned, "At last, my love has come along."

"This can't be happening," Vivian shook her head as if to clear the haze of sleep from her mind.

"But it is," Cooper said, the hand gripping her waist flexing to feel the supple curve of her body.

Her pupils dilated, black and lush with heat, and she let out a nervous laugh. "I mean, I would swear that's Dash and the Danger Boys up there."

Cooper had no idea who that was, but he stole a glance over his shoulder at the band. "But one of them is a chick. Playing the drums. With pink hair. That's kind of hot."

"Oh my gosh, then it definitely is them," Vivian exclaimed, laughing. "I can't believe it. Only Miles would have the number one rock band in the country playing his wedding reception."

"What was your wedding like?" Cooper wished he

could call the words back the instant they left his mouth. He cursed silently as the happy glow died out of Vivian's eyes. Great seduction technique, Casanova. Bring up the failed marriage she ditched you for!

But before he could change the subject, Vivian shook her head. "Nothing like this. My wedding was . . . an event. Everyone who was anyone was invited. All my society friends, my parents' business partners and investors. It was more of a board meeting or a country club social than a wedding."

"Sounds like a blast."

A corner of her mouth kicked up. "No, it wasn't fun, but then, it wasn't meant to be. It was meant to show off who we knew, how much money we had, and how much power my parents wielded. Now this wedding . . ."

With a sweep of her arm as they circled past the wedding cake, a multi-layer confection of curlicued white frosting, filigreed gold leaves and blue flowers made of sugar, Greta said, "This wedding is a reflection of the personalities of the bride and the groom. If you'd never met Miles and Greta and somehow stumbled into this wedding, you'd get a good idea of who they are and what's most important to them."

Their next turn around the dance floor swung them past the receiving line by the tent door, still lively with congratulating guests, hugs, and joyous greetings. "Family and friends," Cooper agreed.

Vivian nodded. "And making sure we all have a fabulous time. Miles and Greta pull everyone they love into their orbit, spreading the wealth of their happiness and letting the rest of us bask in the reflected glow. It's not a bad deal, especially when you're low on glow of your own."

Glow was one thing Vivian Banks had never lacked. Although now that Cooper had his arms around her and an ironclad reason to be studying her closely as they danced, he could make out some small changes to the face that had been etched in his memory. Vivian had always been bubbly, with all the charm and fizz of a glass of champagne—but faint new lines beside her eyes and a slight translucence to her skin gave Cooper's dance partner a more reserved, mature look.

This was a woman who had lived, not a girl with her whole life still ahead of her. Cooper couldn't help wondering exactly what cares had put those shadows under Vivian's eyes.

It didn't matter, he reminded himself. It was none of his business how her life had gone once she chucked him out of it. His only business with Vivian Banks was a quick and dirty seduction.

Steering back on course, he murmured, "As far as I can tell, your glow hasn't changed in ten years. You're as beautiful as ever, Viv."

He expected a pleased smile or a blushing laugh—anything but the unmistakable skepticism that tightened the corners of Vivian's shuttered eyes. She tripped, throwing them off step for half a second, but it was enough to turn their easy, sensual dance into something mechanical and awkward.

"Sorry about that," Vivian murmured, still pale as sea foam. "At least I'm still as clumsy as ever."

She acted as if she didn't believe him. How could she not know how beautiful she was?

Frowning, Cooper tightened his grip on her and drew in a breath to ask what the hell happened to turn a confident, vivacious girl into the somber, withdrawn woman before him. But the music died, and Vivian pulled away with an air of relief. She used to love dancing, too.

Cooper fought down his growing awareness of the mystery of Vivian Banks. He didn't want to see a mystery. All he wanted to see was Vivian, naked and splayed over his sheets, reaching for him with a sultry smile.

"Excuse me," Vivian said, her gaze landing somewhere in the vicinity of his chin and sticking there. "I should really go see if the bride needs any help with anything."

"I'm pretty sure the wedding planner and Greta's mom have everything in hand." Cooper studied her downcast eyes and nervously twisting fingers. "But sure, let's go talk to Miles and Greta. I have a little something for them, anyway."

She hesitated, confirming his suspicion that she'd suggested helping Greta at least partly to get away from him. *It's not going to be that easy*, Cooper wanted to tell her. As if she'd heard his silent promise, Vivian blew out a breath and nodded. "Okay, lead the way."

Triumph smoldered in his chest like a white-hot coal. *Oh, I'll lead you, all right. Straight to my bed. And after tonight, I'll never think of you again.*

After tonight, I'll finally be free of you.

Vivian steadied herself and commanded her heart to stop racing like a runaway horse. There was no way Cooper's compliments and smiles meant what she wanted them to mean. He'd always been a charmer, when he wanted to be—and from what she'd read in the gossip rags over the years, he'd honed that ability to razor sharpness as his sud-

den, stratospheric wealth propelled him into the highest
society.

*He didn't mean anything by dancing with you, or hold-
ing you close*, she scolded herself silently. *He's being . . . if
anything, he's being kind.*

Vivian had no illusions that a man like Cooper Hayes,
so powerful, adventurous, and handsome, could ever be
interested in a woman who had done nothing with her life.
A woman who wasn't suited to anything other than playing arm candy to a rich man.

Well, she was through with that life. Even if that's what
Cooper wanted from her, Vivian was done being the
silent accessory to someone else's exciting life of action.

She wanted her own life. And she was finally in a position to start working to get it.

A burst of optimism warmed her belly, unfamiliar and
lovely enough to distract her through the first round of hugs
and congratulations with the bride and groom. She tuned
back into the conversation just as Miles clapped Cooper
on the shoulder and said, "So. Are Greta and I flying off
for this fabulous honeymoon you've arranged in my helicopter? Or are you going to try to convince me you won
the bet?"

Vivian stole a glance at Cooper, whose brow had lowered like a storm cloud. "Don't make me take those tickets back," he growled, only half kidding.

"What bet?" Vivian caught the quick look exchanged
between bride and groom.

"Nothing," Cooper cut in, glowering at his oldest friend.
"Miles is being an ass."

The groom raised a brow. "At least I'm not a sore loser."

"I haven't lost anything," Cooper insisted. "The dead-line is past. I won."

"Debatable," Miles said, an amused glint in his eyes. "Are you sure you're being honest with yourself? Think about the exact terms we agreed on, and you might real-ize you're mistaken."

Totally lost, Vivian looked to Greta for help. The bride leaned in conspiratorially. "Miles bet his billionaire bache-lor groomsmen, that if they came to Sanctuary Island and helped him out with a few wedding-related tasks, they'd find their lives changed forever before he said, 'I do.'"

Vivian couldn't help but smile as a rush of love for this special island filled her. She'd adored Sanctuary from the moment she stepped off the ferry for her first visit to meet her childhood friend's fiancée five months ago. "Sounds like a sucker's deal to me," she observed.

Switching his narrow glare from Miles to Vivian, Coo-per demanded, "What do you mean?"

"I can't imagine anyone spending time on Sanctuary Island without falling in love," Vivian said, picturing the calm, glassy surface of Lantern Lake in her mind.

A short, charged silence followed her words, and when she replayed them silently, she had to fight down a flush. "With the island," she hastened to add. "Everyone who comes here falls in love with Sanctuary Island. Is what I meant. At least, I certainly fell in love with it."

"Oh right!" Greta seized on the subject change. "How did escrow go?"

Rock solid satisfaction expanded Vivian's ribcage with pride. "Like clockwork. Have I mentioned that I can never thank you enough for your help with the Lantern Lake cabin?"

"A few times," Greta said, laughing and rolling her eyes fondly. "Here and there. I'm so glad it worked out!"

"You bought property here?" Cooper asked, looking at her askance. "I never would've thought you'd leave New York."

The words sent a chill through her that had nothing to do with the wintry wind whipping the over the waves outside the glass walls of their tent. "There's nothing for me in New York. Not anymore."

A strange expression came over Cooper's face, something like recognition firing in his eyes. "Sometimes the only way forward is to leave everything you know behind."

She stared up at him for a long, suspended moment, the connection between them as strong and real and tangible as it had ever been when they were young. He was so magnetic, his presence sucking the very air from Vivian's lungs and leaving her shaky with the knowledge of how much she still wanted him.

"I tell you what," Miles interrupted, amusement coloring his deep voice. "Let's table the bet for the moment. We have a party to enjoy, and Greta and I have a honeymoon adventure to embark on, thanks to you. We can settle the bet when we get back in two weeks."

And with that, he whisked his bride onto the dance floor for their first dance.

"I won't still be here in two weeks," Cooper protested, scowling after his friend.

His words pierced right through Vivian's heart with a dart of regret, but she ignored it. She couldn't be silly enough to hope for more time with Cooper. But she couldn't stop herself from saying, "That's too bad, since winter just started for real. Sanctuary Island is supposed to be very beautiful in the snow."

That brought Cooper focus back to her, sharp and intense enough to make Vivian's nerves spark. "As beautiful as Central Park in the snow?"

Nostalgia fluttered in her chest, memories as delicate and worn from repeated handling as the pages of an old love letter. "Beautiful in a different way. Wilder, more solitary. More peaceful."

"You never used to like being alone," Cooper said, studying her.

Vivian tried to laugh. "Thanks for making me sound like the original party girl."

He stared down at her face, and Vivian had to fight not to squirm under his scrutiny. What did he see? Could he read the years of her marriage in her eyes, the constant whirl of empty social engagements and crowded parties where she'd been surrounded by people, yet totally alone?

She wasn't sure she could bear to try to explain how much her battered heart craved actual solitude—as if being truly alone would glorify her loneliness somehow.

But Cooper didn't push her. Instead, he smiled and arched a brow in that invitation to sin she remember so well from their school days. "Speaking of parties," he purred. "Let's get this one started, shall we?"

Vivian had never been able to resist Cooper Hayes, and she didn't intend to start tonight—when it was almost certainly the last night she'd ever spend with him.

And it was a magical night, by anyone's standards. He introduced her to his friends, the other groomsmen, and she introduced him to the friends she'd made during her extended visits to Sanctuary Island. They didn't talk about the past, or their families, or her marriage.

The dinner, catered by the Firefly Café, was course after course of spot-on, perfectly prepared Southern classics. In between the fried chicken and cornbread, there was dancing to the pared-down strains of a band of rock gods turning jazz anthems into pure, liquid sex.

Vivian savored the strength and warmth of Cooper's muscular arms around her as they swayed to the music. Everything felt surreal, like a dream or a fantasy, and when he leaned down to whisper in her ear, she couldn't hold back a luxurious, full-body shiver.

"You were made for dancing, Vivian. I love the way you move."

She tipped her head back and blinked up at the brilliant explosion of stars through the clear glass of the roof. "I can't believe this is happening. I can't believe we're both here, like this."

I've missed you every day.

Vivian bit her tongue. She didn't want to say anything to break the spell—especially not something guaranteed to remind them both that they could have been together all along . . . if she hadn't been such a coward.

"I learned to believe in destiny while I was traveling." Cooper's voice was dark with some emotion Vivian couldn't name. Then he smiled, seductive and dangerous. "I learned to respect it. Because when the universe gives you a shot at something, you take it—or you regret it forever."

The idea struck a chord in Vivian's chest. She met his gaze with all the boldness she could muster, heart thundering with nerves and anticipation. "Then we definitely shouldn't let this moment pass us by."

Satisfaction blazed bright in Cooper's eyes for the rest of the evening, even as they saw the bride and groom off in their luxury helicopter then headed down to enjoy the bonfire on the night beach.

The rest of the party guests began to trickle home. And as the bonfire blazed high, casting a red and orange glow of heat over the few remaining wedding guests huddled in Adirondack chairs around it, Cooper said, "I want to see this house you bought."

After one too many champagne toasts, Vivian's blood felt heavy and warm in her veins. She rolled her head on the wooden lounge chair to peer through the shimmery darkness at him. His face was half in shadow, half lit by the hissing, popping bonfire, but she could easily make out the broad, hard-muscled shape of his shoulders and arms, and the taut twist of his trim waist.

He waited patiently, watching her as she stared at him, and Vivian felt a rush of heat that had nothing to do with the bonfire. "It's not a house," she said breathlessly. "It's more of a cabin, really. Very small, a little bit of a fixer upper, but lovely views of Lantern Lake."

Cooper propped one elbow on the arm of the chair and rested his chin on his hand. He'd lost his black bow tie at some point in the evening, and the top two buttons of his white shirt were undone, exposing a narrow V of tanned skin. "You know, I've been all over this island in the last couple of weeks, and I don't remember seeing a lake."

"It's hard to find," Vivian agreed, with a tiny, secret smile. "Almost as if it's my own private paradise."

Or . . . the private paradise of whoever wound up living there for real.

She ignored the pang of longing. The Lantern Lake cabin certainly wasn't her dream house, or anything. *You can't afford dreams anymore,* she reminded herself. *Not until you prove to yourself you can survive without the help of a rich husband and wealthy parents.*

"Okay, now I really have to see it." Cooper stood and held out a hand to her. "Show me this Lantern Lake of yours. I want to take a look at your private paradise."

The silken seduction in his tone was more practiced than the boy she remembered, but the look in his extraordinary hazel eyes was the same. Somehow, after so long and so much painful history between them, he still wanted her. And heaven knew, Vivian had never forgotten what it felt like to be desired by Cooper Hayes. Everything in her yearned to experience the heady bliss of a night with Cooper once more.

Vivian paused, the cold harshness of reality threatening to pierce the soft shimmery bubble of her fantasy. If she took Cooper back to the Lantern Lake cabin, she had no illusions about what would happen there.

The youthful desire that had burned hotter than the bonfire lighting up the beach was still ablaze between them. In the sheltered privacy of her little cabin, surrounded by nothing but the calm lake, stands of maritime pine trees, and the bands of wild horses who made this island their home, Vivian knew she wouldn't be able to resist Cooper.

She wouldn't even want to.

But after a night of passion with him, what would the morning bring? Because she also had no illusions about any possible future between them. That ship sailed—and sank—a long time ago. Could she bear to go through with tonight, knowing it was the last time she'd ever see him . . . touch him . . . kiss him . . .

When the universe gives you a shot at something, you take it—or you regret it forever.

Vivian put her hand in Cooper's and let him tug her to her feet. "Let's go."

A spark caught and flared in the depths of his eyes, burning hotter than the fire at her back. Vivian's heart jumped and started to pump thunderously in anticipation.

Without another word, Cooper laced their fingers together and pulled her away from the circle of light the bonfire cast over the last, lingering wedding guests. Vivian followed him to his low-slung red sports car, too full of jittery excitement to even feel the chill of the night air.

She couldn't pass up the chance to add new memories to the store of mental images that had gotten her through the toughest times of her life. She'd steal one more night of passion with the only man she'd ever loved—and then she'd open her hands and let him go back to his fabulous life of wealth and adventure.

The life she could have shared with him. The life that would never be hers now.

So she'd take tonight and be grateful, no matter what happened. No matter how much it would hurt to say goodbye to Cooper when it was over.

Chapter Three

Cooper followed Vivian's quiet directions across the silent, narrow island roads. The tension between them hung as thick as the fog over the Scottish highlands where Cooper had done his first off-roading trek.

That battered old Land Rover he'd driven through rushing creeks and up perilous hillsides hadn't been as fancy as his Ferrarri Testarossa, but it had been a damn sight more reliable. As the sportscar's racing wheels spun uselessly against the gravel road at the end of what Vivian optimistically called her "driveway," Cooper spared a brief moment to wish he'd brought the Rover instead.

The convertible churned up the dual ruts of the pitted, pocked drive, curving through a winter forest of evergreen and pine. Its flip-up head lamps were the only light, apart from the graceful sickle of the moon.

Cooper squinted at the pitch blackness outside. "Isn't it a little dangerous, living this far from the center of town?"

A tiny smile curled Vivian's lips. "This from the man who BASE jumped off Angel Falls in a wing-suit, and filmed the entire stunt."

"Not dangerous for me," Cooper argued, peering through the small windshield and wincing at the grating scratch of something sharp along the car's undercarriage. "Dangerous for—a woman living alone."

Vivian's smile widened fractionally, as if she'd heard the concern Cooper didn't want to feel, much less speak aloud. "Don't worry. Sanctuary Island is very safe. We have our own Sheriff's department, but about the only calls they ever get are kids trespassing on the horse preserve and people running the one traffic light in front of the bakery on Main Street."

He wasn't sure he liked that. Aside from the obvious dangers to a woman alone, cut off from easy access to emergency services, there was the personality angle. Viv had always been an extrovert, quick to laugh, the life of every party, surrounded by friends and admirers.

"I just can't picture you being happy to sit alone in an empty house in the middle of nowhere," Cooper said bluntly.

She turned her head slightly, as if glancing at something outside the passenger window. "I don't mind a little alone time, these days."

There was something in her voice, some heavy meaning too vague for Cooper to grasp, and before he could ask about it, Vivian clutched his arm in excitement.

"We're here! Slow down, this is a good view of the property."

The Ferrari growled its way out of the woods at the top of a small hill, the beams of its headlights reflecting off the mirrored surface of a secluded lake. Set against the meandering shore, amongst the reed grass and cattails, was a small clapboard cottage. Warm golden light spilled from the lamps on either side of the door, like a beacon calling them home through the darkness.

Shaking his head at his own ridiculousness, Cooper caught sight of Vivian out of the corner of his eye. Face lit by a soft smile, her midnight eyes seemed to reflect the twinkle of the stars over the lake. She looked more like the girl of his memories now than she had all evening.

"Beautiful," he told her, eyes never leaving her face.

"Isn't it?" She sighed, her gaze roaming almost hungrily over the tiny homestead spread out at the foot of the hill. "The minute I saw it, I knew I had to have it."

Forcing himself to look back at the property, Cooper acknowledged the magnetic attraction of the place. Even with the epic distraction of the woman next to him, he could feel the familiar tug of interest, the spark of desire to explore. He wanted to hike around the lake, climb a tree and see the view from up there, poke through the little, old cabin and get a sense of the people who'd lived there before.

Maybe he'd even get a sense of the woman who lived there now, he reflected, carefully navigating the end of the drive and parking in front of the porch. As clear and vivid as his memories of Vivian Banks had always remained, he had to admit she was more or less a mystery to him now.

Heart thumping with all the anticipation of an undiscovered country, Cooper followed Vivian up the rickety porch steps. He barely noticed the peeling paint on the doorframe and the sad creak of rusty hinges before Vivian shut the door behind them and Cooper made his move.

With a low sound of need, he pinned her against her own front door, caging her in with his larger body. Cooper stared down at her, blood rushing fast and furious in his veins and throbbing between his legs. Vivian blinked up at him, her irises a slim purple band around pupils wide with shock or desire. Or a combination of the two.

"Don't you want to see the house?" Her voice was a husky whisper in the dark, like velvet stroking his skin.

"I've got everything I want right here," Cooper said, with a deliberate grind of his hips that made her gasp. He ignored how right the words felt, how true they seemed, in favor of dipping his head for a deep, persuasive kiss.

But he didn't need to do much persuading. Vivian met him heat for heat, bite for bite, moan for moan. The fire between them seemed never to have gone out—it had only been banked, live red coals waiting for a spark to flare into the kind of scorching heat Cooper thought he could die from.

When Vivian clutched at his shoulders and twined one lithe leg around his, Cooper groaned and got his hands under her hips. He lifted her up until she locked her ankles behind his back and the force of his body pressed her into the door. She curled her arms around him and buried her face in his neck as he tunneled his hands under the filmy material of her bridesmaid dress.

Vivian had never liked wearing tight, confining pantyhose, even in the dead of a New York winter—and, in that, at least, she hadn't changed. With a growl of appreciation, Cooper got his hands directly on the smooth, heated silk of her bare skin.

He ached to be inside her, to experience the tight clasp of her body and the surging waves of her response. In the past, he never would have taken her this way, rough and ready and up against a wall—but he'd been young, then. Young, trusting, and innocent enough to want to cherish every breath Vivian Banks took.

Older now, more experienced and more confident, Cooper was no stranger to the quick and dirty encounter. He knew exactly how satisfying it could be, how much pleasure he could give a woman in this position.

But some tiny corner of him, some remnant of the romantic idiot he used to be, forced him to ask, "Is this okay with you?"

The look she flashed him made everything in his body tighten. "Everything. Anything. Just don't stop."

Maybe it was greedy. Maybe it was shortsighted. Maybe Vivian was the worst kind of fool—but she couldn't bring herself to believe she'd ever regret stealing one last night of passion with the only man she'd ever loved. Even knowing he didn't love her back, and never would again.

And somehow, the knowledge that it was the last time freed her up to be as brave and adventurous as she'd been as a girl, before the reality of her life taught her to keep her head down and do her best to be invisible. When Cooper stared deep into her eyes, she knew he saw her. And instead of feeling exposed or vulnerable, Vivian reveled in it. She was alive, with Cooper Hayes's superheated, muscular body keeping her pinned to the front door like a butterfly on a card, and when he moved his hips like that . . .

Vivian shuddered, her eyes fluttering closed as black starbursts exploded across her vision. Her body, which she hadn't thought twice about in years, came to shivering, gasping life in Cooper's arms. Yes, she thought in dazed answer to Cooper's question—this was entirely okay. Okay didn't come close to covering it.

The first time against the door didn't last long. It couldn't. They were too hungry, starved for each other. The second time, on the stairs up to the small, single bedroom, was full of laughter and cursing as they fumbled for balance and leverage against the hardwood risers and railing. By the time they finally fell into her bed, the soft, clean cotton sheets were a cool and welcome relief against their fevered skin. Vivian pulled Cooper down until his body covered hers, a wall of muscle and bone keeping the future at bay. She turned her head far enough to peer through the gauzy white curtains at the subtle violet shade of the lightening sky. Dawn was coming.

Squeezing her eyes shut, Vivian craned her neck to press her kiss-swollen lips to Cooper's.

"You're not too tired?" His low voice rasped over her nerves, making her shiver.

"One more time," she replied, and he met her lips with a deep groan of need.

The third time was slow, every touch and caress whispering over Vivian's sensitive skin. With moans and sighs, she urged him to hurry, to give her what she needed, but Cooper rose over her on his strong arms and stared down implacably. His eyes burned with determination, iron control hardening his jaw, and Vivian knew he intended to take her apart piece by piece. Surrendering to it, she tilted her head back and rode the waves of sensation until she broke on the rocks, shattered and completely undone.

Finally sated, Cooper collapsed beside her and fell asleep instantly. She forced her heavy eyes to stay open for a long moment, long enough to trace every line of Cooper's face. Men were supposed to look softer, more boyish in sleep, she thought drowsily. But Cooper didn't. Even the slackness of sleep couldn't erase the hardness from his face. He'd changed.

Well, so had she. She was stronger now, in some ways—and honest enough with herself to admit she was a total mess in other ways.

And as she drifted off to sleep, Vivian was aware of a sharp pain in her chest at the knowledge that they'd never have the chance to get to know one another as they were now. Because she couldn't afford the distraction while she worked toward her independence . . . and because Cooper didn't care to know more than her body.

Too bad accepting that she deserved this pain didn't seem to lessen it at all.

Chapter Four

As usual, Cooper came awake in a rush of total awareness of his surroundings. He'd worked hard to overcome waking disoriented—the occupational hazard of world exploration. No matter where he was, from a hut in the Andes to a villa in St. Moritz, Cooper had trained his brain to keep track. He hated being off balance when he opened his eyes, so before sleep, he fixed an image of his current location in his mind's eye . . . but last night, he'd had other things on his mind.

Those other things came back to him in a rush of awareness of the slender, naked, feminine body curled warm and close beneath sheets soft from repeated washing. Vivian. The memories of the night before crashed over him and headed straight for his morning erection. He wished he could be surprised that last night's marathon sex hadn't gotten this woman out of his head, but he wasn't. There was something about Vivian that hooked him, drawing him to her like an addict to a bottle of bourbon.

And what advice would he give a friend trying to kick an addiction? Cold turkey, baby.

Just as he was trying to get up the energy to haul his ass out of the warm bed and into the frigid morning air of the bedroom, Vivian stirred beside him and made a soft smacking sound with her lips. Cooper couldn't help but grin. She'd always been a cute sleeper. Back in the dorms, he used to wake her every morning by raining kisses over her forehead, cheeks, closed eyelids . . . she'd furrow her dark brows in confusion, and he'd kiss the sleepy frown away.

He shifted uneasily, trying to avoid the swell of tenderness the memory evoked. The sheets slid over his skin, and for the first time, he saw the room in the light of day. The bed was an old four-poster, obviously solidly made since it had withstood their combined efforts to break the thing the night before, but enough scars and nicks marred the gleaming cherrywood headboard to tell him the bed wasn't new. But it wasn't an antique, either, the kind the Banks family had used to decorate their ancestral pile in Westchester County, outside New York. And the sheets . . . they were frayed at the edges, faded and worn. Cooper, who'd slept on some high-thread-count Egyptian cotton in his day, could tell that these weren't that fancy. He frowned a little as he ran his hand across the surface of the covers draped over his hips. Why wouldn't Vivian Banks have the very best?

The mystery of how she'd spent the last ten years tugged at Cooper, but he shoved it away. So Vivian was living more simply than she'd been brought up, or than she would have with the rich society guy she'd married. Even the super wealthy liked to take a vacation from their lives and rough it, now and then.

But as he took in the rest of the room, Cooper felt his eyebrows climbing toward his hairline. The curtains at the window were tatty and full of holes, as if moths had gotten at them. The scratched hardwood floor was covered by an old, stained hooked rug in faded reds and blues, and the ceiling sagged in one corner with a worrying crack running down the plaster wall beside the window. The window's panes sparkled, though, the rising sun beaming through the polished glass. So she'd been here long enough to hire a cleaning lady, he assumed.

Stop it, he ordered himself, pushing down the covers and sliding from the bed to find his clothes. He cursed silently when he realized they were all downstairs—or, more likely, scattered along the stairs themselves, marking the path they'd taken from the front door to the bedroom like a trail of breadcrumbs. A gust of frigid air whistled through a crack in the window frame, chilling him completely. Cooper paused for a long heartbeat, staring down at the warm, cozy nest of the bed. Vivian's black hair tumbled across the pillow, a tendril curling loosely around her bare breast. All Cooper wanted was to reach down and feel the texture of that saucy curl, then climb back in bed and wake her up with a kiss.

But that wasn't the plan, he reminded himself. Come on, bud. Cold turkey, let's go.

Putting one foot in front of the other, Cooper made it all the way to the door. Unable to resist, he took one last look over his shoulder at the woman he'd once loved more than his own life . . . and encountered the vivid indigo of her eyes blinking drowsily back at him.

"Are you leaving?"

He froze, caught out, but anger rescued him. This was his revenge, to seduce her and leave her flat. He'd earned this moment with years of pain and bitterness, and he'd be damned if she made him feel guilty about it. Proud of the cool dispassion of his tone, Cooper said, "It's been fun, but I've got things to do. Places to be. You know how it is."

The flash of pain before she lowered her lashes was exactly what he'd expected to see, but it didn't give him the satisfaction he'd hoped for. Despair and fury collided in his chest like Godzilla and Mothra. But before he could do more than suck in a breath to lash out, she lifted her gaze to him. Carefully open and free of accusation, Vivian tugged the sheets up to her chest with innate dignity. "Okay. Thank you for a nice evening."

She could've been in her mother's tastefully decorated parlor, politely saying farewell to one of her parents' pre-approved dates. Fury achieved a sudden advantage over despair, sweeping through Cooper with an intensity he'd never experienced. He'd come here to repay Vivian for the hurt she'd dealt out, not to feel guilty for hurting her.

"That's it?" he demanded, putting his hands on his hips, careless of his nudity. "Thanks, and see you around?"

"Well." Vivian's eyes dropped. "I don't imagine I'll be seeing you again anytime soon, but yes. Essentially."

Galled past the point of self-control, Cooper stalked back over to the bed and stared down at her. "Last night was better than 'nice.' Admit it."

A hot rush of blood to her cheeks chased away the remnants of sleep. "What do you want me to say?"

Kneeling on the bed, Cooper loomed over her, fascinated by the way she melted into the mattress, as if she couldn't help herself from yielding to him. "I want to hear that you never had it so good. Come on. Tell me it was ever once that good between you and your husband."

Vivian stiffened. "Ex-husband," she reminded him tartly. "And he's got nothing to do with this. Don't be gross."

He shrugged, straddling her thighs and trapping her under the tight sheet. "So I want to know the man you ditched me for was a loser in bed. Sue me, I'm human."

If he hadn't been scrutinizing her face, studying every minute shift and tightening of muscle, he would have missed the brief flare of intense emotion before she dropped her lashes once more.

"If I told you that no one has ever come close to touching me the way you do, what would happen?" Vivian asked quietly, her fingers still and tense on the coverlet. "You'd still walk out that door and never come back. And I'll still be here on my own, the way I deserve."

Cooper had always hated being predictable. "What if I stayed?"

He hardly knew what he meant, the words almost as a big a surprise to him as they obviously were to Vivian. Her head shot up, eyes wide. "You mean . . ."

Backpedaling, trying to catch his footing, Cooper sat up and climbed off the bed. He needed a little distance. "I mean . . . what's for breakfast? After all the calories we burned through last night, I could stand some pancakes."

Looking as if she very much wanted to interrogate him about his intentions, Vivian dropped the blanket and scooted out the other side of the bed, keeping the high queen-sized mattress between them as a barrier. It didn't make her invisible, though, and Cooper had to fight to keep his eyes on her face with all those glorious curves on full view. "I can do pancakes," she said carefully. "It's the least I can do, as a good hostess, before my guest . . . departs?"

Cooper spread his hands. "Look, I don't know what to tell you. I'm feeling my way, here. Nothing has turned out the way I thought it would, since I first set foot on Sanctuary Island. All I know is that I'm not ready to get out of Dodge just yet."

It looked as if Vivian's ribcage burst free of the bands of tension that had been binding them. She heaved in a great breath, a wide smile brightening the whole room, and for a disorienting moment, everything in Cooper's world dimmed except for her.

"So . . . pancakes," she said, snagging a soft-looking cotton robe off a chair in the corner. "You still like chocolate chips in them, or are your tastes too refined for that now?" Her was voice a little breathless, but happy. Happier than the idea of feeding breakfast to her ex-fiancé really warranted.

"Whatever you've got is fine," he replied absently, his attention on the sway of her hips as he followed her downstairs to the tiny, spic and span kitchen. "I've learned to eat and enjoy weirder food than you could possibly imagine in the last ten years. Actually, I'm allergic to chocolate now. It's kind of a funny story."

He picked up his clothes on the way down the stairs and hopped into his pants while relating the tale of the Aztec chocolate festival to a giggling Vivian. But even as he cracked jokes and made her smile down into the mixing bowl full of pancake batter, Cooper wondered what the hell he was doing.

He hadn't left already because . . . he was probing for a weakness. His revenge idea wasn't going to work if Vivian was prepared to be left hanging after their one night stand. But what if it wasn't a single night? Could he really keep up the charade of falling back in love with her, and play this thing out until it actually surprised her when he picked up and left without a word?

For some reason, the idea of that was sour on the back of his tongue. Swallowing down the sickness, Cooper acknowledged that as much as he hated what she'd done to him, he wouldn't turn the tables and give it back to her, pain for pain. But he could stay through breakfast, and see what other opportunities presented themselves.

Because no matter how sweetly she sighed into his kiss and writhed in his arms, Vivian Banks still deserved to be punished for breaking his heart.

Vivian dropped the whisk into the batter for the third time and bit back a curse as she fished it out with trembling fingers. This wasn't what she'd expected from Cooper. It was almost as if he wanted to stick around. His reluctance to leave the Lantern Lake cabin sent flutters of warmth all through her, and made it extra tricky to concentrate on pancakes. She'd be lucky if she didn't burn all her fingerprints off on the griddle.

But Cooper had requested pancakes, and as she'd told him, it was the least she could do. Heaven help her if he ever realized that no matter what he asked her for, she'd do her best to give it to him.

It was more than the years of conditioning with her

overbearing parents and her demanding ex-husband. When it was Cooper, she actually wanted to make him happy.

"Tell me more about your travels," she said, keeping her back to him as she fiddled with the ancient dials on the gas stovetop. Every time she cooked, she battled the fear that the oven would explode and blow the cabin to smithereens, and her along with it. But so far, it just clicked and sputtered and eventually spat out a few sullen blue rings of flame.

"Not much to tell." She could almost hear the shrug in Cooper's voice. "Been all over, seen a lot. There's still a lot out there left to see, though. Spin the globe . . ."

His voice trailed off, and Vivian was assaulted by a crystalline memory of getting trapped in the university library after the doors were locked. They'd been in the stacks, deep in the dusty philosophy section where no student ever went, and they'd . . . lost track of time. Locked in for the night, they'd run all over the library like kids in a candy store, high on breaking the rules and being in love. When they'd happened on the giant globe in the mahogany and brass stand near the history section, they'd taken turns closing their eyes and spinning it before stabbing a finger down to stop the thing. Wherever that finger landed, that location was written down and added to the list of places they planned to travel to together after college. Cooper had called it the Backpacker's Hippie Honeymoon, and Vivian closed her eyes against the burn of tears. That long lost list—all those places she'd never seen. Had he gone without her?

Unwilling to ask in case the answer was "yes," Vivian cleared her throat and went back to spooning batter onto the hot, spitting griddle. "Think you'll ever settle down?

"Can't see the point of that." Cooper's chair squeaked, and she could picture him kicking back, leaning the chair on two legs the way he always used to do, as if daring gravity to pull him down. "Not when the world's this big and full of interesting stuff. You only get one life."

"True." Vivian shrugged off the lingering desire to see more of the world. Maybe she'd be able to travel one day, after she got her life together. Until then . . . "That's part of why I bought the house here. Sanctuary Island is so southern, so beachy and beautiful, and the people are so friendly and welcoming. Nothing like where I grew up."

"Or where you lived with Richie Rich." Cooper's tone was knowing, sardonic, and Vivian fought not to show any reaction.

"Sanctuary Island isn't like anywhere else on earth," she said with certainty, staring down as bubbles began to form in the glossy surface of the circles of pancake batter. "I only wish I could stay here."

The thud of chair legs hitting the cracked linoleum floor confirmed her earlier vision, and Vivian smiled a little. "What do you mean? You just bought this house. Sick of playing poor already?"

The harsh edge to the words had Vivian tensing, defensive. But he didn't know, she reminded herself. Not yet.

And maybe now was her chance to be the one to tell him. Surely that would be better than having him find out another way.

Right. There was no way this was going to be anything other than humiliating. But even as she steeled herself for the mortifying moment of truth, Cooper blew out a breath. An instant later, she felt his big, warm palm sliding around to cup the bend of her waist. He dropped a soft kiss on the side of her neck, just above the gaping collar of her robe, and Vivian's tongue stuck to the roof of her mouth.

"I'm sorry," he said roughly. "I'm being a jerk. Don't listen to anything I say until I drink at least one more cup of coffee."

"That's okay." Vivian twisted her head to give him a quick smile before turning back to flip the pancakes. "It's not a big deal. I just . . . I didn't buy the cabin to live in. It's more of an investment."

Cooper's hands slipped away, and she immediately felt a chill in their wake. "I never got the appeal of a summer home," he said, wandering over to the coffeemaker to pour himself another steaming cup from the pot. "Doesn't that basically just mean that whenever you have time off or want to take a vacation, you feel like you have to go back to the same place? You'll never see anything new."

He thought she'd bought the cabin as a vacation house. It was a reprieve—but for how long? Swallowing thickly around the white lie, Vivian pointed out, "But if you go back to the same vacation spot year after year, you build relationships there. You make friends you get to see over and over, and you can learn to really fit into the place. It can be a home away from home."

Not really a lie, she consoled herself. She hadn't confirmed that the cabin *was* her vacation home. She'd just argued that a vacation home could be a nice thing to have.

Although, to be completely truthful, she hadn't enjoyed it all that much when Gerald took them back to the Hamptons every single summer. It never felt like home— more like yet another stage where they could play out the elaborate drama of her marriage and Gerald's business dealings.

"I guess. But you'd probably have to have a home first, before you could have a home away from home. Got any sugar?" Before she could caution him, Cooper put his hand on the brass pull of the cabinet over the coffeemaker . . . and the entire cabinet door jerked off its hinges.

"What the hell!" Off kilter, Cooper fumbled with the unwieldy door until it clocked him in the side of the head, then clattered to the floor.

Rushing to his side, Vivian exclaimed, "Are you okay? I'm so sorry, I should have warned you about my temperamental cabinets."

Cooper shook his head as if to rattle his brains back into place. "Cats are temperamental. That cabinet is psychotic. Your house is trying to kill me."

Putting a gentle hand to Cooper's temple, she nudged him to tilt his head so she could examine the red mark left by the falling cabinetry. "Don't be a baby," she said automatically. "You're fine. It's just a bruise, and my house is not trying to kill anyone. It's just a little . . . old. And in need of some TLC."

"I could use some, too," Cooper told her, leaning closer. "You could kiss it and make it better."

Heat rolled up Vivian's spine, tingling and good. "Show me where," she murmured, lifting up on her tiptoes to reach the sore spot on his temple. She kissed where he pointed, her lips following his fingertip from temple to jaw to nose, and finally to the masculine fullness of his bottom lip.

Instead of a kiss, Vivian nipped that succulent bite of flesh between her teeth, light enough to sting the way he liked. The heartfelt growl from deep in his chest was cut off by a grunt of frustration, however.

"What's the matter?" she asked, heart hammering and wetness gathering at her aching center.

"I guess I could get my revenge on your house by watching it burn to the ground," Cooper said, taking her shoulders and turning her to face the smoking, blackened pancakes curling on the griddle. "But then we wouldn't get to have breakfast."

Chapter Five

After breakfast was salvaged and they both found their missing articles of clothing, Cooper still didn't leave. Instead, he asked for a tour of the property.

Something was going on here. Something Vivian didn't want him to know—which, of course, made him want to know more than ever. In the last ten years, she'd become more of a mystery, but her basic tells hadn't changed.

For instance, she always tugged on her left earlobe when she was skirting the truth. If she were wearing earrings, she'd play with them. If not, like this morning by the stove, talking about the state of disrepair of her summer cottage . . . tug, tug, tug.

What was she hiding?

They bundled up against the cold, and Cooper thanked his lucky stars he'd brought his duffel to the reception and left it squeezed into the Ferrari's tight little trunk. He'd intended to fly away from the wedding in Miles's helicopter, just to make a point about winning the bet, so he'd packed up what he brought to the island in preparation.

Vivian plopped a knit hat on her head, complete with hilarious earflaps and a fluff ball on top. The way her eyes sparkled erased the years from her face. "Come on! You've got to see Lantern Lake, it's absolutely glorious."

For Cooper's money, he'd already gotten to see Vivian's "private paradise" the night before, but he was always game for an exploration. "Lead the way."

Every breath fogged the air in front of them as they trooped out the door and down the porch stairs, Vivian carefully guiding him to skip the sagging second-to-top stair in case it wouldn't hold his weight.

Other than a few idle comments about how much the temperature had dropped overnight—or maybe it was the absence of a blazing beach bonfire—Cooper walked beside Vivian in comfortable silence. It wasn't the emptiness of having nothing to say, but rather the fullness of not needing to say anything in order to enjoy one another's company.

Telling himself he hadn't missed that at all, Cooper stared out over the quietly lovely vista of the secluded freshwater lake in the middle of a maritime pine glade. Frost tipped the cord grass and edged the cattails, bending their heavy heads down toward the water's surface. Across the lake, maybe a hundred feet away, a wild horse lifted its shaggy head from its morning sip of lake water and scented the breeze.

Grabbing Vivian's hand, Cooper pointed wordlessly at the animal, who watched them without blinking for a second or two before slowly lowering its dark chestnut head to the water once more.

"They're all over the island," Cooper murmured, gaze resting on the wild horse. "There must be five or six separate bands of horses."

"I love them." Vivian's low voice was surprisingly fierce and raw. Giving her a sidelong glance, he saw that moisture had welled along her bottom lashes, turning her eyes into sparkling amethysts. "They know how to be free."

It was an odd comment from someone who'd grown up a child of wealth and privilege. Vivian's parents had given her every opportunity, every advantage, which gave her plenty of free time to spend on fun. For a kid like Cooper, who'd worked for everything he had, including working two jobs to be able to afford his textbooks and an off-campus apartment even on a full academic scholarship, Vivian had always seemed to have it easy.

He hadn't held it against her, back then. He'd loved her ease—her casual generosity, her willingness to drop everything for the prospect of adventure, her unthinking, simple joy in her own body and what it could feel when the two of them were together.

"What happened?" Cooper asked, before he could stop the words. "In the last ten years, what changed for you? You used to be so . . ."

"Stupid?" Vivian asked, every line of her body tensing into taut, wiry suspense. She reminded him of the horse across the lake, when it first sensed the presence of potential predators. "Weak? Cowardly?"

"No!" Cooper grabbed her stiff shoulders and turned her to face him, but she looked down. The black fringe of her lashes hid her expression. Always hiding from him. "I meant—you used to be free, too. Happy. What changed?"

"You really don't know?" She glanced up from under those lashes, the shine on her eyes making his heart clench into a fist. "Never mind. It doesn't matter."

"It matters to me," Cooper said roughly, not even pausing to question if that was the truth, or if he was playing her. He wasn't sure he could tell the difference anymore. Maybe he never could.

Vivian closed her eyes briefly. "Oh, Cooper. Do you honestly think my life was so perfect back then? When we met, that first day of Professor Engelhoffer's English Lit class—that was the first time I ever tasted freedom. Happiness. Before that . . ."

She shook her head mutely, and Cooper had to fight down the urge to turn her upside down and shake her until the rest of her answer fell out. "I don't understand."

Vivian finally met his gaze head on, no hiding. "You want me to say that it was my awful ex, or the years of loveless marriage, or the scandalous divorce that made me this way. But it wasn't. I was always like this—except when I was around you."

She was giving him too much, every word leeching strength from her as if she'd sprung a leak like the old gas stove in the cabin. Any minute, she'd go up in flames of embarrassment and nerves. But Vivian held her head up and stared deep into Cooper's green-gold eyes. He deserved the truth.

So what if it left her a pile of ashes on the frozen ground?

"You never met my parents," she reminded him, wrapping her arms around herself to ward off the chill. "Maybe you thought . . . I know you thought it was because I was ashamed of you."

Cooper dropped his hands from her shoulders, stepping back. "Can't say I gave it that much consideration."

Vivian averted her gaze politely from the lie. "Well, that's not what was going on. I wanted to elope with you, to run away and leave everything behind, because I knew that if I told my parents about you—if they understood what you meant to me—they'd stop the wedding. Stop us from ever seeing each other again. And I was right."

She swallowed hard at the look on Cooper's face before he smoothed it into distant blankness. "What do you mean?"

"The dean invited them down to talk about donating a new wing for the science building," Vivian recounted, the entire sequence of events engraved on her soul. "They decided to stop in and visit me at my dorm after lunch, but I wasn't there."

"You were never there," Cooper agreed absently. "You'd all but moved into my apartment by that point."

The apartment. A wave of nostalgia swept over her head, drowning her in memories of the grimy little fourth-floor walk-up where Cooper had lived and studied during their college years. A blazing oven in the summer and colder than a freezer in the winter, no kitchen but a hot plate and narrow mini-fridge. "I loved that place," she said without thinking.

"Right." Cooper's cheeks went brick red, in the way that meant he was embarrassed but didn't want to show it. "You loved it so much, you married me and we lived there forever. Oh, wait . . ."

Pain scraped along her nerves, scouring out her ribcage. "No, you're right. I had some of the best times of my life in that apartment, but I didn't want to live there forever. And when my parents got the address from the R.A. on my dorm hall, and confronted me there—" She broke off, overwhelmed for a moment by the image of her expensively dressed parents picking their way through the cheerful clutter of the small studio. The look on her mother's face when she saw how Vivian had been living . . . and when she saw what Vivian was wearing.

"Where was I during all this?" Cooper demanded.

"You were already at the courthouse," Vivian said faintly. "I had class, remember? So I was going to meet you there. I wanted to skip it, but you said . . ."

Her throat went tight, choking off the words, and Cooper's expression went flat and distant.

"I said we'd have all the time in the world to be together after we were married. A few more minutes apart wouldn't matter."

Miserable, Vivian felt her shoulders slump as she nodded. "I'd gone home to change—so my parents walked in on me wearing a white dress and holding that pillbox hat with the veil I bought at that vintage shop on Fulton Street. And they knew."

"So what?" Cooper shook his head, frowning fiercely. "What difference did it make if they knew you were getting married? You were over the age of consent. All you had to do was walk out that door and come meet me."

"It wasn't that simple," Vivian protested. "They're my parents—I grew up trying desperately to make them proud of me, and failing ninety percent of the time. Nothing I did was ever good enough, but that only made me try harder. Until that day."

Cooper's eyes were as hard as moss-covered stones, opaque and judgmental. "They forbid you to marry me. And you caved."

That was the stark truth of it. Vivian wished she could argue, that she could point to some heroic motive, but nothing she said would change the fact that if she'd defied her parents, she would have spent the last ten years a far happier woman. And she never would have hurt Cooper so badly. "I was wrong," she confessed baldly. "I'm sorry. I made the wrong call. If I had it to do over again, if I could go back . . ."

"We can never go back." Cooper cut her off with a sharp, slashing hand gesture before turning and stalking down to the lake's edge.

Vivian watched him shove his hands into the pockets of his well-worn canvas jacket, her battered heart sinking to the pit of her stomach. She'd finally had the chance to apologize to Cooper, and it hadn't made any difference.

Not that she'd truly hoped it would—although she was appalled to discover there was a small, stubbornly optimistic part of her that had held out a slender thread of real hope.

That part was crushed, now, trembling under the weight of the past and all her many bad decisions. Leaving Cooper at the altar had only been the first of many . . . but it was the one she regretted the most.

"All you had to do was walk away from your parents," Cooper said. He could feel her hovering behind him, but he kept his gaze on the placid surface of the misty lake. "But you walked away from me instead."

She took a few steps closer. "At the time, I didn't think

I had a choice. It was so ingrained, the need to obey my parents and follow their rules. To not rock the boat."

"You were already planning to rock the boat," he pointed out. "You knew they'd hate it if you married me, that they'd never think a low class scholarship punk like me was good enough for their perfect debutante daughter."

Vivian paused at his side, her posture defeated. When she smiled, it was more of a grimace. "I had enough courage to go behind their backs—barely. But I didn't have the guts to defy them to their faces."

"They're your parents," Cooper ground out. "They would have come around eventually."

She was quiet for a long moment, nothing but the gentle lap of water on the lakeshore filling the air. "Maybe your parents would have, in a similar situation," Vivian finally said, choosing her words carefully. "But mine wouldn't. Trust me on this."

Cooper wanted to shake his head and deny it. The whole idea of parents—whose whole job was to love and care for their kids—being so unforgiving and so unwilling to allow their daughter to pursue her own happiness . . . it was completely foreign to the way Cooper grew up. His parents never had any money, but their house was full of love and laughter, until his dad got sick.

Breathing out the grief of that with the ease of practice, Cooper slanted a look at the woman beside him. Her classically perfect profile was as familiar as the shape of his own hand, but had he ever truly known her?

"For a long time, I wondered why you left," he said. "We were in the middle of senior year, but you even transferred to another school to get away from me."

She sighed. "My parents insisted. And I didn't transfer. I just never went back and finished my degree."

Some of the leftover anger and betrayal from that time period colored his voice when he asked, "Did they also insist that you marry that other guy? Whatever his name was."

"Gerald Findlay."

The name was almost familiar, but he was distracted from placing it by the realization that Vivian hadn't answered his actual question. Cooper glanced at her sharply, narrowing his gaze on her guilty face. "Are you serious? You let your parents pick out your husband for you?"

She squeezed her eyes shut and wrapped her arms around her torso, as if the wind had just kicked up. "I didn't think it made any difference. If I couldn't be with you, I thought it wouldn't matter who I actually married, and I might as well make my parents happy."

"Lucky guy." Cooper felt an unwelcome stab of sympathy for the poor schmuck who'd married into that dysfunctional family mess. Had the guy thought he was getting a wife who loved him?

But Vivian was shaking her head, a small and completely humorless smile flattening her mouth. "Believe me, Gerald didn't care. I looked the part, and I expected nothing from him, which left him free to get back to go back to what he really loved—his business dealings. Which was the reason my parents wanted me to marry him, in the first place. They wanted to get in on his investment scheme. I was basically collateral. I didn't know it at the time but they were on the verge of bankruptcy, and Gerald offered them a way to hold onto their lavish lifestyle."

The offhand way she said it, as if she hadn't expected more from her parents, made Cooper frown. "Is that why you divorced him?"

That wary prey look came over her again. "I divorced him because he abandoned me. Three years ago. You really . . . you never heard about this?"

Dread crept up the back of Cooper's neck. "What should I have heard?"

Under the cold-reddened cheeks, Vivian looked pale and wan but she squared her shoulders. Tilting her chin up determinedly, she said, "It was all over the news for a while, because so many people were affected."

"By your divorce?"

Vivian blew out a gusty breath that fogged the air in front of her. "No. By the fact that Gerald's investment company turned out to be a sham. He fled to the Maldives with the cash, after cleaning out everyone who invested with him."

Reeling with shock and sudden recognition—he had heard the name "Gerald Findlay" before—Cooper said, "Including your parents?"

She flinched, but kept her voice steady as a rock. "Actually, no. As it turned out, my parents were in on it with him. They steered their wealthy, high society friends to invest with Gerald . . . and when it all came crashing down, they were safely ensconced in a penthouse in Moscow, sitting on piles of money. They sold out all their friends and cashed in, then retired to a country with no extradition to the U.S. So they can never be forced to return. They didn't leave me much, but everything I had went to paying back the victims of their fraud."

Speechless, Cooper could only stare at her. While he'd

been off making his fortune and enjoying it while seeing the world, she'd been used as part of a negotiation between her crooked parents and crookeder husband, then abandoned by both to face the wrath of the people they'd duped.

No wonder she seemed more guarded than he remembered. But she wasn't hiding from him now.

In fact, Vivian pulled her shoulders back and lifted her face to his as she said, "So there you have it. I broke my engagement to the penniless man I loved and married the rich guy my parents wanted—and now here I am. I own nothing more than the clothes on my back, and you're a billionaire with the freedom to do and be whatever you want. I could almost laugh at the irony, if it weren't the life I have to live."

Shaking his head as if that would re-order the pieces of information that this revelation had shattered, Cooper said, "What do you mean, you own nothing? You just bought this cabin."

Sadness and longing darkened her eyes to the color of the night sky after a storm. "With Miles and Greta's money. They loaned me the down payment, and I got a loan from the bank—that's what I was doing the other night, that made me miss the wedding rehearsal. The cabin doesn't belong to me . . . but it is my future. I'm going to fix it up and flip it, and hopefully make enough money to buy the next place. And so on."

"You're doing the renovations yourself?" Alarm tightened Cooper's chest. He'd seen the rickety state of the cabin, but . . . "I assumed you'd be hiring contractors and handymen to do the work."

"I don't have the money for that." She smiled, and it was

only a little shaky at the corners. "Don't worry, I'm looking forward to it. I spent most of my marriage decorating and redecorating our house, and I borrowed a few DIY books from the Sanctuary Island library. I'll be fine."

She would be fine, Cooper decided on the spur of the moment. He'd make sure of it.

"I have a proposal for you," he told her. "And this time, you're not walking away from me before I'm done with you."

Chapter Six

The word "proposal" rang oddly in Vivian's ears, everything else fading out around it. "What?" she asked, sucking in a breath and half expecting him to go down on one knee.

Instead, Cooper put his hands on his hips and turned to survey the exterior of the cabin with a critical eye. "How much did you borrow to pay for this place?"

Vivian didn't like the skeptical tone. But as she followed his gaze, taking in the dilapidated side view of the front porch, the disreputable missing shingles from the roof, and the general air of being down on its luck, she couldn't blame Cooper for turning up his nose at the old place. But Vivian had vision, and if she squinted, she saw the cabin as it could be—bright lights shining from the windows, a curl of smoke seeping from the chimney, and a fresh paint job would work wonders to turn this house into a home.

"I didn't borrow more than it's worth," she assured him,

biting her lip when it sounded as if she were trying to convince both of them. "It's going to be someone's dream home, I'm sure of it."

She ought to know. It was *her* dream home. But she had to sell it. That was the plan.

Until Cooper Hayes tilted his head and said, "I want to make you an offer. Right here, right now."

Caught off balance, Vivian stammered, "What kind of an offer?"

"A generous one." Cooper's mouth quirked up, and he named a figure that was five times the amount Vivian had paid for the cabin. Her eyes felt like they would pop out of her head as she mentally tabulated how quickly she could pay back the Harringtons and the bank, with enough left over to fund her next house flipping project.

"But . . ." She struggled to control her lungs, which wanted to hyperventilate. "Cooper, that's too much. I can't accept."

Annoyance creased the corners of his eyes. "My money is as good as anyone's. At least I came by it honestly."

He meant it to sting, and it did. But Vivian couldn't let emotion or personal need into this conversation. "I didn't tell you all that stuff about my parents and Gerald to make you feel sorry for me, and I won't take advantage of . . ."

"What?" He lifted a brow. "Our relationship? We don't have one. Our history? It sucks. You're not taking advantage of anything except a solid opportunity. This is a business deal, plain and simple."

Vivian blinked away the burn of his cool assessment of their relationship. *Message received, Mr. Hayes. Last night meant nothing to you. I mean nothing to you.*

But if that were true . . .

"Why are you doing this?" she demanded.

Cooper shrugged, pacing a few steps along the lakeshore as if he were restless. "I don't know, I like it here. Sanctuary Island is pretty, the people are nice, some of my best friends have fallen for local girls . . . it makes sense to establish a base camp somewhere. Might as well be here."

Vivian narrowed her eyes. "What about all that stuff you said, when you thought this was my vacation home? You sure weren't interested in having a base camp then."

"I changed my mind."

Breathing deeply through her nose, Vivian turned to look at her cabin once more in the harsh, unforgiving mid-morning light. Temptation prodded at her to accept, arguing that she'd never get another offer this good.

"There's only so much of a fight I can put up, here," she said absently, her imagination already working on the list of supplies and tools she could buy with the purchase money.

"I'm not sure why you're fighting it at all, to be honest."

"Would you believe it's been a long time since anything surprised me in a nice way?" She glanced over her shoulder at him. "I started to get used to bad luck."

Cooper smiled, slow and predatory in a way that pumped adrenaline into Vivian's bloodstream. "We'll see if you still feel lucky when you hear my conditions."

Cooper had learned to trust his instincts over the years, to let the universe guide him. The universe had led him to his best friends, his most memorable experiences in foreign lands . . . and it had also led him back into contact with Vivian Banks.

There was something between them, and he needed more time to figure out what it was. Other than the obvious, he acknowledged silently with an appreciative scan of her lithe, slender form. They'd always been compatible in bed, and when they first knew each other, they'd been compatible everywhere else, too.

Things were different now. They were both different people, a lot of water had passed under the bridge—so much that maybe it had flooded and washed the bridge out completely.

But maybe not. He looked at Vivian now, hope and apprehension warring in her eyes, and he knew he wasn't ready to walk away. Did that mean he was giving up on his revenge?

Not entirely.

Cooper smiled, and it must not have been a very comforting grin because Vivian immediately looked wary. That was okay. She should be.

"What conditions?" she asked cautiously.

He stuck his hands in his pockets and cracked his neck lazily. "I think the amount I'm offering buys me input into what renovations you do."

She nodded slowly, the line of her shoulders relaxing slightly. "That seems reasonable."

That was because she hadn't heard the kicker. "I'll also want to oversee the renovations personally."

Vivian's jaw dropped for a bare instant before she closed her mouth with a snap. "You mean, you want to stay on the island so you can order me around and watch me work?"

"Not exactly." Cooper sauntered closer, feeling like a lion stalking a gazelle when she quivered in place, clearly fighting the urge to fall back. "I want to stay here . . . in the cabin. With you. And I want to help with the work."

That wrinkle he'd always adored appeared between her black brows. "You want to pay me a fortune for a fixer-upper, and then you want to do the fixing up yourself?"

Not quite ready to admit that he wanted to spend more time with her, Cooper shrugged again. "Sounds like an interesting project. And who knows, maybe that's what's always been missing when I've bought a place to live before—maybe if I get my hands dirty and make it the way I want it to be, it'll feel more like a real home."

Her deep blue eyes softened, and Cooper knew he had her. "That makes sense. Although, in the interest of full disclosure. . . . it doesn't always work that way. I did a ton of work on the Westchester house where I lived with Gerald, and it never really felt like home."

A complicated blend of triumph and jealousy went through Cooper in a confusing rush. He chose to focus on the victory of getting his own way with Vivian. "Great. I'll call my money guy and have him start the paperwork. In the meantime, what's the first item on your punch list?"

Vivian held up a hand to stop him. "Wait. Before we shake on it, I have a condition of my own."

"I'm not a business shark like Miles," Cooper said, amused. "But even I have enough savvy to know you're not really in a position to add conditions of your own to this deal."

"Nevertheless." Vivian set her jaw stubbornly, even as a light flush pinked her cheeks. "I have to say this, because we need to be clear. You're buying this property, and the right to help fix it up. You're not buying rights to anything else . . . including me."

This time, it was Cooper who almost took a step back. He felt like she'd smacked him across the face. Voice low and dangerous, he said, "Is that what you think of me? That I'm trying to buy you?"

The blush across her cheekbones intensified, but she didn't back down. "No, actually."

"If you recall," Cooper pointed out tensely, "No money changed hands before last night."

"And I'm not saying I don't want a repeat," Vivian replied, tilting her head up challengingly. "But I've had enough of my body being used as a bargaining chip in a business negotiation. If I sleep with you again, it'll be because we both want it. Not because I owe you anything, or because I'm obligated to in any way. I have to be crystal clear about that . . . not just for me, but for you. Because I know you'd never be comfortable with anything less."

All Cooper's indignation drained out of him, leaving behind nothing but a strange pride in the way Vivian was handling this. She'd been through a lot since he last saw her, but she'd come through the fire strengthened at the core. He held out a hand, and when she clasped it to shake, he pulled her in close.

"I agree to your terms," he murmured into the soft tendrils of black hair fanning across her temple. She smelled like wood smoke and lavender. "Does that mean we can't seal the deal with a kiss?"

A slow, sweet smile curled the corners of her mouth. Those lips were made for smiling, Cooper thought. And for kissing.

In answer to his question, Vivian stretched up to press their mouths together, the heat of the embrace shocking in the morning chill. Hunger roared through him, but Cooper could control it.

Now that he knew this wasn't a one-time deal, and he'd have weeks or months . . . however long it took to fix up this crazy little cottage, to sate his need for Vivian Banks. And when they were through with the renovations, he'd finally be through with her.

Right?

Chapter Seven

The next two weeks passed quickly. The days were full of learning things like how to patch a roof together, and evenings spent curled up on the second-hand couch that was the only living room furniture. Vivian hoped Cooper would let her stick around after the renovations were done, at least long enough to help with the interior decorating, but she was afraid to bring it up. Things were good between them as they worked side by side and slept tangled in each other's arms. She didn't think she could bear it if the answer was "no."

Not that Cooper gave her reasons to doubt him. If anything, he seemed intent on protecting her happiness rather than tearing her down.

"Can you hand me that hammer?" he asked absently, sprawled on his stomach below the peak of the roof, surrounded by piles of replacement slate shingles.

From her position on the ladder, Vivian could reach the

spot it had slid to if she stretched, but the zipper of her puffy down vest caught on the edge of the roof.

"Whoops!"

Cooper's head shot up, concern darkening his handsome features. "Never mind! Stay put, I'll get it."

Vivian unhooked the zipper and rolled her eyes. "I can do it, just give me a minute."

"No need. Just hang out on the ladder. It still feels steady, right?"

She hid a smile, fond exasperation tickling at her. "Yes. The ten-pound bags of mulch you braced it with are holding. Honestly, Cooper, when you said you wanted to oversee the renovations, I didn't imagine that meant you'd be doing them all yourself!"

"You've helped." He hooked the hammer with his foot and inched it up the roof to where he could grab it. Holding it aloft triumphantly, he wiped a trickle of sweat from his forehead with the back of his wrist. It was another mild winter day on Sanctuary Island, and working on the roof in the afternoon sun made it seem almost hot.

Not that Vivian had been allowed to do much actual work.

"Sure, because standing on a ladder and doing nothing is really helpful," she grumbled.

"You made me lemonade," Cooper pointed out. "And brought me lunch."

"I'm supposed to be learning about home repair and renovation, not how to be a waitress!"

"Learn by watching," he said firmly, going back to his careful placement of the dark grey stone tiles. "I don't want you scrambling around up here. You could fall."

"So can you. But I already know how useless it is to

mention that fact." She sighed. "Useless is basically my middle name."

"Don't say that," Cooper mumbled around the nails he'd stuck in the side of his mouth until he needed them. "You're not useless. I'm here to help, so just accept it. You don't have to do this all on your own."

A wave of warmth swept through her, but right on its heels was the old, familiar clench of guilt. She should be on her own. It's what she deserved.

Cooper's eyes narrowed as if her negative thoughts were written on her forehead. He propped himself up on one sweatshirted elbow and pointed the hammer at her. "Stop it. Seriously. I can't take that guilty face. What do you have to feel so guilty about anyway?"

She could hardly believe he had to ask, but . . . "Um, disappearing on our wedding day without even leaving a note?"

An odd look came over his face. "You really still feel bad about that."

Bad didn't begin to cover it. "It was the worst mistake of my life. And it led to a whole host of other mistakes, terrible choices and stupid decisions, and I feel guilty about all of it. All those people my parents and Gerald defrauded—some of them lost their life savings."

"Yeah, and you spent your life savings trying to pay them back," Cooper argued. "Even though you had nothing to do with the crime."

"I should have known what Gerald was up to. How could I not have realized something was wrong?" She shook her head, hands tightening on the top rung of the ladder until the rough metal tread cut into her palms. "The truth is, everything was wrong back then. I couldn't pick out that one criminal thread of wrongness from the mess of the rest of my life."

Cooper's eyes flashed, and he began the slow, precise process of making his way across the slanted roof toward her. Vivian swallowed, nose and eyes burning, and wished she had the inner fortitude to laugh off the memories and assure him she was fine.

Instead, she waited mutely until Cooper had inched close enough to put his arms around her. As steady as the ladder was, Vivian sighed with relief at the strong, sure grasp of his arm. She dropped her head on his shoulder and tried not to unbalance him.

"Viv," he said tenderly, in a tone that threw her back ten years into the past, when everything had been simple and she'd still had hopes about how her life could turn out.

"Hey, come on now." Cooper's long-fingered hand, rough with new calluses, cupped her chin and lifted her face until he could kiss her. "You're fixing it. Maybe not literally with a hammer and nails, like you thought—but you've taken major steps to fix your life. You should feel good about that."

Tears choked her for a moment, and when she could speak again it was more of a croak. "How can you say that? You, of all people. You know how much I deserve to be punished."

The whole world slipped sideways for a horrifying instant of vertigo that made Cooper clutch at Vivian more tightly, certain that the roof was caving in or the ladder was toppling to the ground. But when he sucked in oxygen and steadied himself, he realized it wasn't the roof or the ladder that had shifted.

It was his reality.

Every moment of anger, every bitter recrimination he'd leveled at Vivian in the years since she walked out on their future . . . and nothing he'd said or thought could match the ways she'd punished herself.

"You told me once that you married Gerald because you'd already given me up, so it didn't matter what happened to you. But it was more than that. You were punishing yourself for what you did to us."

He saw the truth in her eyes before she gave a short, ashamed nod. "Every day I stayed with him was like being in prison. It was awful—but I couldn't leave. It was like making reparations, like penance. I thought, if I stayed with him even though I was miserable, then maybe eventually I'd earn forgiveness. But it didn't work, because the person whose forgiveness I needed was you. And you were gone."

"Oh, Viv." Heart ripping in two, Cooper pressed his mouth to her forehead and tried to control his breathing. "Sweetheart. We need to get down off this roof."

She sniffled. "Sorry. I know you were hoping to get this finished today."

"Stop apologizing," he growled, then blinked at himself. But he meant it. "The roof isn't important. What's important is that I need to hold you right now, if not sooner, and I don't want a ladder and the threat of a fifty-foot drop between us."

Giving a watery laugh, Vivian nodded once and let go of him to grasp the sides of the ladder. Cooper watched her make her careful way down the rungs, only the glossy black hair on top of her head visible. Every inch of space separating them felt wrong all of a sudden, and he hurried down after her.

When they were both on solid ground, Cooper wasted no time pulling her into his arms. It was colder in the shadow of the house, but he didn't think the chilly breeze was what made Vivian tremble against his chest.

He could sympathize. He felt a little on the shaky side himself when he thought about how intent he'd been on punishing Vivian when he first saw her again after all those years apart. All those years, which he'd spent getting rich and seeing the world—and she'd spent miserable and trapped in a loveless marriage by her scheming, opportunistic parents.

"I'm sorry," he said, the words ripped from his gut.

"Hey." Vivian leaned back enough to lift her face to his. "If I'm not allowed to apologize anymore, you definitely aren't! Especially since you haven't done anything wrong."

Maybe not, but he'd sure thought about it. Shame curdled in Cooper's belly. "I should have known you wouldn't just leave me. I should've looked for you, made sure you were okay. Instead, I went off and made my fortune . . . and you lost everything."

Vivian shook her head, her brows wrinkled in concern. "Cooper. Don't blame yourself. I certainly don't. And anyway, I might have lost a few things along the way, like my horrible ex-husband and the fantasy that my parents loved me and cared about me . . ."

"And all your money," Cooper reminded her.

She laughed. "And all my money. But I found a couple of important things, too. Like my self-respect. And the strength to pick myself up and start over—that one was a nice surprise. I didn't know that about myself, that I was capable of that kind of resilience."

"You should be proud of yourself," Cooper said, fierce

protectiveness expanding his rib cage with every breath. He hated it that Vivian had ever been made to feel like less than the strong, amazing woman that she was. "I'm proud of you, if that means anything."

"Of course it does!" She blinked up at him, dark violet-blue eyes wide with something like shock, mixed with trepidation. "Cooper, you're everything. The last couple of weeks with you . . . that's my latest and best discovery. That the past doesn't have a stranglehold on us. Because if you can forgive me for what I did to you, then maybe, just maybe . . . there's hope for the future."

She stopped as if she'd run out of words and breath, and the expression on her face made Cooper want to shout and rage and tear down the world with his bare hands—because Vivian Banks should never look at Cooper Hayes like that. As if she didn't know that she was everything to him, too.

Cupping her face between his hands, Cooper did his best to drill every word straight into her heart. "Vivian. I forgive you. I do. We were just kids, and the pressures your parents put on you . . . it must have been overwhelming. They sound like master manipulators, and you were so young, so sweet, so hungry for love. Your parents knew that, and they used it against you. It wasn't your fault."

Joy lit her eyes like sapphires, but she shook her head. "It means more than I can tell you, to hear you say that. I've wanted your forgiveness for a long time. But I can't put all the blame on my parents. As you pointed out, I could have stood up to them. I wish I had. Every day and every night of my marriage, believe me, I wished I had the guts to tell them all to go to hell."

She shuddered, darkness moving through her like a

cloud passing in front of the sun. Cooper tensed, his muscles going tight and battle-ready as every part of him ached to fight off her demons. But then she smiled, and the sun came out once more.

"Just knowing you've forgiven me is the greatest gift, Cooper. I can hardly believe it."

The adrenaline in Cooper's bloodstream converted to hunger in the blink of an eye. "Believe it," he said, bending to sweep her up into his arms and hold her high against his chest.

Vivian didn't even tense at the abrupt move—she only sighed happily and melted against him, winding her arms lazily around his neck. "I'll try," she promised, pushing her face into the side of his neck and inhaling as if she liked the smell of sunshine, male sweat, and roofing dust. "But it might take a while."

She shot him a glance from beneath her lashes, and Cooper realized what she was really asking. A sense of rightness steadied his steps as he carried her around to the front of the cabin, heading toward their warm, soft bed. "Take as long as you need," he told her seriously, laying her down on white cotton sheets that already smelled like the two of them. Like home.

Vivian caught her breath. "You mean . . ."

Leaning over her, Cooper smoothed back a lock of her hair and brushed her bottom lip with his thumb to make her shiver. "I mean, we have time. I'm not going anywhere anytime soon. And neither are you."

And as they sank into each other, Cooper tried to lose himself in the moment. Because the moment was wonderful, heat and tightness and the kind of pleasure that turned a man inside out . . . but in the back of his mind, the past lurked like a cancer, sending our tendrils of black poison.

He still had questions, things he wanted to know but hesitated to bring up because he didn't want to cause Vivian any more pain than she'd already suffered. Now wasn't the time, anyway. They'd made enough progress for one day.

Cooper forced the questions down, focusing on the sweet taste and eager response of the woman in his bed. They had time. He'd make sure of it.

Chapter Eight

Vivian scraped one last curl of flaking paint off the porch railing and blew out a breath. She paused for a minute to wipe her forehead and smooth her flyaway hairs back into the hasty knot she'd twisted it into after the long—shared, delicious, knee-weakening—shower that morning.

Since she'd stopped, it was a perfect time to check her messages. Vivian pulled her phone from the pocket of her sleeveless down vest to see if either the bank or the title company had returned her emails. There was a notification from her bank, and she clicked it quickly only to frown at the news that it would take several days for Cooper's check to clear. And there was still no news on the status of all the ownership paperwork.

"What's the matter?" Cooper called from the yard, where he was working on scraping and sanding down the front door, which they'd taken off its hinges and rested on a pair of sawhorses in preparation for repainting the cabin's trim a bright, happy red.

Vivian slipped the phone back into her pocket. "It's kind of crazy that I could deposit a tiny check for not much money and have it all available immediately—but when it's a lot of money that I really need, it's going to take another week."

"Whatever you need the money for, I can cover it," Cooper said.

Vivian went still. She didn't want to offend Cooper, and she could tell it meant something to him that he'd pulled himself up by his bootstraps into the financial stratosphere, and that he could afford to buy her anything she wanted. But at the same time, she didn't want to set a precedent she wouldn't be able to live with.

"That's sweet of you," she told him sincerely. "I truly appreciate the thought. But it's important to me to be independent."

Cooper frowned. "You always shared whatever you had with all your friends at school—buying rounds of drinks, picking up the tab for lunch. What's the big deal about me helping you out now?"

"I don't want to owe you anything." Vivian's fingers cramped, and she realized she was clutching the metal-handled scraper too tightly. Uncurling her fist, she set it gently down on the railing.

"I'm not going to collect on you," Cooper protested, starting to get frustrated. Worse than the irritation, though, was the hurt Vivian could see lurking in his hazel eyes. "What do you think, I'm going to take it out of your hide? If you insist on it being a loan, that's fine—I know you're good for it, since I already cut you a check."

"That's different! I'm earning that money by renovating and selling you the cabin, which you will then own free and clear. It's straightforward, simple, clean. I can live with that."

Something flashed across Cooper's face too quickly for her to read it, and when he opened his mouth, she held up a hand. She was determined to get this out on the table between them. Any future they might have depended on being up front about this.

"What I can't live with," Vivian said, "is another man thinking he owns me because I don't have the means to make my own way in the world."

Cooper's mouth shut with a snap, the muscle behind his jaw ticking for a second before he rounded the sawhorses and stalked across the yard toward her. When he was close enough to touch her, he leaned his arms on the railing she'd been scraping and stared up at her. His voice was low and serious when he told her, "I would never think that."

Softening a little, Vivian leaned over the railing to hug his shoulders. Cooper rested his forehead between her breasts, his breath hot through the waffle print of her thermal shirt. "I know, Cooper. I promise, I'm not confusing you with my ex-husband. But money . . . it changes people. It changes relationships. And if we want this one to work, we have to be honest about how we're feeling about all the issues that crop up. Money is only one of them, but it's a big one for me."

Vivian held her breath a little, the way she had every time she'd mentioned the possibility of a future together over the past two weeks, and once again, Cooper didn't disappoint her. He tilted his head up and reached over the railing to wrap his thick, muscular arms around her hips.

"You're right. We should talk. There's something I have to tell you."

From the guilty glint in his hazel eyes, Vivian had a sinking feeling that she wasn't going to like it. The buzz of the phone in her pocket felt like a reprieve.

"Hold that thought." She straightened up and fished out the phone. "It's the title office! I have to take this."

Cooper's eyes went wide and he shook his head, making a grab for the phone, but the woman on the other end of the line was already speaking. Viv swatted at him and turned away, tuning out Cooper's antics and trying to focus on what Janine was saying.

"I was surprised to get your email." Janine's nasal voice filtered through the phone speaker. "Seeing as how the paperwork was signed on Monday. A representative for Mr. Cooper Hayes took care of it."

"Oh. He didn't tell me." Vivian glanced over her shoulder at Cooper, who grimaced and palmed the back of his neck.

"Well, it hasn't been processed yet, but everything is in order," Janine said briskly. "A copy of the deed was overnighted to you, I'm surprised it hasn't arrived yet."

"Island mail service can be a little unreliable," Vivian said absently, her brain working overtime. "What do you mean, the deed was overnighted to me? Shouldn't you have sent it to Mr. Hayes's attention?"

"What?" Janine sounded confused. She wasn't the only one. "We're talking about the property at forty-two hundred Lantern Lane, correct?"

"Yes."

"Whew! For a second, I was worried I'd sent your deed to the wrong address. What a mess that would have been."

"You mean Mr. Hayes's deed," Vivian corrected her, heart fluttering in her ribcage like a wild bird trying to get free.

"Hmmm. Nope, no, I've got a copy of the paperwork right here. The property at Lantern Lake is in your name, Ms. Banks. Mr. Hayes signed a quit claim and transferred the property to you on the same day that he became the owner."

The instant Vivian dropped the phone from her ear and clicked it off, Cooper was vaulting up the porch steps and rushing to her. "I can explain."

"You put the house in my name," Vivian said blankly. "You paid me five times what it's worth, and you didn't even want it for yourself?"

"I got what I wanted." Cooper reached out, and felt his entire body unclench when Vivian didn't pull away. "More time with you. A second chance. That was worth a hundred times the amount I paid for the house. A thousand."

But Vivian was shaking her head. "Cooper, you can't—you can't just give me this house. It's not what we agreed. I mean, thank you. I know you meant well, but . . ."

"You love this house!" Cooper knuckled under her chin, lifting it to get a look at her eyes. They were damp and wide, conflict darkening the irises to deep violet. "I knew from the first night, when we drove over the hill and you looked down at the property. This is your dream house. Or it will be, with a little more hard work and a lot of love. Don't be mad at me."

Her mouth twisted. "Of course I'm not mad. You're right, I love this house. It's beautiful, the lake renews my soul every time I look at it, I have friends on the island,

and this house is where you and I reconnected—but I can't let you give it to me."

Cooper's heart froze, ice prickling at the inside of his chest. For a horrible moment, it felt like she wasn't rejecting the house. She was rejecting him, and everything he could offer her. "Vivian. I want you to have it."

Something like sympathy lightened her gaze for a moment before she firmed her mouth and shook her head regretfully. "I know. But I can't accept it. And I'll tell you why, but you're going to wish I hadn't. It's not a pretty story."

Cooper framed her face between his hands, a frown tugging at his brows. "You know you don't always have to be pretty and sweet and perfect for me, right? I don't have some standard in my mind that I'm always holding you up to. I want you exactly as you are. The real Vivian."

Pain tightened the corners of her eyes. "Not everyone in my life has been so accepting, or so forgiving."

Cooper swallowed down the simmering anger in his gut and led her down to sit on the porch steps. He pulled her in close to his side, wrapping an arm around her shoulders, and waited.

It took her a moment to speak, as if she were gathering her courage, and when the words finally came, they were halting and slow. "My parents sent me off to Gerald with nothing. No college degree, no money, and no way to earn any. I was supposed to be his entrée into high society, the visible and tangible proof of my parents' support so the three of them could fleece the wealthiest people in their circle. But I didn't know that at the time."

She paused, ducking her head to her raised knees, and Cooper wound his fingers into her tousled black hair, aching for her. "You don't have to tell me this. I'll take the house back. I'll do whatever you want."

"Thanks." Vivian shuddered once, then raised her face to his. Her eyes were red, but dry. "But I think I do have to tell you. What happened back then—if I let it be a secret, then it will become a wall between us. And I don't want anything to separate us, not ever again."

The passion in her voice reached deep into Cooper's chest and stirred an answering hunger. Not just for her body, but for her spirit and her heart, and for every moment of their lives that they would still get to spend together. He could only be grateful that she was strong enough to remove this last obstacle.

"Back then," she continued, steadier now. "I was a mess. I'd left the love of my life behind without a word, and now I was supposed to be someone else's wife. Gerald was—well, he was a businessman, first and foremost. He was very clear about his expectations for me. I was to be beautiful, to maintain my weight and fitness level, to wear the clothes he bought for me, and to smile at every dinner party, every charity benefit, every afternoon tea at the club. And I was to keep my mouth shut, or there would be consequences."

"What consequences?" Cooper heard the growl in his own voice, but he couldn't tamp it down.

Vivian closed her eyes briefly. "You have to understand, Gerald didn't love me, and he knew I didn't love him. He didn't care—I was an asset, a prop in his con—but he knew he could use it. He knew I'd been told to do whatever he said, and I think it was clear to him that I was completely powerless. And he also knew that if I stepped a foot out of line, all he had to do to punish me was to demand his rights as a husband."

Cooper felt himself turn to stone. His muscles locked down and his lungs seized up. He barely had the breath to wheeze, "What?"

"Gerald told me up front that he wouldn't touch me," Vivian said bluntly. "Unless I broke the rules. Believe me, I learned the rules by heart, and I followed them to the letter."

"So he never . . ." Hope punched Cooper's heart like a heavyweight champ going for the KO. It wasn't as if he'd imagined that Vivian had never had sex with her husband. He'd assumed they did—but to find out that sex had been used against her like a weapon . . . it made Cooper's skin crawl.

Vivian looked away, toward the lake. "Only a few times. It wasn't—he wasn't violent, or anything. It could have been much, much worse."

Sickness rose like acid in the back of Cooper's throat. "Oh, Viv. Don't. What happened to you was bad enough. Don't downplay it by playing what if."

She shook herself as if she'd walked through a cobweb, short and frantic, then went on. "And when I was good, he bought me things. Lavish gifts, fur coats, a sailboat . . . why didn't I get on that boat and sail away from him?"

Cooper, who'd been screaming that same question inside the locked box of his head, gritted out, "He kept you dependent on him. It sounds like he practically brainwashed you, Viv. Like some damned cult leader or something. He had you in his clutches, and he wasn't about to let you go."

She nodded. "That's exactly how it was. I felt trapped. I *was* trapped, by my own inability to pick myself up and escape. There were no guards, no chains, nothing keeping me there. Why didn't I leave?"

Finally, for the first time since they'd started this awful, heartrending conversation, Vivian broke. A sob clawed its way out of her throat and her shoulders hunched. Cooper's heart tore right down the middle, jagged and nasty. He got both his arms around her and lifted her into his lap so they could press as tightly together as possible.

"You survived," he told her fiercely, his mouth against the side of her head and her tears soaking his shirt. "That's all that matters. You made it."

"And I found my way back to you," she choked out, her fingers clutching at his collar. "And miracle of miracles, you forgave me. Even though, by rights, you should hate me."

The words struck him like a frying pan to the head. He *had* hated her, almost as much as he'd loved her. The things he'd planned to do, to hurt her the way she'd hurt him . . . "You told me once that you married Gerald because after you left me, you thought it didn't matter what happened to you. But Vivian, it did matter. And no matter how angry I was when you left, or even how mad I still was ten years later—I would never, ever have wanted you to go through that."

Vivian gave him a watery smile, swiping at her nose with her sleeve. "Well, I got through it, and now we're together. All I want to do is forget about it and move on with my life. But you can see why a big, lavish gift from the man I'm involved with is a little bit of a trigger for me."

"Yes, absolutely. I'll take care of it." Cooper made the

promise without having to think about it. Now that he knew the whole story, most of his attention was on making the connections as the final pieces of the puzzle slotted into place. "You paid back Gerald's investors . . ."

"By selling off the boat, the furs, the jewels—all the gifts he'd given me. The government repossessed the house and property, everything that was in his name, when Gerald fled the country. But the gifts were mine, so I used them to pay back Gerald's other victims." She grimaced in disgust. "I wouldn't have wanted to keep that crap anyway. Too many reminders."

"So you ended up with nothing," Cooper said slowly, a flame of rage kindling in his belly. "While Gerald basically got away scot free. And now he's living the high life . . . where?"

"The Maldives, last I heard." Vivian shrugged, and Cooper frowned. He couldn't believe how casual she was about this. "No extradition to the United States, and a dollar goes a long way there. He can basically live like a king without lifting a finger for the rest of his miserable life."

The injustice of it burned through Cooper's insides. "We can't let him get away with this. He's a criminal, he should be brought to justice."

After I have a short, sharp chat with him about the way a man should treat a woman like Vivian Banks.

But she was shaking her head decisively. "No, it's over. Let Gerald spend his dirty money. It won't make him happy. He's a very unhappy, twisted person at heart and nothing can change that."

"Maybe not, but I'd lay big odds on being able to make him even more unhappy." Cooper bared his teeth, already making plans. "I can ask to borrow Miles's helicopter—

they get back from their honeymoon today, right?—and we'll fly from here to the closest airport where we can charter a plane. Quick hop to the Maldives, I'll grab Gerald, and we'll have the whole flight back to the loving embrace of the criminal justice system to get a few things straight."

Vivian stood up so quickly, she almost overbalanced. But when Cooper reached a hand to steady her, she stepped away from him, eyes wild. "No! Cooper, what are you saying? You can't be serious."

"Deadly serious." Cooper stood too, the buildup of energy and emotion shoving him to his feet. "I'm not talking about assassinating him, much as I might like that. No, I'm just going to drag Gerald Findlay back to face trial for his crimes. It's better than he deserves, but at least it's something."

"And what if I ask you not to go?" Vivian hugged her arms around her ribcage, her cheeks pale. "Please, Cooper. If you ever loved me, if you've truly forgiven me, put this idea out of your head."

Cooper stopped and stared at her. This woman, who'd been wronged in so many ways, was still going to stand there and defend her villain of an ex-husband? She really was too good, too sweet—she needed to be protected. That feeling crashed into the guilt Cooper still carried for his own intent to punish her, and the fact that he hadn't rescued her. The compulsion to move, to go, to get out of here and do something, overpowered him.

He shook his head, fists clenched and muscles jumping with tension. "No. I can't let this go."

Chapter Nine

Vivian felt cold all the way to her bones. Was it going to snow? Or maybe it was only that she stared at Cooper, standing on the Lantern Lake cabin's porch steps mere inches away, and she'd never felt further from him.

"Please, Cooper. Don't do this. I'm begging you."

His lip curled. "You're begging for the freedom of the man who essentially held you prisoner for years? He doesn't deserve your loyalty, Vivian."

A shockwave exploded through her. "I'm not loyal to him! I don't care if he lives or dies. I'm begging for *my* freedom—from the past, from my memories and mistakes. What's done is behind us. Can't we leave it there and move forward?"

Cooper stepped off the stairs and began to pace along the front of the porch. "How can you move forward, knowing your parents and Gerald are out there, living the high life and not paying for what they did to you?"

"Because getting revenge is the last thing on my mind!" Vivian threw up her hands in frustration. "Honestly, I don't have the energy to spare for it. I've got this house to renovate, my finances to straighten out, and the chance at real happiness with the long lost love of my life. Why would I want to spend a single second on the past, when the future looks so bright?"

Cooper scrubbed both hands over his short, buzzed hair. "I can't get the image of him lying on some beach somewhere out of my head. It's making me crazy."

Frustration and disappointment made Vivian's voice sharp. "Well, you're certainly acting crazy! Charter a plane and fly to the Maldives. And for what! We're here, we're alive, we're free, we're together. If that's not enough for you . . ."

The echo of her own words stopped her. Maybe it wasn't enough for Cooper. Maybe she wasn't enough.

"We'd be together either way," Cooper argued. "Come with me, we'll see this thing through together."

Feeling as if she'd swallowed an ice cube, too big and too cold and hurting all the way down to her gut, Vivian shook her head. "If you're determined to go galloping off on some revenge fantasy, leave me out of it. I spent too many years punishing myself for my mistakes instead of realizing that I still had a future. I can't live like that anymore. I don't want to, and I don't have to. Not even if it's the price for being with you."

Cooper stared at her, all emotion wiped from his handsome face, and he said nothing. The silence stretched between them, tangible as the whistle of air through an empty canyon, and Vivian's hopes evaporated under the winter sun.

He was going to leave. Cooper was going to go and do this hate-filled, violent thing, instead of staying here and building a life and a home with Vivian.

"It's your choice, if you want to go," she forced out, her tight throat making her voice scratchy and low. "I would never try to take your choices from you. But I have a choice too—and I choose not to be a part of it."

And with that, she turned on her heel and walked up the steps and into the house he'd given her, leaving Cooper standing outside in the cold.

Vivian couldn't bear to watch him walk out of her life, and know she'd lost him for the second time. But she heard the distinctive roar of his Ferrari's engine growing fainter through the trees, and she sank down onto her threadbare sofa and wept.

A long, cold night and lonely morning later, Vivian had to face the truth. Cooper was gone. No doubt halfway around the world by now, and when . . . *if* he came back, she didn't know what that would mean for their relationship. Did they even have a relationship at this point? She'd called him the love of her life, but he hadn't said "I love you" in return.

Instead of torturing herself with doubts and worries, Vivian hauled herself out of bed and put on her work clothes. She might as well get the porch stripped of paint. That would be a better use of her time than sitting around feeling sorry for herself. She was sick of self-pity.

But it was hard not to feel sad when she pushed aside the plastic they'd covered the front door opening with to keep the heat inside. It was hard not to mourn for what might have been as she trooped outside and saw the half-stripped front door lying abandoned on the sawhorses.

Vivian gave herself a moment to bite her lip and remember the companionable contentment of working alongside Cooper, turning this house into a home through the sweat of their brows and the blisters on their hands. Then she pulled up her socks and switched gears. Getting the door repainted and reattached to the house was a higher priority than the porch railing.

She worked feverishly for a while, and the hard, physical labor helped to blank her mind and calm her mood. Underneath the surface calm, a deep well of sadness lingered—but Vivian found she could ignore the urge to dive into it, so long as she kept herself busy.

So she got the door stripped in record time, sanding down any rough patches and buffing away the dents and scuff marks of years of hard use. It was almost therapeutic, she reflected as she smoothed her palms over the clean, bright wood. A little love and attention, and this door was like new again—but even better than new, with the weathered patina of experience.

I want to be like that, Vivian reflected. *I want to shed the rough, ugly scars of the past and let my experiences give me a glow.*

With Cooper, she'd begun to believe in the possibility. And standing on the shore of Lantern Lake in the sparkling cold of a frosty winter morning, Vivian realized she still felt it. Even if Cooper never came back, she would be okay. Would she be as happy as she could be with him? No. But she'd survive, and even find contentment and peace.

For a woman who'd spent years defining herself as part of a couple—one deliriously happy and one the exact opposite—it was a revelation.

Taking a break between sanding and carting out the paintbrushes and cans, Vivian turned on her phone. She wanted to call the title company back and get the ball rolling on transferring the property back to Cooper's name.

But before she could find the number for the title company, Vivian's eye caught on an email from a Janine Turner. Was that the name of the woman who'd helped them with the property paperwork? Vivian clicked into it and felt equal parts of confusion and joy expand her lungs like a pair of helium balloons.

She was so engrossed in puzzling out the meaning behind the title rep's email, she didn't register the growl of a fine-tuned Italian sports car engine until it was almost on top of her.

Phone in hand, Vivian whirled to see Cooper unfolding his tall, broad-shouldered body from the driver's seat. He looked rough, a scruffy growth of beard darkening his jaw and purple bruises under his eyes telling of a sleepless night—but he was still just about the most welcome sight Vivian could imagine.

"You didn't leave," she said, immediately wanting to smack her own forehead. "I mean, obviously. You did leave the house, but not the island. Or the country. Or—can you help me out here, please?"

Cooper came around the front of the car, but kept his distance, as if he wasn't sure of his reception. He smiled slightly. "When I left here yesterday, I intended to fly out immediately. I wanted to round up the posse and ride out after justice—but when I went to ask Miles if I could borrow his helicopter, it hit me."

"What?" Vivian held her breath.

Palming the back of his neck, the way he did when he

felt uncomfortable, Cooper shot her a sheepish look from under his brows. "I was planning to ask to borrow the helicopter—which meant on some level, I'd already admitted that I'd lost that bet, or else I'd be on my way there to take possession of *my* helicopter."

Vivian felt more at sea than ever. What did this have to do with anything? "The bet?"

He stuck his hands in the pockets of his rugged canvas jacket. "Miles bet me that if I came to Sanctuary Island, I'd fall in love before he ever said 'I do.' And he was right."

Heart in her throat, Vivian swayed closer to him. "Oh?"

Cooper nodded slowly, never taking his eyes off her. "The first moment I saw you again, walking down that aisle toward me like a fantasy I thought I'd given up on, it all came rushing back. Hell, maybe it was there all along, buried under layers of hurt and resentment. But Miles was right. I love you, Vivian Banks. I loved you when we were dumb kids, and I love you even more now that we've found each other again as adults. I even loved you when I hated you. You're it for me—and you're all I need."

With a glad, inarticulate cry, Vivian dropped her phone and ran to him. Cooper swept her up in his strong arms, spinning them around in the sunshine. Laughing and crying, and kissing him through both, Vivian managed to mutter, "I love you, too. What took you so long?"

"I had a few things to arrange." He let her slide down his body until her shoes crunched into the frosty leaves and grass. "And no, not one of those things was a sudden trip overseas to play vigilante."

"Good," Vivian said fervently, tightening her arms around his lean, hard-muscled waist. "Thank you."

Cooper grimaced. "A long night of driving around this island made me realize I've got some stuff to work through. Like my tendency to want revenge for the past instead of letting myself enjoy the present and plan for the future. In this case, I was partly so fired up about getting back at your ex because . . . well, originally, I planned to punish you instead. I was going to sleep with you and then walk away— but that backfired when you opened your arms and let me go . . . and I discovered I wasn't ready to leave. And then when I found out what happened to you while we were apart, well. I have some guilt to work through about not finding you and helping you, and that might have played a part in my revenge fantasy, too. Like I could make up for not being there for you back then."

"You can make up for it by being with me now," Vivian said urgently. "Cooper, that's all I want. For us to be together. Everything else will work itself out."

Love and desire warmed Cooper's hazel eyes in the instant before he covered her mouth with his for a deep, searching kiss that only ended when a distant buzzing filtered through Vivian's hazed brain.

Sucking in oxygen, she turned her head in search of the source of the odd noise. A few paces away, her phone lay vibrating amongst the fallen leaves. And that reminded her of the odd email she'd received right before Cooper showed up.

"Speaking of working things out," he said, a mischievous grin curling his lips. "I told Janine to call this morning to finalize the paperwork."

Vivian scooped up her phone, and sure enough, it was the title company. "That poor woman. We must be running her ragged."

Arching a brow, Cooper tilted his head. "We don't have to make the change. I'm fine with things as they are."

In answer, Vivian hit the 'talk' button, her eyes never leaving Cooper's. "Hi, Janine? So sorry for all the confusion. Yes, I want to transfer ownership of the Lantern Lake house into both our names. Cooper Hayes and Vivian Banks. Together. Final answer. Thanks."

She hung up, blood bursting with joy. The possessive edge to Cooper's jaw and the soft tenderness in his gaze both combined to steal her breath. "It's a big step," she said huskily. "Owning property together. A lot of responsibility."

"We can handle it," Cooper said confidently, wrapping his arms around her from behind and turning them so they both could gaze up at the ramshackle, partially renovated cabin. "We're all grown up now, we know how to see something through."

The enormity of what they were doing hit Vivian suddenly, sending a wave of fear through her. "And you won't miss roving all over the world, footloose and fancy free?"

She felt his big chest move as he shrugged. "We can still travel. There are lots of places I want to kiss you—the top of the Eiffel Tower, in the shadow of the Parthenon, under an arch at the Alhambra . . . the list goes on and on. And when we're done making out around the globe, we'll come back home."

"Home," Vivian echoed, perfectly content in the circle of Cooper's arms, with the whole world at their feet and the promise of many happy years to come.

The future had never looked so wonderful.

Epilogue

A year and a half later . . . .

Miles Harrington stood up and tapped his wood-handled knife against his Mason jar of champagne. Up and down the rough-hewn picnic tables laden with wedding cake and hurricane lamps, the guests quieted. Their happy faces turned toward the best man expectantly.

"Good evening, everyone—and what a glorious evening it is, here at the edge of Lantern Lake." Miles nodded toward the mirrored surface of the water, lit by floating paper lanterns. All was serene and calm on this warm June night, the fresh island air broken only by the sounds of laughter and the clink of glasses.

"If you don't know who I am . . . well." Miles paused, smiling slightly. "If you don't know who I am, you probably don't belong at this wedding."

"Because only a wedding crasher wouldn't recognize

the great Miles Harrington!" Zane Bishop heckled from further down the table where the wedding party sat.

Miles sent him a mock-stern glare. "As an old family friend of both the bride and the groom," he said repressively, "I'm relatively certain I know every single one of you out there. Some of you, ahem, Zane, I know things about that you might prefer to keep private, so perhaps you should shut your mouth for the rest of this toast."

"Please, you think this man has any secrets?" Zane's wife, Felicity, shook her head in fond exasperation, and distracted her husband with a kiss when he would have responded. Zane subsided good-naturedly, waving over his shoulder for Miles to carry on. At only four months since their wedding, they still definitely qualified as newlyweds. With his black bow tie undone and hanging around the open neck of his tuxedo shirt, Zane looked as disreputable as ever—but there was something settled and happy about him now that hadn't been there before Felicity came into his life.

Miles decided to cut him some slack. "As I was saying, I know all of you. And I know you all join me in wishing the happy couple well. Leo summed it up best in the poem he wrote for the occasion. I won't attempt to outdo his eloquence."

The auburn-haired lord dipped his chin modestly, his other arm firmly around the shoulders of his bespectacled, and very proud, fiancée. "You're doing fine, old thing," Leo called with a smile bright enough to outshine the strands of round bulbs strung overhead.

Miles toasted him briefly before turning to gaze down at the happy couple seated to his left. "To Cooper and Vivian," he said, his voice ringing out over the water.

"Together, the way they should have been all along—but even better, I believe, for having spent those years apart."

He studied the way Vivian melted into her newly minted husband's side, independent enough to be comfortable leaning on him. And he saw how still Cooper went every time he met his wife's happy smile. The wanderer had found his true home at last.

And that's what Miles wanted to talk about, after all. "As I look around this beautiful place, the hidden lake and the cabin Cooper and Vivian poured hours of work and their whole hearts into so that they could be married on its front porch . . . what I really want to toast is Sanctuary Island."

A murmur of appreciation swept through the crowd like a warm breeze. Smiles were shared and hands were clasped as every person there acknowledged how lucky they were to live in such a special place.

"Almost two years ago," Miles continued. "I met the love of my life here."

He looked down at the woman seated beside him, his throat going warm and tight with emotion. Greta pursed her lips at him, her cheeks pink with a healthy glow . . . and probably a bit of embarrassment at all the eyes on them. But Miles couldn't help it. He'd built his family company into a multi-billion dollar international corporation—but there was nothing he'd done in his whole life that made him prouder than being Greta's husband.

Scooping up her hand, Miles brought her fingers to his lips for a kiss before facing the crowd once more. "Six months later, I made her mine. And I also made a bet with the groom, and my fellow groomsmen . . . I bet that if they spent a few weeks on Sanctuary Island, they would find their lives changed forever, for the better. I don't want to stand up here and take credit for the incredible happiness of my friends—wait. Yes, I do."

Everyone laughed and a few people shouted, "Hear, hear!" while Zane balled up his napkin and tossed it at Miles's head. Smoothly ducking the flying linen, Miles raised his glass. "But I can't take all the credit. Most of it goes to Cooper and Vivian, for finding their way back to one another and being smart enough—and brave enough— to take their second chance and make the most of it. The rest of the credit goes to Sanctuary Island itself. This place taught me and my friends to believe in love. To believe in our ability to woo and win the women of our dreams. To believe in happily ever after."

"To Sanctuary Island!" the crowd cried, applauding and cheering and toasting the moment with deliciously crisp sparkling wine from a nearby Virginia vineyard. Cooper stood to shake Miles's hand, but Miles used the grip to drag him into a hug.

"I've never been so happy to lose a bet in my life," Cooper said, as he drew back to pull Vivian to her feet. She was radiant in the ivory silk dress Felicity had talked her into wearing. The simple, clean lines suited her far better than the sumptuous frills of the ball gown she'd worn at her first wedding.

"I've never enjoyed winning more," Miles replied, with a sharkish grin. "And I'm very accustomed to winning."

Throwing her arms around his neck, Vivian leaned up to whisper in his ear. "You can joke all you want, but you *are* a big part of the reason tonight is happening. And I'll never forget it."

Miles cleared his throat and set one of his oldest friends

back on her heels. "It was my honor and my privilege. Our families have known each other a long time."

Internally, he winced at the mention of Vivian's reprehensible parents. Should he say he was sorry they couldn't be there to witness their daughter's happiness? Not that they deserved to be there, or would appreciate it the way they should.

But Vivian's bright indigo gaze never dimmed. "Family is what we make it. I know that now. Cooper is my family, and so are you. And I know we'll continue to be close for years and years to come."

The band struck up the opening notes of "At Last My Love Has Come Along," and Vivian slipped away for her first dance as the wife of the man she'd loved for so long. Miles watched the way Cooper whirled her around the floor, effortless and slow, their gazes catching and clinging in a moment so intense and private, Miles had to look away.

His own eyes found his beautiful wife regarding him with a mixture of joy and understanding that took his breath away. "How's Rosie?" he asked, his heart quickening at the thought of their baby daughter.

Greta snagged her phone off the table and showed him a picture. "Sleeping peacefully, as of five minutes ago. Lavonne said she missed us at bed time, but she settled for an extra read through of *In the Night Kitchen*."

Miles had to laugh at the image of his tiny daughter honing her negotiating skills on her babysitter. They'd hired his assistant, Cleo's daughter, to travel with them to Sanctuary Island for the wedding, knowing they wouldn't be able to fulfill their wedding party duties and take care of an energetic fourteen-month-old girl. Lavonne was as

terrifyingly competent as her mother. Miles knew Rose
was in good hands, and he'd looked forward to a night out
with his gorgeous Greta—but he hadn't counted on how
much he'd miss their nightly ritual of bath time, followed
by story time and snuggle time.

"And how are you?" he asked his wife, leaning in to
brush a kiss at her hairline while she absently scrolled
through a few more pictures of their daughter.

"Happy," Greta said, putting the phone down and smiling up at him in the way that never failed to send his blood
racing. "Happy for Cooper and Viv, happy to be here for
them, happy to be here in general. Just happy."

After surviving a life-threatening childhood illness,
Greta had steeped herself in gratitude for every moment
of the life she felt lucky to still be living. Being with her
had given Miles a new appreciation for life's many joys,
from the huge and all-encompassing like the arrival of
their precious Rosie, to the tiny and mundane. Like a dance
by a lake on a starlit night.

Standing, Miles held out his hand to lead Greta down
to the dance floor where other couples were beginning to
join the newlyweds. It felt amazing to be able to pull Greta
into his arms, to feel the warm, trusting weight of her
against his chest as they swayed together.

"My lonely days are over," Miles murmured, echoing
his favorite line of Coop and Viv's song.

"Not just yours—the lonely days are over for every one
of your closest friends!" Greta laughed, cupping the back
of his neck and nuzzling a kiss under his jaw. "The question is, who are you going to fix up next?"

"I think my matchmaking days are over. I'd rather
spend my time showing our daughter the flowers in her

great-grandmother's garden that inspired her name . . . and making love to my wife."

He felt the shiver that raced over Greta's skin. "That sounds good to me," she said, breathless enough to make desire surge through Miles.

"Let's leave the romance to the magic of Sanctuary Island," he whispered. "This place doesn't need our help to make people fall in love."

Miles twirled Greta into a spin and then dipped her low and laughing over his arm. The stars twinkled overhead, reflected in the smooth waters of the lake and in the fathomless happiness of his wife's eyes. The air smelled sweet and green, lush with growing things and alive with the breeze rolling in from the ocean beyond the pines. In the darkness beyond the flickering lanterns, wild horses ranged free along the sands and the people of Sanctuary Island lived out their lives . . . and, if they were very lucky, found true and everlasting love.